Also by Eileen Lottman

The Brahmins
After the Wind
Summersea

She and I

Eileen Lottman

William Morrow and Company, Inc.

New York

Grateful acknowledgment is made for the following excerpts:
"I Love You," Cole Porter, copyright © 1943 by Chappell & Co. (renewed). All rights reserved. Used by permission.
"Smoke Gets in Your Eyes," music by Jerome Kern and lyrics by Otto Harbach, copyright © 1933 by PolyGram International Publishing, Inc. (3500 West Olive Avenue, Suite 200, Burbank, CA 91505). Copyright renewed. International copyright secured. All rights reserved. Used by permission.

Recognizing the importance of preserving what has been written, it is the policy of William Morrow and Company, Inc., and its imprints and affiliates to have the books it publishes printed on acid-free paper, and we exert our best efforts to that end.

Library of Congress Cataloging-in-Publication Data

Lottman, Eileen.
    She and I / Eileen Lottman.
      p.   cm.
    ISBN 0-688-10175-5
    I. Title.
    PS3562.O79S54   1990
    813'.54—dc20   90-47771
                                          CIP

Printed in the United States of America

First Edition

1 2 3 4 5 6 7 8 9 10

BOOK DESIGN BY ROBIN MAKIN

*This novel is dedicated
to my daughter, Jessica*

Some of the places in this novel are real,
but all of the characters are fictional.

Contents

Contents

Pushing
the Frontiers
of Surgery

(from *The Washington Post National Weekly Edition*, March 7–13, 1988)

Baltimore——— . . . "I am willing to take any reasonable risk to separate Siamese twins because of the grotesque future they face," says Surgeon General C. Everett Koop, who has separated three pairs. "These are always terrible ethical decisions, but they have to be left in the hands of the surgeons who can determine what the best possible result will be."

In one famous operation, performed in 1976, when Koop was chief of surgery at Children's Hospital in Philadelphia, he separated babies sharing a heart. One died. "For one to live, one had to die," Koop says. "The heart really belonged to one child and not the other, but it was a very difficult operation for me. . . ."

• • •

From *International Index to Periodicals* (*July 1931–June 1934*) under listing "Siamese Twins": **see monsters: double**

Home Again

I wake suddenly from a doze on the couch and there is my mother's taste in furniture all around me again, and outside the window day or night it is still Sioux City, and if it weren't for the television flickering in front of me, I'd think I'd never left home. For a terrible, sinking moment I worry that maybe living in New York and Boston and finding my true love—oh, yes, I still believe that's who he was—was all a dream, or one of my wishful imaginings. But there is the television—so this is now, and I am reassured. I did get away from here.

It's a black-and-white movie about New York. I've been there. They're going to meet at the top of the Empire State Building. I've been there. I've been kissed like that. I've had a life of my own. Somebody wonderful has loved me.

My sister, Sheila, is very fat now, and I've stayed slim, which makes her madder than you can imagine. We lie side by side on an extra-wide couch. She drinks more than a fifth of vodka a day; she's trying to kill us. Good luck to her. It's taking a hell of a long time.

During the day I watch movies on the VCR and sometimes try to read a novel, while She and my mother play endless games of Spite and Malice, and if you knew them, you wouldn't be surprised that it's a game of double solitaire.

Late in the afternoons, She often gets testy and tries to pick a fight, but by then I'm feeling kind of quiet and bluesy and sort of numb from the alcoholic fallout coursing down the old bloodstream—I wonder if I could complain to the antipollution people, and I wonder what good that would do—well, I don't rise to her bait and pretty soon she passes out.

We have two identical television sets and they're never tuned to the same channel. In my opinion, the greatest contributions of mankind to civilization are earphones and remote control.

My mother spends most of her time on the phone telling anyone who'll still listen how sorry she feels for herself. My dad is very old now, but he still works long hours and goes to a lot of lodge meetings and we hardly ever see him. My sister snores loudly all night while I watch the late show and the late late show.

This book is the last burst of energy I ever intend to expend. I've been talking all my life about writing a novel; well, here it is. All the events and characters are purely fictitious, ho ho.

1

We Are Born

Sometimes I think I can remember back to the very beginning, when I felt safe. Sheila's moist, warm breath and steady pulse were the rhythm of my universe, the sound of her heart beating and her bubbling mouth noises, even her crying must have assured me, lulled and satisfied me. Deep in the primal gut we shared was a special knowledge. Other humans are born with the fearful shock of being thrust out, alone—they say it's what makes them sing the blues and yearn all their lives for That Certain Someone. Loneliness is a terrible thing, they say. I wouldn't know. It sounds like heaven to me. Loneliness . . . solitude . . . I long for a taste of loneliness; solitude is the most beautiful word I ever heard.

But in the beginning it must have been a comfort. She was always there, part of me. We were yanked out onto a cold delivery table into blinding light and the callous scrutiny of medics, like everyone else in these times, except that we had each other. It must have been that bizarre and special grace at the very start, before I understood anything, that supplied me with the fundamental sanity I'd need to deal with all the shit that was going to be my life with Sheila.

All the family pictures show us standing together like best friends: in the summer with our little white dresses exactly like Shirley Temple's (my ruffles edged in blue, Sheila's in red); in the winter with snow-encrusted mittens and bright cheeks. Sheila is always on the right (left as you face us) and I'm on the left, smiling at the camera, squinting in the sun. More often She is smiling and I seem to be nursing some grudge. There are no newspaper clippings in the albums. Go to the library if you want to see all that. In our family we pretended that we were normal.

Bella posed us, taking infinite care, and Daddy hunched over the bulky folding Kodak with the sun behind him—there is his shadow to prove that he was there. The thick black album pages are crammed with photos, each glued down with four gilded corners: baby pictures (fully clothed), little-kid pictures, self-conscious preadolescent pictures, high school graduation and college fooling-around pictures—even a wedding picture—and never once can you see, in the photos that were saved, that we are slightly flawed.

We were born in Sioux City, Iowa, on August 15, 1927. It was the same year Lindbergh flew the Atlantic; we created somewhat less of a stir. (When the Lindbergh baby was kidnapped a few years later, I was sure we were next, but our mother comforted us: "No one would want *you*," she said in a tone of such conviction that it reassured us absolutely.) From time to time—birthdays, mostly, and slow weeks for news—we showed up in Sunday rotogravure sections and certain so-called ladies' magazines, some scientific papers, and even books, under headings such as "Twins, Conjoined,"

"Siamese Twins Born to Jewish Couple Thriving in Midwest," and other lurid and/or scholarly titles. None of them, of course, tells the truth. How could they? Truth and reality are not on the list of things my family deals with. Facts to us are nothing more than no-see-'em gnats on a summer night, sometimes pesky but best ignored.

My guess is that my mother's first words were, "Why did this have to happen to me?" A more maternal person might have put it differently, such as: "Why did this have to happen to them?" but we can't all be natural mothers. Shortly after we were born, one columnist with nothing better to write about speculated that a condition such as ours might be due to the mother's uncertainty about whether she really wanted to become a mother at all. This, the columnist suggested, could bring about the birth of unformed, malformed, half-formed, or otherwise uncertain babies. Any woman, this man warned, could find herself giving birth to monsters if she wasn't really one hundred percent mother material. Bella had in fact admitted to a flattering interviewer that there had been times when she wondered whether she should have gone on the stage instead of settling down. Not that she regretted for a minute the fulfillment of every woman's fondest dream—a loving husband, home, and the blessed miracle of children!

Surely she must have wanted desperately to be rid of us. If we didn't have the grace to die on our own—and we were very healthy, shared liver and bloodstream and all—we could at least be sent off to a permanent playpen somewhere, out of sight and mind.

Bella-known-as-Billie had been the belle of every ball since her seventeenth birthday, only a brief five years before. Now she had been put through living hell, and for what? The pain must have been awful, since we are joined side to side and it was hours before they realized there was a problem and cut her open to get us out. And now, on the most dramatic occasion of her life, this monstrous excretion from her body was getting all the attention.

I reconstruct the scene from later familiarity with the principals:

Bella lies back on the starched hospital pillow, which sets off dramatically the brave circles of rouge on her pallid cheeks. Her voice trembles, still weak from the suffering he has put her through. She opens the subject mournfully. "We have to find a place for them." It's almost a whine.

He misunderstands, nods. "A bigger crib," he agrees. "It'll be all right."

Her huge green eyes take on a feverish light. Her Cupid's-bow lips aren't smiling. Maybe she moans a little to remind him which of them is going through this ordeal, after all.

"No. Away . . . away . . ." When he still doesn't understand, she spells it out: "A place where they would be better off, happy . . . with people of their own kind—a special place where—"

I like to think he cuts her off right there. "Absolutely not," he says. He did stand up to her sometimes; and surely that once—that crucial one time that I am imagining—he prevailed. "These are our children and we will take care of them." I believe that he might have said that, or something close to it.

Then she whimpers bitterly, "You don't care anything about what happens to me." A tear rolls down her cheek and she turns her exhausted head on the pillow, away from him. He can't stand it when she won't look at him.

He reaches for her hand. She begins to cry hard, harder, hysterically. He rings for the nurse, which is not what Bella wants. She shrieks at him, "Freaks! You gave me freaks! You've ruined my life!"

When the nurse comes in she gets a hypo, and by the time she wakes up all the world is talking about how heroic and beautiful she is. The reporters wait outside her room and a radio network has brought in microphones and miles of wire to send her happy, tremulous voice around the world.

All her life Bella has yearned to be famous, to be a movie star or at least on the radio, and suddenly she is getting more attention than Gloria Swanson, whom everyone says she resembles somewhat. She is lying in bed surrounded by American Beauty long-stemmed red roses and is about to be interviewed, and photographed, her every word translated into foreign languages. So she puts on lipstick and combs her hair (a little spit curl in front of each ear) and the nurses help her into a new pink satin bed jacket. She poses for the photographers, looking gallant and beautiful and wan. As for us, we are no more than two squally faces swathed in blankets in the arms of two nurses standing too close together. They are smiling for the cameras.

The doctors are also interviewed. Can they be separated? No. Perhaps someday science will discover how to divide one liver into two; already they are experimenting with transplanting certain organs from newly dead bodies into living ones, although it looks like it may be easier with a heart, even, than a liver. They have hopes that it could only be a matter of time.

As babies, we learned to sit up (in tandem—it must have been grotesque), stand up, and walk—the usual things at about the usual time. It's all documented in the University of Iowa medical files. I was faster at learning to speak; Sheila was quicker at grasping for things. She was the pretty one, with black shiny curls and clear white skin, and deep sparkly eyes that caught the light and made it her own. The *Chicago Tribune* once said that "the livelier of the twins gives the impression of having a source of illumination within herself, to dispense as she chooses." She shone on anyone whom she would charm and just about everyone fell for it. I personally never saw Sheila's eyes, except in a mirror, at an angle.

Our mother wouldn't allow the word *freak* to be spoken in

her hearing. If she did hear someone say it, she'd moan loudly and sometimes she'd actually faint, neatly drawing attention away from us and onto herself.

I think Bella is a beautiful name—it even *means* "beautiful"—but she was modern, American, a good-hearted flapper, a party girl who got stuck in a nightmare. Let's say this for her; she was a good sport. Everybody always said that about Billie.

2

When We Were Little, Billie Sometimes Danced for Us

When we were little Billie sometimes danced for us. She wound up the Victrola, rolled down her hose, and did a wacky, energetic, giggly Charleston. If she was in a really good mood, maybe she'd run upstairs to get the pink garter with the rosebud on it, pull it over her foot and up just under her round plump knee. I could see a face there, a sweet little face with two dimples for eyes, quite merry when she danced, but when I told my mother that I saw a face in her knee, she said I was being silly.

She had energy and spirit, and when she was performing, flushed and smiling, her hair bouncing red-gold in the light from the window, I felt privileged to be a momentary part of her real life, where the fun was. We were suddenly important; after all, without an audience, how can there be a show? I could imagine the whole living room filled with people sitting just as Sheila and I were, staring open-mouthed in

23

rapt appreciation of her beauty, her style, her liveliness, her talent. We applauded when our mother took her bows (who taught us that?) and she threw kisses at us. We clapped and called for more, more, but she would always stop too soon, claiming to be winded despite her famous pep. Then she'd sit down with us and start talking about stuff that she wished could happen.

They would design costumes. "Pink," Billie said, "with tulle and little sparkling stars all over the skirt. You'd carry a wand and Sandy could have a halo."

This game did not interest me. I'd stare off into space, or open one of the storybooks I always had with me. (I was born knowing how to read. Sheila had to struggle with syllables and sounding out words and it took her forever. And even when she learned, she didn't care for it.)

"I want a wand *and* a halo," She whined, and Billie laughed as if She had said something clever.

"My, you'd be so famous," our mother sighed. "If your daddy would only let you. But Daddy knows best, and he makes a very good living, so we don't even really need the money. Do you know how much money Shirley Temple makes in just one year?"

"How much, Billie?" Sheila would prompt. Give that girl a cue, out will spit the straight line every time. She learned it at her mother's dimpled knee.

"A lot, honey. A lot, lot, lot. More than most grown-ups make in ten years, maybe."

"I want to take dancing lessons," She sniveled.

"Well, don't you think I want that for you too? Just like every other little girl your age whose daddy can afford it?" A loud, piteous sigh. "Well, maybe one of these days. But first you and Sandy have to get a little stronger on your legs. C'mon, let's do the exercises!"

Up we'd get, me grumbling and reluctantly putting down my book. And all through the drill, left foot stretch, step back, lift and turn together, right foot stretch, step forward, lift and turn together, over and over and again and again . . . all through it, Billie would be talking about how we could wear pretty costumes and delight vast audiences and become the most loved and highest paid little girls in the world ("twice as much as Shirley Temple; after all there are two of you") if only Daddy could be made to understand.

"And you can call yourselves anything you like. Everybody changes their names when they're on the stage or in the movies. Theda Bara spelled backwards is Arab Death—"

"No it isn't!" I yelped excitedly, having spelled the words backward faster than a whip. But my mother didn't like to be interrupted and was not the slightest bit interested in spelling, even though she'd brought it up in the first place.

". . . and do you think that's Fifi D'Orsay's real name? It certainly is not! Now, how about Melody Starr—that's a name I made up myself. Do you like that? Melody Starr. The Starr sisters, Melody and . . . who? What's a name that goes with Melody?"

Sheila thought hard and seriously. I was pretending I was somewhere else (a skill I got better at as years went on). Billie considered aloud. "Dawn . . . Gwendolyn . . . Melissa . . . how about that? Melody and Melissa Starr? I think I like that best."

"I get to be Melody," Sheila put in promptly.

"If your sister doesn't mind," Billie answered, and at that point, as I remember, she got bored with the whole thing and turned us over to Helen, the "girl." Helen came from a farm near Otoe, Nebraska, and she worked for us for room and board and four dollars a week. She got Thursday evenings and all day Sunday off. There was a Depression and she was lucky to be with such a nice family, even though her dad thought Jews were heathens. She had to go all the way home on the bus every Sunday just to prove to him she was still alive. I loved Helen. She was kind and kept *True Confessions* magazines in neat stacks under her bed and sometimes she would polish our fingernails light pink. Once when she was drying us after our bath, she hugged me for no reason, without hugging Sheila.

Listening to my mother gossiping with her friends, I came to the conclusion that everyone thinks everybody else is peculiar. So if people stared at us, whispered about us, and even pointed at us, they did it to each other, too. Could be the way we were dressed or our manners or something one of us said; could be a lie someone told about us, or maybe one of our skirts was hiked up or my sock had a hole in it. Sheila's socks never got holes.

Trying out our first roller skates one day, we spotted Mrs. Goldman coming down the street in our direction. She was staring, as if she was trying to solve one of those what's-wrong-with-this-picture contests. She stopped and we had to, too.

"Hello, girls."

"Hello, Mrs. Goldman."

"Hello, Mrs. Goldman."

"How are you girls today?"

I let Sheila answer. "Just fine, thank you."

"And how's your mother? I haven't seen her since canasta on Tuesday."

It was my turn. I tried to be polite. "She was constipated for three days, but this morning she took an enema and now she's fine again."

Mrs. Goldman turned deep red and burst out in an explosive guffaw, which she tried to hide. She hurried on past us.

"What a dumb thing to say," my sister told me disgustedly.

"Why?" I thought Mrs. Goldman wanted to know how Billie was so I told her. Why was that wrong?

"You're just supposed to say, 'Fine, thank you.' "

"All the time, no matter what?"

"Yes, dummy."

"Well, then why do people ask?"

She just pushed off on the skates and of course I had to go along. The world was full of booby traps.

But most of the time there was home, where it was cozy and relatively safe, with smells of ironing and pot roast, Billie's Kool cigarettes, and Helen's Evening in Paris perfume, the worn yellow-green linoleum floor where we played while Helen peeled potatoes, shucked corn, put up fruit, in a pale green housedress patterned in lovely sprays of fading lilacs.

Home was my beloved Nancydoll, who—wonder of wonders—had no twin. This anomaly was the result of our third birthday, when I opened my blue-ribboned box to find a doll exactly like the one She had just taken into her arms from her red-ribboned box. My spontaneous reaction was to throw the doll as hard as I could against the nearest wall. Her head broke open with a terrifying crunch, and plaster crumbled all over her nice blue dress. Billie and Daddy were furious, but darling Aunt Mitzi had a sudden wonderful leap of imagination, and the next day there was Nancydoll, unique and all mine, and a whole day newer than She's silly Melody and her dead twin.

Home was the only place that had a little wooden stool next to the potty. When She was on the toilet, we faced the braided rag rug and the bathtub, but when I was on it, we had to face the wall. (Public toilets were a terrible problem; there was almost never room for the one who had to stoop down waiting, and they were almost always dirty. Billie had taught us that we had to put paper all over the seat before we used it, which made it slippery and tricky not to splash all over your own or your sister's leg.) Home was listening to Eddie Cantor on the radio Sunday nights with Daddy and Billie. Sometimes we sat on Daddy's lap.

Home was also where I spent hours and weeks and finally

years building my own world, a miniature village set out in the backyard in the dirt where no grass grew, between the hollyhocks and the storm-cellar door. I made houses and stores and a library and school and church from cut-up cigar boxes. Carefully bent hairpins stood streetlight duty at every corner, burnt kitchen matches tied together with black thread were my telephone poles, and real toy cars plied the carefully planned streets, which were swept by toothbrush every day. My dream was a car for every driveway, but the only way I could get them was if a boy gave me one of his old ones, and they would only do that if you showed them your underpants, so I didn't have very many cars. Sheila never wanted to show her underpants, and every time I started negotiations for a used car, She'd threaten to tell. There were no dolls to represent people in my town—the inhabitants existed only in my imagination, where no one else could see them. I never told their names aloud.

Whenever we moved to a new house, I rebuilt my town from scratch, improving the layout and design. I had urban planning down to a science before it was a science.

She loathed playing in the dirt, but in return I let her dress me up in high heels and Billie's old evening gowns for endless hours of parading around the house from mirror to mirror. We had equal time, except when one of us was being punished. Then the bad one, usually me, would have to give over some precious time to doing what the other wanted.

Sheila had two best friends, Bubbles and Edie. The three of them, dragging me along, would play dress-up in someone's attic (our own or our aunt Mitzi's were the best, but Bubbles had some good stuff in hers, too) or they'd have one of their stupid tea parties, with Kool-Aid or cocoa in doll-size cups, or they'd flop on someone's bed and giggle and chatter about weddings and clothes.

Then She'd have to spend an equal amount of time doing what I wanted to do; crouch in the dirt playing in my little village, or sit and read, munching apples. Solitary things. No talking. She and I had pretty much stopped talking to each other by the time we were in second grade. We'd only fight and hurt each other, and anyway, I wanted to pretend I was *really* alone, and that, I presumed, meant silence.

We had identical Orphan Annie watches and a chart on the corner of our dressing table, where we kept careful track of how many hours we spent doing what She wanted to do and how many hours were mine. We fought about that more than anything. I still say She owes me several years of hours.

On Saturday mornings we went to the library, where kids were allowed to check out four books each week. I tried to make them last the whole time, but that was hard, even though I got to read Sheila's, too. For a long time I had to read them out loud to her. Sometimes she wouldn't take out any books, or only one or two, just to rile me, and she'd always try to pick stuff I'd hate. Animal stories made me cry, so there was almost always a book about a lost and mistreated dog or a wolf with his leg in a trap. I cried a lot anyhow, not even knowing why, so when I had a reason I was practically unstoppable. But I read them all; it never occurred to me not to.

How did I know the world would hurt us? I didn't learn that from books, but I knew it. The troubles that befell people in stories had nothing to do with us. I could be a princess locked up in a tower all alone or a ragged, cold, and hungry girl selling matches to stay alive or the beaten, miserable puppy who would save his cruel master's life . . . and I'd shiver and feel their pangs. But the worst time was when the story was over. Being alone in a tower or on a snowy corner of a heartless city or trapped in a burning barn couldn't be nearly so bad as never being alone at all. Nobody wrote stories about that.

I tried not to hate people, because it wasn't their fault. One day, Marilyn Pickel's mother and our mother drove down to Omaha for a shopping trip and they dumped all three of us at Aunt Mitzi's house. We played Pick-Up-Sticks and Marilyn cheated. She moved a stick with the one she was trying to pick up and She and I both saw it, but Marilyn wouldn't admit it.

"You're a cheater, Marilyn Pickel," She told her.

"I am not!" Marilyn looked like she wanted to go home, but too bad, she was stuck there and it was our aunt's house and we didn't like cheaters.

"We both saw you, Marilyn," I said.

Marilyn's face got blotchy red and she kicked the little colored sticks all over the floor in a sudden rage. "You're ganging up on me because there's two of you, and it's not fair, you're just freaks anyway and everybody knows it!"

"Take that back," She said furiously.

"Freaks! Freaks! Nobody would play with you unless they had to! You ought to be in a circus instead of out in public, where you make people sick to look at you!!"

"Aunt Miiii . . . tzeeeeee!" She hollered, but it wasn't necessary. Our aunt had heard the raised voices and was standing, as still as a statue, in the archway of the living-room hall.

"What did you say, Marilyn?" gentle Aunt Mitzi asked in her composed, rocklike, elocution-trained voice. She would do her duty, wherever it led her. Everyone always said that about Aunt Mitzi.

"They said I cheated, but I never," Marilyn blubbered. "I want to get out of here, I want to go home, I want my mother!"

"Your mother isn't here. She left you in my care. It looks like I'm going to have to teach you some manners. Didn't your mother ever tell you not to call people names?"

Marilyn just sobbed.

"We don't use words like that, Marilyn. That is a very foul and filthy word to use about anybody, and I am going to wash your mouth out with soap so you'll never, never forget that."

"You're not my mother!" Marilyn shrieked as dear Aunt Mitzi pulled her along by the arm. "You can't do this to me! I'll tell my father!"

"Your parents will be grateful to me if they've got any sense. You'll never insult people again, if I have anything to say about it. I don't want to do this, but it's for your own good, Marilyn."

She dragged Marilyn up the stairs and into the bathroom, with us following right behind, excited and, I have to admit it, thrilled. Aunt Mitzi took a washcloth and soaped it with Palmolive until it was green and foamy, and then she forced Marilyn Pickel's mouth open and she jammed the washcloth inside. Marilyn gagged and choked and tried to kick Aunt Mitzi's legs, but my father's sister was no dope. She had sagely stepped to the other side of the basin for this operation. Sheila and I could only watch in awe.

"Now, will you remember never, never to use that word again?" Aunt Mitzi asked quietly as Marilyn spat and fumed and vomited into the basin. What a dummy—she tried to wash her mouth out with a glassful of water, but that only made more suds. She nodded her head, yes, yes, yes, I'll remember, I'll remember, I'll remember.

My sister wouldn't talk to Marilyn the rest of the day, but I felt sorry for her and gave her some Smoker's Breath Drops from Uncle Iz's drawer, to get the Palmolive taste out of her mouth. Then I tried to read her a story, but she was crying too hard and fell asleep on the guest room bed.

When our mothers got back, Aunt Mitzi told Mrs. Pickel straight off what had happened, without using That Word. Mrs. Pickel apologized for Marilyn's bad behavior and I had the feeling old Marilyn was going to get it again when she got home, for embarrassing her mother. That, I knew very well, was the most unforgivable sin of all.

31

Lying in bed that night, feeling just generally sad, it occurred to me that Marilyn had been punished for the wrong crime. We *were* freaks, after all, and how was she to know That Word wasn't permitted in our family? Her cheating in the game had been completely overlooked! It certainly was a damn difficult world to figure out. I'd never get the hang of it.

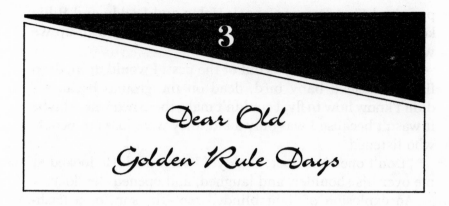

3

Dear Old
Golden Rule Days

Daddy and Billie, with traitor Helen right behind them, prodded Sheila and me out of our room, down the stairs, and into the living room. The stained-glass window high over the front door had turned sinister during the night; shards of sun glinted through the green and purple—they were evil eyes, warning me not to dare the unknowable fate that waited beyond the threshold.

Somehow, I had to make them understand that we weren't ready, would never be ready. It was wrong and cruel to send us out there. Oh, please oh please ohpleasepleaseplease let me stay home and read my fairy-tale books!

I knew with a dreadful clarity that the world outside would hurt us more than God had.

Sheila was so thrilled and excited she was trying to skip down the stairs, yanking and pulling at me until I felt dizzy. She just couldn't wait (as Billie couldn't) for the long-promised First Day of School. Helen and Daddy and Billie kept saying how wonderful it would be, how grown-up we were now.

They were pushing us out of the nest. I would drop, drop like a smashed baby bird, dead on the ground because I didn't know how to fly. I couldn't make them hear me. Maybe it wasn't because I was only a kid; they were just not people who listened.

"Don't open the door, Daddy!" I screamed. He looked at me over his shoulder, and laughed, and opened the door.

An explosion of light blinded me—the sun, or a flash-bulb—and when my vision cleared the whiteness had turned our own front yard bleak and unreal. The oak tree bent down to shake sharp-clawed tentacles at me. Our big rubber-tire swing had been transmogrified into a silently jeering, hollow, toothless mouth. The photographers crowded around us and snapped pictures and reporters yelled terrible questions. (We were used to that; on our birthdays, Helen would always bake two cakes, one for the children and one for the reporters.)

Suddenly and urgently, I had to go to the bathroom.

I pulled on my mother's hand, but she only clutched me tighter and yanked me along. "I gotta go, I gotta go!" I told her over and over, louder and louder, until finally it registered. She left off smiling for the cameras and looked down at me, seriously annoyed.

"You just went. It's just nerves," she said. "And you can hold it till you get to school."

"No! No!" Everybody in the whole school would know where we were, what we were doing! "No," I whimpered, and to my own surprise I was sobbing.

They were not my everyday tears. Desperate and terrified, those tears are here in my eyeducts today, ready to erupt again with frustration and outrage and helplessness, with the knowledge that disaster could be averted but will not be. I was powerless, but THEY could change everything, if they would only hear me, listen to me, care enough. And, already, I knew they wouldn't.

I still cry sometimes for that little girl whose only way of dealing with betrayal was to fear that she might wet her pants.

Everything was new and uncomfortable: little white socks, shiny stiff brown oxford shoes, matching plaid cotton dresses with starched puffed sleeves. Billie had tried the old ribbon trick when she should have known from experience that it wouldn't work: a huge red satin bow for Sheila's thick black curls, to bounce and divert attention, and a huge blue satin bow for me, an attempt made to secure it with bobby pins, even as it started its inevitable downhill slide along my intractable mop, to be lost forever before the hour was out. But on the first day of school, a blue satin ribbon would be sacrificed to Billie's concept of Fair and Equal Treatment for Both My Girls. Handkerchiefs, embroidered by Aunt Mitzi, each saying MONDAY in a different color, were tucked into the cuffs of our starched balloon sleeves.

And after all that trouble, this: one twin smiling gaily and pirouetting for the photographers as best she could, blowing kisses and touching the hem of her skirt in a hint of a curtsy, bucking for immortality in the roto pages of the *Des Moines Sunday Register;* the other red-faced and shrieking at the top of her lungs, kicking and flailing out and trying to sink through the sidewalk to China rather than go along nicely with her sister to school. How sad for the pretty one to be stuck forever with that. How embarrassing for the parents.

The photographers pulled their heads up from under their black hoods and stood silently waiting for me to stop. I guess the country was depressed enough without having to look at pictures of a five-year-old mutant having a tantrum. I finally ran out of tears. They were no use. Billie dusted me off and yanked my hair up as tightly as she could twist it in the

35

ribbon's grip. My cheeks were dried and my nose blown, and the four of us were heading off toward the school, Daddy holding on to She's hand and Billie gripping mine like a wolftrap clamped down on a rabbit. We all looked over our shoulders, back at the cameras, when they asked us to, and the pictures show a happy family ("normal in all but one respect": *Omaha World Herald*) on the first day of kindergarten in September 1932.

Daddy was late for work on account of my carrying on, so he had to leave us at the corner, hurry back to get the Dodge, and drive downtown to his office. Billie said goodbye to us at the corner, too, and went back home with him. Sheila pulled me along. The morning was cool and a few bright yellow leaves had already fallen. As we came closer to the grim brick school, kids converged from every direction, all spiffed up and walking funny in new brown shoes.

She got us inside the gate and into the line at the big open door on the right that had G I R L s carved over it in stone. The boys were making a lot of noise and pushing each other over at B O Y s. A bell rang from inside the building and the line started moving, with some of the bold sixth-grade girls jostling and giggling shrilly. A tall blond girl we didn't know dared our next-door neighbor, Margaret Ann Garrity, to touch us, and she did it, as if she were touching a hot potato, and that sent a whole bunch of the girls into loud, mean laughter. I wanted to die. Anyway, I realized that I no longer had to pee; my mother had been right about that.

The inside of the building smelled like paste and ammonia. The biggest woman I had ever seen stood in the hall and said, over and over again as the girls laughed and squirmed and darted past her, "All first-timers into this room. The rest of you go to the room you were in last spring. All first-timers into this room. Kindergartners, into this room, please." I thought it was nice of her to say "please," since grown-ups don't have to be polite to kids. The boys were crowding into the same hallway and going into the same rooms as the girls and I wondered why they had to enter through a different door. It must have something to do with penises, but what?

The kindergarten room was big and sunny and there were a lot of little chairs in a circle in the middle. She and I pushed two chairs together and sat down. Two mothers had come all the way into the school. One of them smiled at us. My sense of doom deepened. The windows were open, and I thought about leaping through one of them. I would have to drag Sheila with me, and it would be awful; everyone would look at us. We were on the ground floor, anyhow; I'd probably only break a leg instead of dying, or, worse luck, She would break a leg and I'd be just fine.

Our teacher turned out to be the huge lady who had stood at the door. She said her name was Miss Peterson. She welcomed the mothers and then told them they could leave. The boy next to me blushed as red as the stripes on the flag when his mother kissed him before she left. It was the first time I ever thought about other people having troubles like mine— embarrassment troubles. I looked over at him sympathetically, but he just stared down at the floor.

Nobody paid any attention to us after all. I guess the kids all had their own terrors to cope with. Conjoined twins are nothing special when you're five years old; what you care about is what's going to be done to you next.

Miss Peterson talked about hanging up our "cloaks" and keeping crayons neat and the need to pay attention and other things I've forgotten, and then she held up a large card with the letter *A* on it and asked if anybody knew what that was. I nodded and said, "A." Everybody turned toward us and stared. Sheila jabbed me in the arm, furious. For a couple of years after that, until the rest of the kids caught up, I had to pretend in school that I couldn't read.

One day the elastic in my underpants was loose and I guess I kept hitching them up; I wasn't aware of it until first

Tommy Moran and then some of the other boys started imitating me and snickering. My sister told them to stop it, then she hauled me up to the teacher and whispered that we needed a safety pin and could we be excused; then we went to the girls' room and I pinned them up. It never would have occurred to me to do that. My impulse was to throw something hard and sharp at Tommy Moran.

There was a secret code for getting along in the world and Sheila had the key to it, but I did not.

When I balked at going to another birthday party with the same kids and the same games and the same stupid competition for the same prizes or when I begged to be allowed to read instead of going to someone's house to play or when I told the truth in answer to practically any question, Billie would say in exasperation, "Why are you always trying to be different? Why can't you be like everyone else?"

But I wanted desperately to be exactly like everyone else, to be a normal person, to know the code and never do or say anything wrong, to be interested in the things everybody else seemed to care about, to smile all the time as if I were happy. I knew being popular was the most important thing in the world, but popularity coming to me was in the same odds group as being uncovered as the real heiress to the British throne. Of course I wanted friends, but I was forever saying things that other kids found weird and mockable, and grownups never knew whether I meant to be funny or couldn't help it.

I tripped over things and bumped into people and my knees were always scabby and I broke my front teeth and frequently spilled my milk.

"Klutz," my mother would say reflexively, as long as there were no gentiles within hearing distance. "Klutz," when my mind was on something else and I forgot to tie my shoes; "Klutz," when I dropped something or stumbled going up the stairs or set the table wrong. She said it louder when friends were around, because such a good mother certainly didn't want anyone thinking it was her fault I was so clumsy and awkward. I could understand that.

Sheila, on the other hand, always said things that people felt comfortable with; there were no surprises when She opened her mouth. She could turn staring, gawking, snickering strangers into friends (of a sort); She was the one who deflected most of the stones thrown thoughtlessly or otherwise by people I wanted to kill. She could talk about nothing forever and not get bored, her table manners came naturally, and she never got her clothes dirty unless I made her sit in the dirt. Everyone liked her, except me.

4

Your Ice-Cream Cone Dropped

The boys from Immaculate Conception, which shared the same square block our school was on (the playgrounds were back to back, with a fence between), worked for days to build a solid snow barricade. They had a major supply of snowballs stashed back there, some of them pure ice. It was dangerous to leave school. Most of the girls were running every which way, giggling and screaming. The boys from our school were fighting back in small, quickly organized groups, taking shelter where they could.

In the middle of the barrage of snowballs, I heard Corky Geoghegan yell out, "Look! Here come the freak sisters! Double points! Double points if you hit the two-headed monster!"

"Just pretend that nothing's happening," my sister ordered. "It's our own corner and we have a right to cross here. Come on."

She yanked me into the line of fire. Snowballs pelted my back and my arms and legs; I kept my whole face ducked into my muffler, eyes tightly shut, as we made our wild, awkward dash. The boys loved to see us run; they laughed like the hyenas in Frank Buck's *Bring 'Em Back Alive* movies. Suddenly I was hit with a terrible, reverberating crack at the back of my head. I yowled with pain, but She dragged me across the street and finally out of range. She started stomping through the knee-high drifts (no self-respecting kid ever walked in snow that someone had already trod) and I had to go along or fall down in defeat.

"Shut up, crybaby," she said. "You're the biggest baby I ever saw."

My head hurt badly and there was cold wet snow down the back of my neck and then there was something else dripping: globs of bright red blood staining the snow alongside our galosh tracks. "Look!" I screamed, and then my bawling began in earnest. She got scared too, and we hurried home.

"Billie! Helen! Sandy's bleeding! And I got hit, too!" She shouted as we slammed through the kitchen door.

Billie telephoned for a taxi (damn the expense!) and took us to the doctor, who said I didn't need stitches and then poured on a lot of painfully stinging iodine at the back of my head. Billie asked us who did it and we said it was the Catholic boys and she said one of those little mackerel-snappers must have put a rock in the snowball meant for me. Then she said, "Well, we'll just forget it ever happened. We don't want any trouble."

"Klutz," my sister said when we were alone. "Why didn't you duck?" She knew how to seize the advantage in the fierce ongoing competition that made up our lives. We were lying down because my head ached so much, and She was furious at me, I guess because she didn't want to be in bed in the middle of the day.

She was convinced that not only was I clumsy, ugly, and

41

friendless, but I was also the stupid one. Do you believe it? I did, at the time. She was very convincing.

One late summer afternoon, Billie gave us each a nickel to get ice-cream cones. It meant walking down the hill past the Krausses' barking German shepherd, but Billie said his bark was worse than his bite—not that Schnapps had ever actually bitten anybody, as far as we knew, not yet, anyway.

"I'd better hold both nickels," She said as soon as the screen door closed behind us. Her hand came around in front of me, palm up. It was pink and offensively clean.

"I can hold it myself," I told her. I reached into the pocket of my pinafore and guess what, it wasn't there. How could I have lost it already? Of course she felt the panic that shook me, and when my step slowed, hers did too.

"You lost it already!"

"I did not."

Now I was frantically searching my other pocket and staring at the ground along the brief path we had traced. Tears torrented up inside me. I tried to concentrate on not letting them spill out.

"Well," my sister pointed out dolefully, "I guess you just don't get any." She pulled at me and I went along, miserable and sniffling. I didn't care about the ice cream; it always gave me a stomachache anyway. I just hated being such a klutz.

"Oh, shut up, crybaby. C'mon!" She tried to pull me along the sidewalk, but I just wanted to sit down and never move again.

"Oh, look what I found! Another nickel! Now I've got two. Tell you what I'll do, I'll give you one if you stop crying."

I looked at her hand again, at the two buffalo glinting in the sun. "That's my nickel," I said, breathless with indignation. "How'd you get it?"

"Wouldn't you like to know!" She laughed. She started to

skip, which is hard to do when you've got another person hitched to your liver. It made me feel like throwing up. But fury took over from self-pity and at least I had stopped crying. "Anyway, it's not yours. It's mine. But I'll buy you an ice-cream cone," She said magnanimously.

It seemed all the same to me, so I agreed and we started down the hill, walking slowly in the heat, in and out of the shade cast by the trees. The afternoon had the rotting-flower scent of summer's end.

Thoughtfully, She said, "If I buy you a cone with my nickel, what will you give me? I know—you can drink my milk tonight." Milk stuck in my throat like viscous glue, and if I did manage to swallow it, I'd get terrific gas pains and diarrhea. The same thing happened to my sister, but everybody knew milk was good for kids, so every night at dinner we had to sit at the table no matter how long it took until we finished one full glass each. It didn't help that the glasses were blue and had Shirley Temple's picture on them. You couldn't imagine Shirley Temple ever letting a fart.

"No, I won't," I told her. "I don't want your nickel. You stole it from me anyway."

"Well how'd I do that, if you're so smart?"

"Right after Billie gave them to us, when I was finishing my chapter and you got mad 'cause you had to wait a couple of seconds. I wasn't paying attention and you took it right out of my pocket. You're a robber, Sheila Lazarus, and you're going to go to hell. And I don't even want any goddamn ice cream."

"Swearing. You're the one who's going to H E double L. Everybody knows swearing sends you right there. And if you don't want any ice cream, I'll just put my extra nickel in the bank."

We had to quicken our steps just then to try to get past the Krausses' yard without Schnapps hearing us, but he began barking ferociously as we scooted as fast as we could, semisideways, like two horrible giant crabs scuttling along the sidewalk. Mrs. Krauss was in the yard trimming back the bleeding-heart bushes, and she looked up to see who was riling her dog. "Hello, twins," she called out in her heavy accent. "Don't run, you frighten Schnapps! Don't run, little Jew-girl twins! Don't run!" But we were safely away and just had time to catch our breaths before turning into Birdsall's.

"One chocolate double-dip, please," She told Jimmy. I felt tears roiling up again. I tried not to make a sound, but She knew.

"Oh, and you'd better give me one for my crybaby sister, too."

I stood silent and humiliated.

"Here," She said loudly. "I'd better hold hers, Jimmy, because she might drop it. She's always dropping everything." She held out her hand with the two nickels in it. Jimmy Birdsall took the money and gave her two cones heaped high with cool, luscious rich-brown chocolate scoops generously overflowing the crisp waffled cookie cones.

She licked all the way around the edge of the ice cream so it wouldn't drip, the way Billie had taught us. Billie always licked our cones before she'd give them to us. She had a huge red tongue that swiped away half the ice cream, and then she'd laugh because she had put one over on us. Now I watched in the mirror behind the counter as She did the same to one cone and then the other. Her tongue was small and darted like a snake's instead of scoop-shoveling as Billie's did. When she was done, the edges of the ice cream where it fit into the cone were neat and not about to drip. Not on her, anyway.

We walked out of the store. I reached out for my cone, but She said, "I'd better hold it for you till we get up the hill. You might trip or something."

"I won't," I promised. "Give it to me."

"Will you drink my milk at dinner?"

I thought of trying to swallow her milk as well as my own, and I shook my head. "I can't."

"Well, what am I supposed to do with two ice-cream cones, then? I'm not going to carry yours all the way home!"

"I don't know," I said miserably. It was hard walking up the hill, which was pretty steep. I felt weary deep down in my bones, and I wasn't even eight years old yet.

"Well, I'll give it to you anyway," she said with a sudden burst of generous spirit. "Just a present, okay? You don't have to do anything for it. I'll just hold it till we get up the hill and then you can have it, okay?"

"Okay," I agreed. I didn't care anymore. It was boring and I was hot and wanted to get home to another chapter of *Alice in Wonderland.*

Suddenly She stumbled, nearly pulling us both down. One of the cones went flying and landed pointy side up, splat in the middle of the sidewalk. We stared at it.

"Oh, golly," she exclaimed with the phoniest regret you ever heard. "Yours dropped."

I had nothing to say. When we got back to the cool of the house, Billie was in the kitchen making dinner, and Sheila told her that I had dropped my ice cream on the sidewalk. Billie looked at me, but she wasn't surprised. "Why do you have to be such a klutz?" she said with a big sigh. I didn't even bother trying to set the record straight. It was too complicated, and life was too unfair even to know where to start. The only good thing that happened was that She got a stomachache and I didn't, though I had to sit there while she blew out the gas.

My mother's voice rang in my head, growing louder and more painful as I grew: Why do you have to be such a klutz? Why do you have to be so different? Why can't you be like everyone else?

That question was so monumentally unanswerable that my head would spin and I would get dizzy and nauseous, but

she kept asking and pretty soon I started wondering if maybe
it really was my fault. Could I have been such a klutz even as
an embryo that I bumped into my sister with a passion
white-hot enough to weld us together? If so, I was beginning
to know what that passion was. I could feel it rising in me
stronger every day.

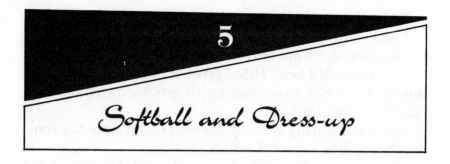

5

Softball and Dress-up

We moved into a new house every few years, just for a change of scene. My mother was restless, and curious to know what it was like to live here, there, or two blocks down the street. We had just rented the big house on Jennings when Sheila decided she wanted her own room. Other girls had rooms of their own, why couldn't she?

I remember Billie looking at her with something like awe. Our Lady of Perpetual Denial was hard put to answer that one. I like to think there must have been one little instant there, one hair's-breadth of a millisecond, when she looked at Sheila and wondered how anybody could be so dumb. Could a nine-year-old possibly not know she was fused at the midsection to another person? Hadn't she noticed? In the glory of her self-absorption, had it truly escaped her attention that there was somebody *there* all the time? Or was She so incredibly simple that she figured grown-ups could unlatch us anytime they were ready?

47

"But why can't I have my own room? Why?"

I was waiting as eagerly as She for the answer.

"Because there are only three bedrooms in this house."

That reminded her. "Helen gets her own room, and she's only the hired girl! How come Helen gets her own room and I don't? It's not fair!"

You could usually get to Billie with that it's-not-fair routine, but it didn't work this time.

"Sheila, sometimes I think you just start things to make trouble. Now, you just shut up, and you too, Sandra!"

No offense meant, and none taken. I hadn't said a word, but equal blame was not something I took personally anymore.

"Anyway, there's four bedrooms. I heard you tell Mrs. Rosen there were four bedrooms in this house. You did, Mama."

"Don't call me Mama. Sounds like the goddamn Swede farmers."

"Billie. You did, you said four bedrooms."

"That was counting my sewing room. I'm going to fix up that little room in the back with chintz curtains and put the sewing machine in there and the ironing board and—"

"You're selfish! You get two rooms and I don't get any! It's not fair!"

"Oh, for God's sake!" That was Billie's usual exit line and she started to flounce out of the room, but this time she must have been struck with the extraordinary denseness of one of her children, and she stopped halfway to the door. She turned back to us. I had been thrown to the floor and She was kicking her heels as hard as she could, one after another, on the hardwood.

"Stop that, you'll ruin the floor. Now, stop carrying on, Sheila, and I will tell you why you can't have your own room. Why you can never have your own room," she added cruelly and, I thought, unnecessarily.

My stomach lurched and I didn't want to listen anymore.

"You," she said, spacing her words like shots from a rifle, "are. a. child. Children. do. as. they. are. told. Your father is the boss in this family and I am your mother, and we tell you what you can and cannot do and I say you can't have your own room."

That was it? That was all? I looked at her in amazement.

"Your big mouth is hanging open," she snapped at me.

"Well, I know it." I shrugged. I waited for her to go on, to say something like: "You can't have your own room and you never will because YOU ARE PHYSICALLY ATTACHED TO YOUR SISTER AND THERE'S NO WAY WE CAN GET YOU APART!" But no.

"I still don't see why I can't have my own room," Sheila wailed.

Billie pulled at her marcelled bob with both hands and then stomped out of the room. My brilliant sister cried for a while, kicked at things, and then got distracted by Bubbles and Edie, who always just walked in and out of our house like it was their own.

Bubbles and Edie and She and I made a peculiar-looking quartet. Bubbles was two heads taller than anyone our age. She was too tall for any skirts her mother could buy in Sioux City, so either her bony knees stuck way out or she wore strangely cut dresses from some Omaha store that stocked tall sizes, which only came in "matron" styles. Bubbles never grew any breasts, and her behind caved in instead of out. Her eyes were bulgy and she had a lot of large teeth, which had food stuck to them until she was fourteen, then bits of lipstick clung there as well.

Edie was soft and round, with tiny little beady black eyes and an extremely small button of a chin framing a very large nose. Her features looked like they belonged to several other people. She was really funny-looking and never got any better when she got older, either, as everyone had hopefully predicted. She had black hair that curled in tight coils around her face. When we were about fifteen, Edie secretly sent away to a store on West 125th Street in New York, which even we knew was Harlem, for some hair straightener. Sheila and Bubbles and Edie locked us all in the Rosens' bathroom for four hours one Saturday afternoon while they gave her the treatment. Some of Edie's hair combed out into the sink; the rest lay like limp snakes along her scalp and forehead. She wore a bandanna to school for two weeks, then one night, as if it had been plugged into a socket, it frizzed back to her normal bride-of-Frankenstein bob. When Edie was born, her folks told everybody they started a "nose bank," and there it was on her father's dresser—a big jar that they put coins in to save up for Edie's plastic surgery. She got the job done during the summer between sophomore and junior years in Central High. I thought it made her face look very peculiar, like a Swedish meatball had been stuck in the middle of a salted herring.

Compared to them, I secretly preferred my own looks: horse face, plastic-rimmed glasses, prominent ears ("big ears are a sign of generosity," Billie would proclaim, staring at me thoughtfully, not having been asked for her opinion), tangled hair, and long, swanlike neck (dead giveaway about my true identity). Individually, my features were passable, I decided; it was only the way they were fighting each other during my growing years that was awful. I had the secret hope that someday someone might find me interesting-looking, as I did myself in the mirror. She, of course, was beautiful.

She and her friends giggled a lot and chattered all the time. They couldn't stand a moment's silence. They spent hours buying makeup at the dime store, snooping in their mothers' dressing tables, trying on clothes and talking about clothes and shopping for clothes and comparing everybody's clothes with everybody else's clothes and imagining clothes

for imaginary occasions. They gossiped and made fun of whoever wasn't there, including each other. I was sure that if I
ever had a friend, I would never talk about her behind her
back. It didn't make any sense to me to be friends with someone you didn't like and admire. I didn't like or admire anyone I had met in my life so far.

Sometimes kids made fun of us, called us names, pulled
their eyes into a slant and chanted, "Siamese! Siamese!"
Once, some boys (all wearing shirts that proclaimed they
came from IMMACULATE CONCEPTION) dared a couple of their pals
to poke us under our dresses to see the place where we were
joined. I was interested in negotiating when Tommy Moran
said he'd show us his weener in exchange, but Sheila hit him
on the side of his head with her three-ring notebook and that
was the end of that. (A couple of years later, Tommy said he
didn't care about that anymore, he'd rather see what was
inside my panties and I said the joke would be on him because girls didn't have anything there at all, but he said he
wanted a look anyway and again Sheila said no and I lost
another chance to see a penis.)

One day when we came into school, I reached inside the
desk and felt something odd. It turned out to be two dolls,
little rubber ones, the kind you could buy for a nickel apiece.
Someone had sliced off the little rounded behinds of the dolls
and glued them together. Snickers from around us let us
know that everyone in the class had seen the person who put
it there and no one would let us in on who our enemy was.

But most of the time people in town accepted us with in-
termittent self-consciousness, as any decent family tolerates
its aberrant members. We were part of the landscape, like the
cornfields on every side as far as you could see, like the silos
and grain elevators that made up our skyline, like the stink of
the stockyards on slaughtering day (Tuesdays), the First
Methodist Church spire, and the A&W root beer stand. People
found it easier to live with Siamese twins than with That Man

in the White House and his New Deal. We were odd, but so was Olaf Anderson, who owned the grocery store on Nebraska Street and always tried to get little girls who came in on errands for their mothers to slip behind the curtain with him into the back room where he kept an army cot and a Franklin stove. So was Mrs. Dodge, who lived next to the cemetery with her windows boarded up, through which she shouted obscenities at anyone walking past, and then you'd see her on the street and she'd say hello and ask for your health in the nicest way possible.

Small towns are full of freaks; people just take them for granted. There were hierarchies of freakiness: Catholics were suspect because they practiced mumbo jumbo, and the Jews were worse because they had killed Christ; Lutherans didn't think much of Presbyterians; Negroes and Indians were pretty much out of sight most of the time, living down by the river in shacks that got flooded out every year in the June rise. There was a Negro boy in our class. He was shy and as nice as he could be. He got stared at as much as we did. He was expelled from high school for accepting five dollars to play basketball over in South Sioux City, Nebraska; that made him a professional, they said, and he had taken a pledge with the rest of the varsity team to stay amateur till graduation. So he never graduated. I still wonder what happened to him.

We played with the neighborhood kids, except on the High Holidays, when they had to go to school and we had to hang around the synagogue with "our own kind." At the Christmas season we were told never to sing the words to the carols, but it was okay if we mouthed the words to pretend we were singing. That way, God would know but the kids around us wouldn't. The older we got the less we were allowed to mix with Protestants, Catholics, Negroes, Indians, farmers, or Jews who lived on the wrong side of town.

The gathering place for our neighborhood was an empty lot between the O'Briens' house and the hill where we collected old Indian arrowheads when there was nothing else to do. As soon as the mud hardened in the spring the softball season was on, and every night in spring and summer and early fall everybody who was allowed out after dinner stayed until it got too dark to see the ball. I saw Tommy Moran swing his bat, hard, at fireflies once on the way home, but I don't think he meant to kill them. He had switched from Immaculate Conception to Bryant School after his dad had a fight with the priest, and I guess I had a sort of crush on him. He had black straight hair that fell in his eyes and round red cheeks, and he was always smiling and laughing and starting things. One day he came to school with his eye black and blue and swollen shut and someone said his dad had beat him up, but Tommy never stopped laughing and making jokes.

On Saturday mornings most of the neighborhood kids would find their way to the lot after chores, and we'd play until our mothers called us home for lunch. (Then of course everyone who had a dime to spend went to the movies.)

"Hey, Sheila! Hey, Sandy! Catch this!" Corky Geoghagen spotted us coming around the corner and hurled a ball straight at us, hard. My sister flinched and ducked, but I got my feet planted fast so she didn't pull me too far over and I caught the ball with a satisfying smack and sting— barehanded, because girls couldn't get mitts for Christmas or birthdays no matter how hard they begged.

"Hey, Sandy! Good catch!" big, gentle Joey McGill hollered from back of home plate. He was almost always umpire because he was considered fair, and anyway, he couldn't hit the side of a barn with his bat if he was standing in a cow stall.

We ambled over. Corky was pitching and Dilly Pickel was up. He swung at a wild pitch and Gloria Keeley, in full catcher's regalia (her brother's), went after it. She missed and a runner took second base.

It didn't matter that the game was already in progress.

There were never enough players to make a full nine on both teams. You could come in anytime and play until your mother hollered for you.

Dilly had struck out. "What team are we on?" I asked Joey.

"Hey, Beany, you want Sandy and Sheila?" Joey called out lazily as the teams changed sides. Beany Pickens, the tallest kid in town, loped in from the outfield and nodded. He was sweaty and smelled like a grown-up.

"Sure," he said. "You can pitch the next inning."

"Which one of us?" I asked.

Sheila kicked my shin. "Me, idiot!"

I waited stubbornly for Beany to say. He just smiled and shrugged. He went over to the grass and sat down with the rest of his team, and we followed.

Now Frankie O'Brien was pitching, and she was a wonder—she could do it overhand like the boys did. Margaret Ann Garrity bunted without meaning to, and the ball rolled to a stop just short of the pitcher's mound, but Frankie and the first baseman both fumbled it and, as her excited teammates cheered her on, Margaret Ann ran safely to first base.

"Okay, Sandy, you're up," Beany said.

I didn't have a position to play; when Sheila pitched, I was an immovable shortstop who could only stand there hoping for a short pop fly to come my way. But I was the one who batted. I could have pitched as well or better than she did, except that we were both right-handed and when I swung my arm for a windup, I'd sometimes end up whacking her in the stomach and then she'd howl and refuse to play. She never appreciated sports much to begin with.

I loved batting. I know for certain that I could have been a great hitter if it hadn't been for Sheila always being in my way. She squealed, "Oh, oh, *oh, OH!*" if the ball looked like it was coming anywhere near us, and she'd dodge and try to pull me down with her, but even so, I managed to hit a lot of pitches with surprising power and a reasonable degree of accuracy.

The first pitch was inside and grazed Sheila on the arm. She screamed and yelled and Joey had to look at her arm and cluck sympathetically and Beany had to ask if she wanted out of the game and Margaret Ann came galloping in from first base to see if she could practice her first aid, which made Beany yell at her because the other team's first base-man, Dilly, ran over and tagged her out, but Margaret Ann started to cry and finally Joey McGill said it was a time-out and she was safe but not to leave first base again, and by then my sister had had enough attention and I got ready for the next pitch. There was a special rule for us: Before we could take a base, we had to be hit twice with the ball instead of only once, because it was kind of hard to avoid hitting us.

The second pitch was high and the third was low and landed hard on my instep, but I didn't make a sound or even limp as we walked to first base and Margaret Ann went to second, still sniveling about injustice when a person tried to do a charitable act.

It shames me to remember that when we played ball, we did it as one person instead of two. We needed to be part of any team so badly that we even let them put in a pinch-runner for us. I wanted to die when I'd have to stand on the sidelines after I'd hit the ball watching some pigeon-toed girl running instead of me. But everybody laughing was even harder to take, and I guess we did run funny.

Being lumped together as if we were one and the same person is the thing in all the world that makes me maddest, because we are very, very different in every way. I am *not* my sister; I'm not anything like her *at all*. The doctors can say so all they want to, but one of the few facts knowable to the human mind is that the medical profession is full of shit.

There are more things in heaven and earth than science is

willing to admit. They think what can't be proved in some lab can't exist, but there we were. And how did they respond to the evidence? By golly, Science wasn't going to be unstrung by a couple of hayseed Hebrew brats in Sioux City, Iowa, females at that. Wildly different as we are and always were, they pronounced us identical. But it must have been obvious even from the start that we weren't products of the same egg at all, couldn't possibly be. Not only do we look very different from each other, our brains and personalities are wildly inimical (if you look that up, the dictionary directs you to see "**hostile**").

In 1833, a Frenchman named Etienne Serres published a paper entitled "Theory of organic development and deformation, applied to the anatomy of Ritta Christina, and to duplicate monsters in general." Ritta and Christina were two unfortunate kiddos who only lived for five months. Serres was trying to discover, sort of holistically, on physical and metaphysical grounds, whether they were one person or two. He came up with the theory that the two bodies had somehow fused in the womb, and that was the cause of what would later become known as Siamese twins. Then holy scientists became more enlightened, poking into the egg and sperm and other places where they weren't wanted, and Serres's theory was set aside as quaint and outdated. The edict came down: Conjoined twins were the product of a single egg never quite separated all the way, the yolk splitting off to make a double. From one egg, out pops a matched set. All conjoined twins had to be of the identical variety . . . except that we are not. I will swear that all the way to my grave and beyond, if necessary.

It shouldn't be so hard to understand how two unborn siblings, having to share the same unwelcoming womb, each growing apace, would struggle and push and shove for space, for survival, and in that cramped, damp formative abyss, become horribly fused together.

It seems to me I spent all my first nine years in a rage, battling with my sibling for room in this world to stand and be myself. It wasn't her fault, of course. *She* had friends. It was pretty obvious the fault was mine, but I didn't know what to do about it except just flail out wildly and furiously.

And then I met Lulu. I had my very own friend, for a little while. It didn't last, and maybe I didn't expect it to, really. But having Lulu for my friend showed me the possibility that I might have a genuine life someday. I might be accepted someday—or even loved!—just for myself.

6

My Friend Lulu

It was the summer between fourth and fifth grades. We were swimming, sort of, at Leif Ericson Park.

The Leif Ericson Municipal Swimming Pool was round, with an underwater observation post in its center. A narrow sidewalk curved all around the pool, with grass on one side and sand on the other. You could lie in the sand and pretend you were on a beach near an ocean instead of dead center in the middle of a vast dull continent. To go in the water, you crossed the sidewalk and walked in grass, automatically brushing much of the sand off your feet. You waded in, and you could stay on the shallow side of the barrier if you wanted to, but the real swimmers glided through one of the gates to deep water. There you swam around and around, or across what we called the moat, to the concrete tower in the center. You climbed up a ladder and stood on the platform just long enough so everyone could see you had made it.

Then you walked through a smelly (chlorine, body odor, dank fetid amoebic fungus) passage and down a narrow, twisty ladder to the strangely echoing core. There were portholes all around, through which you could see people's legs as they swam. Kids' faces floated by, dipping down to leer at you with inflated cheeks and pop eyes, out-of-kilter faces all distorted by the water, made eerier by frames of floating hair.

It altered your perceptions, brought something new and bizarre to the small-town, thought-I-knew-everybody life.

Over on the far edge of the pool there was a slide for little kids, landing them in water about a foot deep. It was marvelously popular until one summer day when a piece of the tin that covered the slide became twisted in such a way that it ripped the bottom out of the bathing suits that skimmed over it. For a while, every little kid in town was running around Leif Ericson with a flap cut loose to expose its little fanny. The mothers, talking among themselves and working on their tans, took no notice until one of the little girls, joining in the laughter at the others, thought to check her own backside and ran screaming and flapping, wild with embarrassment, to her mother. The episode of the tiny bare bums ended in a general melee of mothers shrieking and leaping up to hide their kids in towels the way Adam and Eve supposedly grabbed at fig leaves the day innocence came to an end. There went a whole generation of Sioux City kids who learned one hot summer day that parts of their bodies were something to be ashamed of.

It was a hot day in July when I made my first friend. Every kid in town was at the pool. My sister and I were dabbling around in the water on the shallow side near the gate. The water came about up to where our breasts would be in another couple of years. We could just swim well enough to make it across the deep water to the center island, but the ladder was narrow and we had to climb it in a truly contorted fashion, which we didn't do if there were a lot of people around.

Our bathing suits were the kind that had little skirts, and since we didn't have a bump or lump or any kind of protrusion at all in the place where we were joined together, there was nothing to see, even in bathing suits, but we could feel eyes on us all the time. I think that was the year when Sheila didn't want to go to the pool at all because of people staring, but Billie laughed at her and said it was just silly-girl self-consciousness. She said all girls felt that way when they were nine or ten years old, and just wait till we started to get titties if we wanted to know what it really felt like to be stared at.

So there we were at Leif Ericson pool, just two more kids among all the bobbing heads and shoulders, laughing and splashing and keeping cool by staying in the water all day long. Sheila was flirting with Jerry Fein and Moose Wasserman. They were daring her to swim across the moat or something, and I was looking in the other direction, when an apparition floated by that made me smile. I couldn't remember the last time I had smiled spontaneously, so I knew right away this was something special.

It was Louise Hansen, the Lutheran minister's daughter, floating on her back, alabaster and serene, pretending (with perfect success, I thought) to be a fountain. Elegant arcs of blue water sprayed upward through the generous spaces between her teeth. The center sprays rose in a lovely curve slightly higher than those at the sides; the whole effect was a symmetrical perfection worthy of Busby Berkeley's Dancing Waters in an Esther Williams movie. This living fountain glided by, slowly, almost not moving at all, her pale arms stretched out for balance on the water, her pigtails so blond that even soaking wet they looked like corn silk tassels floating on a summer breeze. As she lay on the water effortlessly spraying thin debonair spouts, Louise was looking straight at me. It was an amazing performance. I felt immensely flattered by her attention.

As I watched, the living fountain trickled out of fuel. Languidly, Louise rolled over, still afloat, and came around again with another mouthful of water, which she again spewed in six graceful and simultaneous arcs.

"That's beautiful!" I shouted at her. She had moved a bit beyond us.

My sister craned to see what I was looking at. "I think it's disgusting" was her considered judgment—as if it should matter to me what she thought. She tried to pull me toward the gate, where some boys were hanging around, treading water and making a lot of noise. But not even the heavyweight champion of the world Joe Louis could have forced me to move an inch just then.

Louise Hansen came to life, languid still, but no longer the alabaster fountain; now she was a blue and yellow and freckled girl my age, bouncing in the water we shared, half swimming (one foot probably propelling her along, touching bottom now and then, the way I swam, too) toward me, grinning with those squarely spaced, cheery teeth. She came right up to me, smiling at *me*, paying not one whit of attention to my sister.

"Hi," Louise said easily, and I thought my answering "hi" was casual enough, if a little on the squeaky side. Then she said, "Want to know how to do that? I'll show you if you want. It's easy."

I couldn't believe my luck. "Don't you have to have—uh—certain kinds of teeth?" I asked her shyly.

"Lemme see."

I opened my mouth for her, grinning to show my own too-prominent front teeth. Louise looked worried. She was standing up in the water now, too, and we were exactly the same height. She concentrated all her attention on my grin. Next to me, my sister snickered.

61

"You could maybe do two," Louise Hansen finally decided.

"I'm cold. I want to go lie in the sand," Sheila complained loudly. I knew better; it was the last thing she wanted to do. Lying in the sand was when people stared at us the most.

"Jump up and down, like this," Louise told her, showing how by scrunching down until her shoulders were under the water, then jumping up (splashing without meaning to), and then quickly scooting down again. "Makes you feel all warm again, honest," she told Sheila in what I thought was a real friendly way.

"Come on, Sandy," my sister said, pulling me away toward the gate, where the boys were all swimming and diving and showing off. But I couldn't be budged.

"Want to see what else I can do?" Louise Hansen asked, laughing out of pure high spirits.

"Sure," I said.

"Come on," Sheila insisted, yanking at me.

"No." I dug in and stood there, arms folded for leverage, waist-deep in the water, tougher than Sheila when I wanted to be, which was now. She gave up abruptly and crossed her arms, too, which was supposed to be a red danger signal, but I ignored her. That suited me just fine. Louise was *my* friend.

But what was this? Suddenly, I was looking at the most amazing sight: ten toes waggling just above the water, painted with sophisticated, go-to-hell daring *blue* nail polish! I was in love. When she came up for air, she was laughing. The sun caught droplets of clear blue water on her pale eyelashes and her cheeks were flushed from the exertion.

"I could show you how to do that," she said. "It's easy."

"We could scare people, just walk around on our hands in the water so all they could see would be our funny feet," I joined in, ecstatic at the fantasy. I would have given anything to be able to do it. If Sheila didn't want to cooperate by holding her breath and waggling her toes, she could drown.

"Sure! I got some more blue polish. If you want to come

to my house, I could paint your toes like mine." She dipped
down in the water so only her head was showing. The sun
had gone past the diving tower. I would have warmed myself
by dipping into the water, too, but She was still standing
there having a pout.

"When could I come?" I asked Louise.

"Oh . . . how about Saturday?"

"Don't you go to the movies on Saturdays?"

"Yeah, but after. Nobody's around at my house on Saturdays. My mother goes to the Ladies' Guild, and my sisters
both work at Sears and my brothers work too, and my dad is
holed up in his study with the door locked, working on his
sermon."

"His sermon!" I was impressed. What would it be like
having a father who told the whole community how to behave? The thought was staggering. My father was hardly
ever home, but when he was, we listened to him. Imagine
having a father who was a Reverend who worked in the
house right where you actually lived all the time—and his
whole job was morals! I looked at Louise with new respect;
painting her toenails blue and making friends with me was
not mere bravado, it was more like a full-scale revolution.
She was some kind of heroine.

"Okay, I'll meet you at the movies and go home with you
Saturday. If I can." This was the most exciting thing that
had ever happened to me.

"Okay," she said. She laughed again and flipped herself
over so that all I had to say so long to were her bright blue
toes. Sheila pulled me away and we sort of dog-paddled, sort
of sidestroked in the tentative swimming style we were perfecting. She didn't say anything, but I could tell she was
furious. More than that, she was determined not to be
dragged to any minister's house, ever. I knew that and was
already thinking of ways to bribe her.

Of all Lulu's dazzling qualities, the most extraordinary
was her ability to ignore my sister. Nothing to it, she said,

living in the shitty parsonage with her folks around all the time and all the goddamn brothers and sisters she had, not to mention the ghosts of all the ministers and their crappy families still haunting the creepy old place, and the moldering dead bodies in the graveyard of the stinky church right next door, a person learned to ignore other presences.

Here are some of Louise Hansen's wonderful qualities:

1. She knew a lot of swear words and how to use them.

2. She was not afraid of anything.

3. Her house was huge and dark and mysterious, and smelled more like furniture polish than pot roast.

4. She didn't hesitate to prowl through her sisters' and brothers' dresser drawers, and she explained to me what the Trojans we found there (in both!) were and exactly how they were used. In this way I learned how babies were conceived. I tried to discuss it with my sister, but she said I was stupid to believe Louise Hansen, who made up terrible things just to get attention, the proof being could I possibly imagine Billie and Daddy doing that, and of course I could not. But even so, I had a strong hunch Louise Hansen knew exactly what she was talking about.

5. My parents didn't like my associating with her.

6. Sheila was just fascinated enough by Lulu's outlandishness not ever to tell on us. She didn't take any part in our adventures, except of course by just being there, and for that I loved her. Sheila, I'm talking about. Can you beat it?

One afternoon Lulu told me she had heard somewhere that there are Jewish men who kidnap little gentile girls (particularly Lutherans) and drink their blood. She said they wear black suits and black hats and have strings hanging out of their jackets, which are used to tie up the little Lutheran girls when they catch them. They have long beards and funny haircuts. Since I was Jewish, maybe I could tell her whether that was true or not.

I was quick to announce with some authority that I had

seen men looking exactly as she described when we visited relatives in Minneapolis. But I hadn't heard about the other thing—not being in danger myself, I supposed no one would have bothered to tell me about it. But there were men who looked like that, and I had no better answer for the strings and the haircuts and the sinister reasons behind the black suits they wore. I'd ask my mother about the kidnapping and drinking blood part.

"Billie will kill you if you ask her that," She said in her most irritating voice of the One Who Knows All. I figured she was jealous of my having such an interesting friend. Why on earth would my mother get angry over a simple question of fact?

Of course, my sister was right. Billie turned livid and shouted at me. (Sometimes when I felt really sorry for myself, I thought that Billie would kill me if it didn't mean that She would die, too.) What she said was, "Don't you ever, ever play with her again!"

Totally at sea, I asked why not.

"Never mind," my mother warned me.

Later, She said to me, rather gently, "See?"

I was crying. I had just lost my best friend, my only friend, and for no reason I could guess. I cried so long and so hard at the injustice of this world that I got a terrible headache. From my mother's response, I could only deduce that Lulu's information must be right. But I never got the chance to tell her.

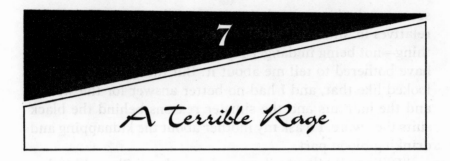

7

A Terrible Rage

Lulu came up to me the next morning with her big friendly gap-tooth grin and I was so glad to see her for a minute I thought everything was all right. But as soon as she got into line with us at the G I R L S door, my sister jerked us around so our backs were to Lulu. She said, much louder than necessary, "We're not allowed to talk to you anymore."

"Huh?" Lulu snorted. "Hey Sandy, what'd she say that for? Hey, Sandy?"

I kicked Sheila's leg hard with the heel of my shoe, and as soon as she got off balance, I turned back around. We were getting a lot of attention from everybody in line now, so She turned quietly, just muttering under her breath.

Lulu's smile was quizzical. "What the hell's the matter with her? She looks like she's got a bug up her ass!" My friend laughed and punched my arm so I'd laugh, too, and I did think it was funny, but just then my heart was flopping over inside my chest and I couldn't even smile.

"My mother says I can't play with you anymore," I whispered. Stupid tears welled up and spilled over before I could help myself. That made Lulu self-conscious, too. Everybody was really staring now.

"I don't care," she snapped with a great show of meaning it. "Who the hell cares, anyhoo? You're nothing but a goddamn circus freak, in case you haven't noticed. Everybody laughs at you, don't you even know that? Who wants to be your friend, not me!" And she ran as fast as she could out across the playground to the sidewalk and around the corner of the school building. I knew she'd keep on running until she rounded the whole block, past our school and Immaculate Conception and the church and the other side of our playground and the B O Y S door, and come up on our line way at the end. I just hoped it wouldn't make her tardy.

I was desperate to talk with her alone. Yeah, sure, alone, ho ho. There was no way I could ever explain to Louise Hansen how much I loved her, how agonizingly unfair life was. My sister was telling all the girls who were now crowding around us that Louise Hansen was a nasty girl and her father ought to wash her mouth out with soap. "My mother won't let us even talk to her anymore, that's what we think of dirty mouths like her," she said. She linked arms with Bubbles on one side and Edie on the other, and when the door opened they marched into the school building like the Three Musketeers, leaving me to sidle along, half behind them and half in the way.

By the time we went out for morning recess, I was seething like the hot lava we had seen in a newsreel about a volcano in Mexico that started on a farmer's field and grew into a major tourist attraction that destroyed a whole town. I hadn't heard anything the teacher said in the classroom, hadn't been able to read my books or listen to the other kids reciting. I had just sat there with fury blazing out of control inside me, fighting back hot tears. I could hardly bear to look over at Lulu, and of course she never looked at me, not once.

67

At recess, She wanted to go on the teeter-totter with Bubbles and Edie on the other end and I didn't care what I did so I went along, but every time our side of the plank came down onto the ground I let it bang, hard, rather than putting down my feet to ease the bump. She couldn't do it all by herself and I just wouldn't do diddely-poop for her or anyone else in this mean and stupid town. We got bumped and bounced and She got madder and madder. I didn't care. It hurt me too, but I didn't care.

"Ouch, my tailbone!" she yelped after one really hard crack against the dirt. (Edie and Bubbles, seeing how uncooperative I was, were conspiring up at their end of the board to let us down as hard as possible. My friend Lulu never would have done such a thing. If she had seen me in that kind of trouble—or any other kind—Lulu would have wanted to help me, not make it worse.)

"Fuck your tailbone," I muttered, between the hard jounces my own was taking.

She gasped. "You learned to talk that way from your dirty-mouth girlfriend. You sound just like her."

Good.

When the bell rang for the end of recess, She and I were on the ground with Bubbles and Edie in the air. I slid off the end of the board, pulling my goddamn sister with me, so that the two ninnies at the other end went crashing down really hard. Everybody knew that wasn't fair—you were supposed to stop halfway down and move off carefully with one foot on the ground, all at the same time so nobody got hurt. But I was glad to hear Bubbles yelping with pain. I was so unhappy and angry that I wanted the whole damn world to fracture its coccyx.

Bubbles was crying when we went inside, so Edie and Sheila told Miss Grainger that I had deliberately jumped off the teeter-totter because I wanted to hurt them. I got punished with a lecture (so embarrassing; you had to stand up in front of the class while she talked about what you did and why nobody should do it and you didn't know where to look; the worst thing you could do was look at anybody in the class, because they'd try to make you laugh and that only led to more punishment), and all the time it was going on, Miss Grainger kept saying that Sheila was not to blame in the least and it was unfortunate that she had to share the punishment, but for everybody not to think she was to blame one whit, because it was Sandra who had misbehaved and to whom this lecture was addressed. All the while it was going on, I couldn't focus my eyes; I saw only my deep crimson rage, spreading and bleeding all over everything. My whole life was a nightmare, and Lulu was right: I was a freak, FREAK, *FREEEEEAAK!*—the whimsy of a malevolent God, a grotesque and disgusting miscreation. I had no right to live; well, that was okay, because who wanted to?

If it weren't for my sister and the monstrous way we were joined, I could have kept Lulu for my friend. I would have sneaked off to see her, lied to my mother, found ways to be on my own the way Lulu did. I would have found lots of friends. Everyone would beg to be my friend because I was so witty and smart and so much nicer than my sister or anyone.

But all the daydreams and imaginings added up to more bottled-up anger, that was all. The feelings couldn't be expressed; the frustration was as much a part of me as Sheila was. I could only cry. I could only stand and be lectured and see everything in blood-red and never, never be able to change anything.

I wouldn't talk on the way home for lunch and I didn't say hello to Helen when we walked into the kitchen. We washed up and sat down at the kitchen table for chicken noodle soup and peanut butter sandwiches. Helen tried to cajole me into talking or smiling, but I was so deep in my own dark thoughts she was like a flyspeck in the distance.

"Well, you sure are the silent one today. Who do you think you are, Charlie Chaplin?"

I heard her, but I didn't care. Sheila poked me. My hand

darted out to grab her fingers and I bent them backward until she yelped. Helen had to leap up from the table and come around to pry my grip loose.

"Sandy! Hey, what's gotten into you, kiddo?" Helen took my chin in her hand and looked me in the eyes, but I twisted out of her grip. Her hand smelled like dishwater, and I hated her, too.

"She's mad because I said her dumb friend Louise Hansen was a dirty-mouth. It's true, too. You should have heard the things she said right in front of everybody at school. And then Sandy used a bad word, too. The worst word there is!" And then She told Helen her version of that morning's events, exaggerated of course and from a point of view you wouldn't recognize even if you'd been there.

"I was so mortified my face turned red and Miss Grainger thought I was going to faint and she kept saying over and over to me and to everyone that I hadn't done anything, in fact I was the best student she'd ever had—well, that's what she meant—and she said I was a really good person and it was too bad I had to be punished because my sister was so bad all the time."

"She didn't say anything like that," I muttered.

"Yes she did! Anyone will tell you. Oh, I was so embarrassed, I wanted to sink through the floor!"

"I wish you had."

"Come on, that's enough of that. Finish your sandwiches. You haven't even tasted your soup! Want me to warm it up for you? Sandy, you've got to eat your lunch, now. This isn't funny."

"I don't want any shitty lunch," I said clearly.

"Oh! Did you hear that?" She was titillated and couldn't help a giggle slipping out.

"Now, hush up, the both of you." Helen sat down in her place again and took a healthy bite out of her own peanut butter sandwich.

70

"Come on," Sheila groaned lugubriously, taking up her burden (me) again. "We'd better get back to school."

"I'm not going," I said.

"Are you sick?" Helen asked. She looked at me critically, checking for signs of fever or spots. "You feel okay, hon? Tell Helen."

"There's nothing wrong with her, but my back really hurts from what she did—"

"Hush up, Sheila. Okay, Sandy, so you got angry and you did something naughty and you got punished, but it's all over now. So how about eating your sandwich and forget all about it, what do you say?" Helen was smiling at me and ignoring She and normally that would have cheered me up, but now all I could think of was hate. I hated God and everything He'd ever made. My pulse was racing and my heart was pounding with the inchoate burden there weren't any words for.

"Come on, we're going to be late," Sheila said irritably.

My heart pounded faster. "Bathroom," I muttered. Sheila heaved a loud sigh and then said, prissily, "May we please be excused?" as we stood up.

"Sure," Helen said. "You okay, Sandy?"

I didn't answer. We went on upstairs and I peed and then She peed and then I started to cry hard, too hard to stop easily, and she said, "Oh God! Not again!" and stamped her foot.

I opened the medicine cabinet and took out Daddy's straight razor and before She had pulled up her panties and smoothed down her skirt I started slashing away at the place where we were joined. I didn't feel any pain, I didn't feel anything but my old rage, going purple now, blending with the blood that poured through our undershirts and skirts and blouses and down our legs into our socks.

Sheila screamed in terror and then she started yelling for Helen. She dragged us to the bathroom door and yanked it open. I just kept slashing and slashing. It was hard to reach just the right place, especially with She jumping all around and screaming and trying to grab my hand. The razor cut through our clothes, drew across Sheila's stomach, leaving a long smooth line that looked like a white-penciled curve line at first. In what seemed slow motion, the mark on her waist and belly and hip widened into a red-crayon slash, and then it started to gush. I cut myself too, hacking away at the skin and gristle where we were joined, but I couldn't get us apart. Helen came running up the stairs. She and my sister were both screaming. Helen grabbed the razor away from me, and suddenly she was all spurted with blood, too. Maybe I was screaming, too, I don't remember for certain.

Helen wrapped us in a lot of towels and then called Dr. Morton. He was home for lunch and lived about three blocks away, so he got there pretty fast. He gave us injections and pretty soon we both stopped crying and fell asleep.

When I woke up, there were bandages all around my hip and my abdomen and my arms. I felt stiff and very peculiar. She was still sleeping, and the last thing I wanted to do was wake her up. We were wound together with ropes of gauze. My anger was gone; I just felt weak and very tired. We were in our own bed and the clock said it was a few minutes after six. The shade was pulled down. Half-light filled the room. I figured we had missed a whole afternoon of school, and I wondered if we would get any dinner or not. I was panicky with anticipation of what Billie and Daddy would do and say. They would be really, really mad at me. I couldn't imagine any punishment that would be bad enough for what I had done. I would have to listen to Billie crying and saying, "How can you do this to me?" I lay there in bed thinking how I had ruined my mother's life, and Sheila's, by being born.

It crossed my mind that maybe if I could hold my breath and not move a muscle or an eyelash, I could make time stand still and thus postpone my retribution. Maybe I would be lucky enough to die. The room was growing lighter—so it was morning, not evening, and a whole night had passed. There was no chance that maybe they hadn't heard about it yet, no chance that I could think of a way to keep them from ever finding out. I was in for it.

Sheila stirred and moaned in her sleep. Then she woke up whimpering. I didn't say anything. Nobody else heard her, so she whimpered louder and finally she was whooping and yelping like a Billy Sunday revival. I just lay there fearing what was going to happen to me now. The door to our room opened. Daddy stood there tying his robe around his middle.

"Good morning, girls," he said. Sheila cried louder, and he came over to the bed and stood over her and said, "Now, now," and she burbled down to a low self-pitying roar. "How about some breakfast? I'll bet you're both pretty hungry!" he said, which was as close as anyone ever came to noting that we had missed our dinner. Sheila just bawled louder.

"Ssh, you don't want to wake your mother, do you?" Daddy said.

"I hurt. Look what she did to me!" Sheila moaned. "I've got bandages all over! I hurt!"

"Yes, yes, well . . ." Daddy muttered. He turned to leave our room. "Let's not wake your mother. She didn't sleep well at all."

My fault.

"Sandy tried to kill me!" She wailed.

Daddy turned at the door and looked right at me. He didn't have hate or anger or pity or anything in his look that I could read. Just my ordinary, everyday usual daddy.

"You can sleep a little longer if you want to," he said. "It's early yet. Just come down when you hear Helen in the kitchen. And don't wake your mother."

Sheila stopped bawling when he shut the door.

"I'm never going to talk to you again as long as I live," she announced firmly. I wish.

I started to sit up, but She groaned and pulled back, so I sank down and waited till she was ready. The cuts were starting to smart terribly, but my fear was worse.

We did get up, finally, and dressed, covering most of the bandages with pleated skirts and long-sleeved sweaters (the clothes we had on the day before had vanished and never surfaced again), and we ate a very hearty breakfast and we went to school as if nothing had happened. We had a note from Daddy for our teacher. It said, "Please excuse the absence from school yesterday afternoon of my daughters, but they were not feeling well. Henry Lazarus." We gave it to Miss Grainger and she didn't say anything and none of the kids asked us what had happened. No one at home ever said a single word about it. Dr. Morton came around a day or two later to change the bandages, and then a week after that Billie took us down to his office so he could take out the stitches, but he never said anything except, "Healing nicely."

Everyone was pretending it had never happened! Except when we were alone—then Sheila bitched about how much it hurt her and how crazy I was. But no one else ever spoke of what I had done. Helen had to give us sponge baths and change the bandages every night for a long time, but she didn't say anything, even when Sheila tried to get her to. She'd just change the subject.

I missed Lulu something awful and every once in a while an unexpected, savage anger would flame up again, making me clench my fists and break out in sweat—and then I'd feel ashamed because I wasn't supposed to think about that. I had acted very wrong, and now I was the only one who remembered that anything had happened at all.

Hey, was I crazy for remembering something that never happened? It was an onerous riddle. When you're ten years old, it is not a possibility that you're the only sane person in your family. I put my mind to other things, and eventually the reality faded for me, too. We had scars, but after a while even I sort of forgot how we got them.

It was a night not very long after that when She and I were awakened by the horrifying sound of our mother gasping for breath. It was loud enough to penetrate the wall between Their room and ours, loud enough to resound through the years until even now I can hear it sometimes when I'm in my old room, waiting to fall asleep.

We sat up and listened in the darkness. Sheila started to keen with low moaning yips of fear, and I tried to shush her so we could figure out what was happening.

Then there were footsteps, running, in the upstairs hall, past our room, to the bathroom and then back, running, *Daddy* running? That in itself was deeply unsettling—Daddy didn't run. Grown-ups didn't run unless there was a fire or they were chasing robbers. If She and I could have turned to each other for comfort, I think that was one time when we might have.

We could see lights on through the crack under our door. "What time is it?" She whispered. She was shaking all over, and I guess I was, too.

I looked at the radium dial of the Baby Ben. "Twenty minutes after three." My whisper was trembly, too.

I had known, of course, that such an hour existed, but only when we were asleep. To be awake at that hour was mysterious and spooky.

"Listen!" She said sharply. Billie was moaning loudly, thrusting out words between the terrifying gasps. She was saying, "Help me . . . help me . . . oh . . . God . . . I'm dy . . . . . . ing!" Then she would gasp again, a long, drawn-out vocalizing on the inhale, gulping air and lapsing again into that horrific cry for help.

She and I got up, put on our slippers and bathrobes. I opened the door a crack and we looked out into the hall, squinting against the light. I couldn't see anything, but we could hear Daddy's voice now, a frantic counterpoint to Billie's rising pitch, although we couldn't make out what he was saying.

75

As distant as the Illinois-Central at first, then louder and more ominous, we heard a siren coming toward us through the middle of the night. People all over town must have been awakened by it, and when it came to our street, it was unbearably shrill and accusing. It stopped right in front of our house, and then its shriek died down to a sigh and was finally silent except for the echo that never did stop.

Daddy flew down the stairs and threw open the front door. She and I crept out into the hall to watch. Two men ran up our stairs, with Daddy right behind them; they all rushed by without seeing us and went into our parents' room.

"Come on." She tugged at me and I let her lead me, because I was weak with fear. We tiptoed down the stairs and stepped inside the dining room, which was just off the front hallway. We went over to the window and I pulled back the drapes a little bit to peek into the alien dark. The ambulance had a red light flashing on top of it. It said ST. JOSEPH HOSPITAL on the side, with a big red cross. I was mortified. Anyone in the whole world could look out their windows and see an ambulance parked right in front of our house, positive proof that we were not perfect. Something was wrong with us.

And then they were coming down the stairs. We stood in the shadows just beyond the hall light. We watched the two strangers coming out of my mother's room, carrying her on a flat stretcher. Daddy was hovering anxiously behind, unable to do anything to help. The men started down the steps, the one in front holding the stretcher high and the one in back stooping to hold it low, so as not to tilt Billie. She was moaning loudly and groaning and gasping and wheezing; clearly, she was dying. They didn't let kids visit in hospitals, so I knew this was the last time I would ever see her. Tears poured down my face and my nose ran. I didn't have a hanky so I was sniffing a lot and She got so disgusted she lent me hers, which was already soaked with tears and snot.

As they neared the bottom of the stairway, I could see

that Billie was tied to the stretcher with a wide band of sheet across her chest. It reminded me of some pictures in her album where she had her breasts all flattened with what she told us was a bandeau. Sometimes we saw Billie's breasts, when she was getting dressed—they hung flat and lifeless, not the way breasts were supposed to look. Sometimes she told us they were that way because of the bandeaux she wore as a teenager, but sometimes she told us it was mother love that made her flat and saggy, because it was so hard for her to feed us when we were babies. It made me swear I'd never feed a baby that repulsive way. I never wanted to have breasts at all if they were going to turn out like that.

As the stretcher men carried her past us, Billie turned her head to look at us. Her eyes were huge and swollen and red and she opened them very wide. On the inhale, she gasped, "It's . . . your . . . fault . . ." and then they carried her away.

My fault. She had been looking directly at me.

I had killed my mother. Helen, in a hand-me-down bathrobe our generous Billie had given her, led us gently back upstairs and tucked us into bed. My sister and I both sobbed desperately, but She fell asleep after a while, her conscience innocent and clean. I lay awake with tears soaking my pillow and running down my neck until it was daylight and time to get up and get dressed for school.

I knew the headache was only a dab of what I really deserved, and anyway I hated to take aspirin, so I didn't tell anyone about it and just let it ache all day. Every once in a while I cried, though, unable to help myself. A couple of kids pointed at me and giggled and She was ready to kill me for shame. Crying in school was a major embarrassment, almost as bad as asking to be excused to go to the bathroom. If the teacher noticed my distress, she pretended not to, I suppose out of kindness.

Billie didn't die. She recovered and came home. Helen packed for her, and she went to Duluth, Minnesota, where there is no ragweed or pollen. I knew that in what she and we all believed were her last moments, my mother had spoken the truth as it is only given to the dying to know and that pollen and ragweed had nothing to do with her agony, although she did feel better in Duluth and from that time on she always left home just before our birthday and spent the rest of August and all of September away, until the first frost or the High Holidays, whichever came first.

8

The Curse

Every now and then, some big-time doctor from New York or Europe would call our folks with a hot new idea on how maybe they could chop us apart after all. My dad didn't want us to miss too much school with a long trip, and anyway, he didn't trust anybody in Europe to be nice to Jews, so he'd say okay if they'd do it locally, and off we'd be hauled to the State University at Iowa City or the Mayo Clinic in Rochester.

For days or sometimes weeks, they'd do anything they wanted with us; vampires taking blood, poking around to see how many holes we had, commenting on our very personal innards and bumps and scars, checking our reflexes with hammers, jabbing us with needles, and demanding samples of everything that moved. Surgeons salivated at the prospect of sinking their knives into us; a thousand doctors asked a million questions, and psychologists made us play with stupid puzzles and games while we weren't supposed to know they were watching through a secret peephole or something. (I thought the whole thing was rather a hoot as long as they weren't actually hurting us, but She was scared. If the authorities didn't know what we were, *what were we?* She needed grown-ups who knew everything.)

There were neurologists and clinicians and famous men with accents, men with beards and men with instruments I swear they kept in the Frigidaire, Ph.D. candidates and blood specialists and biologists and chemists and skin grafters and liver-pudlians, smiling men and frowning men, and a man who's still got my teethmarks on his hand. They all wore white coats; they all had rubber gloves and spatulas and needles and probes and knives and bottles and syringes. Some of them had mustaches, some of them put on phony smiles and talked to us in phony voices.

But the men did not seem to me so powerful and so evil as the women: the nurses—authoritarian, sadistic, brutal, unfeeling stiff-starched harpies who still give me nightmares all these years later. They didn't come and go like the men did; they stayed for eight hours at a time and did things to us—tying us to the sides of a bed, forcing us to eat lumpy slops, threatening to hurt us if we didn't quiet down. How they love vulnerable people, sick people, and children: what satisfactions they get from torture. The word *nurse* makes me tremble.

Rochester was a very strange city. There were underground tunnels between the hospitals and the hotels, always full of sick and deformed people going back and forth; it was like a carnival midway, with most of the attractions on wheels. People propelled themselves or got pushed in chairs, beds, little red wagons, sledges, stretchers, gurneys, and regular hospital beds, and once we saw an elderly man with a neat white beard and no legs being pulled in a dogcart by a Saint Bernard. I never minded Rochester itself—I kind of liked how weird it was—but hold the Mayo! It always ended in disappointment.

When we were eleven, some surgeons in California managed to separate three-year-old twins who were conjoined much the way we were. It was the first successful operation of its kind. We got excused from school and Daddy drove us to Omaha, where Billie and She and I got on a train to San Francisco. We slept in "roomettes" that were wickedly small. Billie had one all to herself and kept complaining that she could hardly turn around in it.

In San Francisco, two doctors in plaid jackets met us at the station and took us to a big stone hospital on top of a very steep hill. All the way in the car they pointed out the sights of San Francisco and smiled a lot, so we would trust them. The doctor in the front rode half turned around looking at us, with his arm over the back of the seat. My blood started pounding because She was getting all worked up about something. She was wiggling around and saying oooo how exciting it was to be there. I couldn't figure out what was going through her pea brain. Did she really think they were going to be able to separate us? Suddenly, I felt frightened and kind of sick to my stomach.

As soon as we were alone in a hospital room, She said that the handsome doctor was obviously crazy about her; did I see the way he couldn't take his eyes off her? She was a great believer in love at first sight, the proof being that she had fallen in love with him, too. His name was Richard Morganstern. She was dying to know if he was married, so I asked him. She thought it was rude and embarrassing, but believe me, at the time he was doing things to us that were much ruder and much more embarrassing.

"Dr. Frankenstein?" said I, all innocence.

"Morganstern," he corrected me gently, all the while probing my personal parts with an icy fork. "Yes, dear?"

"We were wondering if you were married." Behind my

81

glasses I was batting my big brown eyes, but he wasn't interested in that part of my anatomy.

"Sandy!" Sheila said, pretending to be shocked.

Frankenstein gave a little short laugh the way people do just to be polite, and he said, "I don't mind answering any questions you girls have. Why, we're friends, aren't we? Yes, Sandy, I have a lovely wife and three little girls and a boy. All a little younger than you. Hold your arm up high, that's right."

He must have been way over thirty, but that didn't deter my sister. Later, She said (and worse, believed) that it was only loyalty to his family, who didn't understand him, that kept him from telling her of his undying true love, and from asking her to marry him as soon as she got old enough. How would you like to be physically attached for your whole life to someone that stupid?

Well of course the Big Op wasn't going to work this time, either. She and Billie both cried (but I didn't) when, after four days of excruciating and humiliating tests, they told us that the three-year-olds had died, so they wouldn't chance the operation with us after all; just wait, though, in a few more years they might have it perfected. We had been hearing that all our lives. It seemed we were growing just a couple of paces ahead of medical breakthroughs. By the time they really did perfect the operation (and they didn't have a whole hell of a lot of samples to practice on), they would tell us we were too old to risk it. Naturally. I could have predicted that when we were still in our double wicker baby buggy. Even if they had perfected the "procedure" while we were still young and supple enough to survive it—and figured out how to get the blood to circulate in two systems instead of tear-assing around both our bodies through shared veins and jumbled arteries—could we have lucked out in finding two cadavers at the same time with healthy livers in the same blood type? God is very stingy with livers.

We were so frustrated and depressed by the San Francisco letdown that all three of us stopped speaking to each other. Billie cried all the way home and wouldn't even perk up in the dining car, which she usually loved. People walked back and forth through our car just to stare at us—and why not? There we were, the Siamese Jews, the Odd Sisters, in person and in public, hurryhurryhurry, come and look, see this never-ending fascination, this monstrous hilarity, this sight of God's work gone wrong, put here on this earth just to make you quit complaining about your own misfortunes. While one half of this mysterious and outlandish curiosity bawls her head off in a never-ending try for her mother's sympathy, see how the other stares out the window at the fields and railroad platforms trying to pretend she is traveling all alone to a romantic destination. Ah, and don't miss the sideshow, right across the aisle in a cage of her own: the brave, tragic mother, a slightly fading, slightly touched up, still-beautiful peppy lady weeping loudly into a soaked handkerchief, sobs escaping pitifully every time someone walks by.

There was never anything I could think of to say that would make my mother feel better. Anyway, I was mad at her for a long time that year. It was because she knew something she would only hint at, driving me crazy with anxiety and fear. She had called She and me into her sewing room, where she sat in front of the machine pumping with her feet and never looking up from the slacks she was ramming under the needle. She was sewing name tags on everything we owned because we were going to go to camp that summer. We came in and stood there watching for a minute and then she said, "Well, I want to tell you something. Uh. Well, something's going to happen to you, but don't be scared. Helen or I will show you what to do."

Something was going to *happen* to us? Something too terrible to describe? "What? What's going to happen? What

83

do you mean? What do you mean, don't be scared? Scared of what? What's going to happen to us?" We were both thrown into total panic.

Elaborately casual, still not looking at us as she said, "Oh, something to do with . . . becoming a . . . a woman. You'll see. When it happens. No point in worrying you too much beforehand." The needle stabbed madly up and down in a relentless rhythm as Billie's feet propelled the treadle faster than the eye could follow. Zip zip zip around the corners and the name was on. She bent her head down to the needle and bit the threads off with her sharp little teeth.

"What do you mean, becoming a . . . a . . . what do you mean?" She asked, for once as awkward as I.

"Never mind, you'll see. Go on, now, I'm busy. Can't you see I'm busy? I'm not sewing all these goddamn name tags on for fun, you know."

She never looked at us once and that was all she would say. Her lips were pursed up tight. We ran to Helen.

"Billie says something's going to happen to us and you'll show us what to do. What is it, Helen? Show us now. What's going to happen? What's it got to do with being a woman, Helen?"

"Well, it's your mama's place to tell you that."

"She won't tell us. She said you would." In the interest of human knowledge, Helen, a little white lie.

Helen went to her dresser, took out a box of Kotex, showed it quickly, and slipped it back behind her underwear. "This," she said.

We had seen that before. We had seen the Garritys' dog take a bloody Kotex out of the garbage can and run with it, throwing it high in the air and catching it and worrying it with his head tossing back and forth so the gauzy ends fluttered this way and that in the wind. How had it gotten bloody? Maybe someone had been cut and used it for a bandage. What did this have to do with Billie's terrible mystery?

"Well, see, you'll get sick and bleed every once in a while," our farm girl explained. "It's called the curse."

Oh. For the next six or eight months we ran to the bathroom every chance we got to see whether we were bleeding. We kept checking our skirts for signs of blood. The worst thing I could imagine was getting up to recite in school and having everyone roar with laughter because the back of my skirt was soaked in blood. It would strike without warning; it was not called the curse for nothing.

Bubbles got it. She didn't tell us, but her mother told Billie, who told us. "Bubbles became a woman yesterday," was how she put it. Huh? That made no sense at all. Bubbles was exactly the same on Thursday as she had been on Wednesday. But I sneaked a look at her in study hall and I saw that she had her hand in her lap and was sort of patting herself there. Kotex, I realized brilliantly. You put those thick pads there to catch the blood. I shared this insight with my sister as soon as we were alone. She thought about it, nodded, and then told me that she had known that all along and I was really slow to take so long to figure it out.

"Maybe you can ask Bubbles about it," I suggested hopefully. That's what friends were for, I figured.

"Are you crazy? I wouldn't ask her about something so personal! You must be crazy. No wonder you don't have any friends of your own!"

Billie packed all our shorts and blouses and socks and underwear and a box of Kotex for each of us in our camp trunks, along with two little packages holding complicated-looking elastic belts with safety pins hanging down from them. Billie said the counselors would show us how they worked if the need arose. I couldn't even imagine talking to someone I hardly knew about a thing like that.

At the bus station Billie said she envied us, getting out of the hot city. I cried and begged not to be sent away, but she said I was ungrateful. I wasn't the only one on the bus crying, but the woman in charge of the trip made us play games, tell each other our names, and pretty soon there we were, miraculously transformed into happy, carefree campers singing songs of joy and nature.

To the ever-popular tune of "On, Wisconsin":

We're the girls of Council Camp
Way up on the Saint Croix,
The finest camp in all the land
For every Jewish girl and boy.
We laugh, we work, we sing, we play
Through all the livelong day,
Surely it's the finest camp in every way!
(Without a doubt!)

Council Camp was named for its sponsor, the National Council of Jewish Women. The St. Croix River is way up in northern Minnesota. Boys and girls do not attend at the same time. *Surely* is pronounced "Shirley."

"Oh God! Look at them! They're stuck to each other. Oh God! It makes me sick to my stomach!"

"If my mother knew there were freaks at this camp, she never would have made me come."

"Does it hurt?"

"Can I see it?"

"How do you go to the bathroom?"

"If I was joined to my sister that way, I'd kill myself."

"Oh, they love each other. They're so close, they never go anywhere without each other! Har, har, har!"

"Here come the monsters! Run, everybody!"

The cook came out from the kitchen to stand with her hands on her grossly larded hips and just stare at us until the camp director made her go back inside.

We had a special bed. Everyone else had narrow cots. There were six girls in a cabin.

86

"I guess you girls won't be able to ride horseback, will you?" (This from our teenage counselor, trying to be straight-forward and, I guess, kind.)

"Not unless you've got Siamese horses," I said, to be rewarded with a quickly stifled giggle and momentary approval.

My sister just smiled and smiled. She answered all the questions ingenuously. I couldn't believe they didn't see right through her treacly Rebecca-of-Sunnybrook-Farm act: "Oh, it's not so bad, except sometimes, but I only tell my *friends* what it's really like . . . do you want to be my friend? You don't have to pay any attention to her. . . . No, it doesn't hurt, except sometimes. . . . I'll show you, maybe, if we get to be really good friends. We could go riding if we wanted to, but you see, I'm allergic to horses. . . . What a pretty blouse you're wearing . . . my best friend at home, Bubbles, has a blouse about that color, but not nearly so pretty . . ." And soon enough even the snobbier girls found themselves drawn into Sheila's web.

The curse hung over me all that summer and ruined any chance of a good time. I didn't dare go too far from the latrine, where I kept on checking for blood every half hour, oftener if Sheila would let me. I absolutely refused to go on an overnight hike, which was supposed to be the high point of the summer. My sister was so mad at me for that she screamed and had a tantrum right in front of the whole camp, but she could turn herself blue and dry up and be a dead appendage I'd have to carry around for the rest of my life if she wanted to—there was still no way I was going on any goddamn overnight hike and sleep in the woods with no privacy and no plumbing. All the counselors tried to make me go, but I held out against bribery, threats, cajoling, scolding, public humiliation, private heart-to-heart chats, and even being called a bad sport. I wouldn't budge.

I cried at night and during rest hour and sometimes in the

middle of archery or crafts or lunch or campfire sings. I begged and begged to be allowed to call my mother, and when they finally said I could, I wept and pleaded with her to let us come home, but she said no, she was doing what was best for us. I cried some more and kept dragging She to the latrine to see if the curse had struck yet. I developed horrible stomachaches but didn't tell anyone, especially not She, who would have said it was my own fault and I deserved it.

I was suffering from another inexplicable ailment, besides Fear of The Curse. I guess you could call it homesickness. We had been away from home before, on trips to hospitals or relatives, but always with Billie or Helen. Now we were on our own, more or less.

I knew that my only hope of ever finding a place where I belonged was to leave home and family, but here I was flubbing my first chance. Did this mean I could *never leave Sioux City?* Never flee the duck pond to find other swans? Would homesickness for the very home that made me sick keep me prisoner and miserable all my life? No! I thought of the movies about New York and wisecracking career girls and handsome men who stood on penthouse terraces and said, "Someday all this will be yours." That was my real home. Movies and books told me that somewhere in this world people were loving and bright and kind to each other. I'd just have to do the best I could while waiting to grow up, and for the near future just try to keep my distance from overnight hikes, girls my age, and organized religion.

But time doesn't move when you're a child; summers in particular are endless, especially the bad ones. I think it must be part of the theory of relativity that the older you get, the faster time goes, until near the end the chapters get shorter and the calendar pages get blown away in an ever-speedier swirl. But being a kid is Chinese water torture. Drip. Drip. Drip. Drip.

The summer did come to an end and, sobbing and snarling, I survived Council Camp. I had ruined my sister's summer, too, and for that I was really sorry, although nobody believed me when I said so. I was in for a lot of lecturing about good sportsmanship and taking the bitter with the sweet. Helen made me cry by putting her arms around me and saying she was glad to have me home. Then she had to do the same for Sheila, of course.

She got it first, in the first week of January. I remember thinking it was an auspicious way to start the new year, although I didn't really know what I meant by that. It came at night, and She got me up to go to the bathroom. We were both scared and excited to see the trickle of blackish-red running down inside her leg. We got out the sanitary belt and Kotex and between the two of us figured out how to put it on her. We used a washcloth to scrub her leg and her pajamas and then the floor, where she had leaked. There was some on the sheet, too, so we scrubbed away at that and just hoped we had gotten it all out. Then we rubbed the washcloth with soap until all the telltale red came out. We put her damp pajama bottoms over the foot of the bed to dry and we slept way over on my side, hoping all would be dried and blameless by morning. She cried herself to sleep that night, but when I asked her if it hurt, she told me to shut up and mind my own business.

I started wearing Kotex all the time, just in case. I bought it out of my allowance. I didn't mind spending the money as much as I dreaded having to tell Mr. Vandervelt what I needed. When a teenage girl came into the drugstore and spoke so low he couldn't hear her at all, he automatically handed over a box of Kotex. When the boys came in blushing and whispering, he either sold them Trojans or told them they were too young and sent them home.

I had a small inauspicious period, finally, but the second one brought with it crippling cramps that plagued me every month for thirty-five years.

We didn't have to go back to camp the following summer. I did something very daring—I flunked geometry. Since I had never gotten any grade other than A, it was clearly deliberate, although no one seemed to have figured that out. But mission accomplished: We got to stay home, go to summer school for two hours in the mornings, and hang around the Leif Ericson pool every afternoon. It was a huge improvement over the previous summer. She didn't mind, either, because boys were starting to come around and show off for her.

It was becoming an established fact that She was the pretty one and I was the clever one. I could do crossword puzzles faster and find more short words out of a long one than anybody. I wrote poems and had one published (Billie sent it in) in *Child Life* magazine.

"Sandy's the clever one," everyone said. (Sheila's the pretty one.) Well, Sandy wears glasses and has big ears and protruding, cavity-prone teeth, she's always got scabs on her knees, and she's getting rotten posture from trying to hide her developing breasts. Sandy's hair is always tangled and all she wants to do is read books; she says awful things to people—later, she won't wear a girdle, and refuses to make polite small talk at luncheons—but she's clever. That was my redeeming social value, my only virtue. Sheila was adorable and charming and easy in company and privy to the secret code for doing and saying the right things, and I couldn't be like her even if I tried—and I did try, now and then. But there was solace in being the clever one. It made me a possible candidate for survival. Even Billie was sometimes proud of my cleverness, although it wasn't the particular asset she would have chosen for a daughter of hers.

In my late teens, I read a very sophisticated book about a family I would have killed to be part of, a family that held intellectual discussions, owned walls full of books, loved each other and said so out loud. Being brainy was an asset in that family!

But in the story, one sibling lovingly told another that a remark he had made was "merely clever." What did that *mean*? It was God giving me a sock in the eye: *being clever was not a good thing*. Cleverness was an affliction, like an artificial limb, the story went on to say, and drawing attention to it was in the worst possible taste. My one asset in life was in bad taste. An affliction. I had been found out.

The worst of it was that even after rereading that paragraph a hundred times, I *still* didn't know what was meant by "merely clever."

Oh, of course I had been warned not to be *too* clever; the boys didn't like girls who were too clever, and if the boys didn't like you, then your sister would have to drag you along on her dates and you'd wish you were dead. So I had to keep a lid on my brain; I had to watch my vocabulary and keep my edgy sense of humor mostly to myself. I had thought my consolation would be a better world of interesting people somewhere who would appreciate me someday because I was so very clever. And then this!

An affliction, in bad taste. That was me all over.

I started thinking about ways to commit suicide, but it would only have been doing my sister a big favor; they would simply cut me loose and stuff me underground somewhere. She would survive, alone, and with my luck she'd become a famous ballerina.

But the world took a convoluted spin, just in time to save me from total despair, and here is the worst confession I have to make, even taking into account what happened later:

World War Two was the best time of my life.

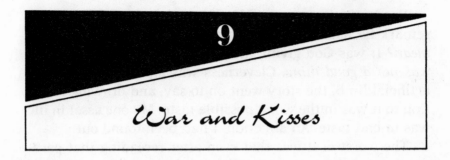

9

War and Kisses

I got my first kiss in the backseat of Moose Wasserman's father's Buick. Four of us were just riding around aimlessly one spring evening after dinner; Moose had picked up Syd Finkelstein, and when they turned up Grandview Boulevard, we happened to be out on the porch swing and they asked if we wanted to go for a ride so we did. Syd started joking around about why didn't we go up to see the view from War Eagle's grave and we all giggled a lot and Moose drove up there and parked.

Tradition decreed that Jewish kids parked up at War Eagle's grave and the gentiles went to the Floyd Monument. Sergeant Floyd was the only person who died on the Lewis and Clark expedition; his appendix burst. I never did know who War Eagle was, but his grave was a nice quiet clearing on a kind of bluff, high enough so you almost didn't smell the river.

Moose and Syd climbed into the back with She and me, and we were joking around, pushing and laughing, self-conscious because this was our first time parking and I don't think even the boys were sure what was supposed to happen.

We didn't even pretend to look at the famous three-state view (flatlands of Nebraska to the west across the river, flatlands of South Dakota to the north, flatlands of Iowa behind us). She and Moose got very quiet all of a sudden, and then Syd's arms went around me and he put his face down close to mine and gave me a long, dry kiss.

I don't know what I expected to feel. It wasn't loving or even particularly friendly. Syd Finkelstein was no Charles Boyer. But suddenly my mind let go, stopped functioning entirely in the rush of longing, of need. I was parched, a castaway long adrift, he was fresh water. My body stretched to press against him, every cell wanted to mate. Passion came as a great surprise to me. When the kiss broke off and he looked at me from only inches away, I was shocked because Syd Finkelstein's face was suddenly a miracle, the most beautiful thing I had ever seen.

Hormones were jumping like Jolly Time popcorn in parts of my body I didn't want to know about. My blood was pumping so fast I thought I might be swooning—certainly, I felt like lying down at once. I couldn't think, didn't want to; all I knew was that this amazing, extraordinary creature found me attractive. Me!

I pulled him down and we kissed again, and this time I pushed his mouth a little bit open with the tip of my tongue and he seemed to melt into me, liking it. He liked it. He liked me! I shuddered with the amazing news.

I didn't know or care what She and Moose were doing over on their side. Probably the boys had planned this. Probably they would tell everyone the next day that they had kissed us and we were "easy lays." Or worse, P.T.'s. Prick

93

Tease. If you let a boy do things you were an easy lay, and if you didn't you were a P.T. It had seemed a simple enough choice before that night; with no one storming the barricades, my moral convictions were as intact as the rest of me. Now in an instant I understood about the headlong, heedless rapture that led all the girls in Helen's magazines into shame, degradation, and motherhood. I was faced with the grand dilemma. I knew what ecstasy was, and passion and love. Yes, of course, love. It was clear to me that I could never find another boy or man so exciting and admirable in every way as Syd, no other would ever rouse me as he was doing this very minute. I would love only one man all my life. Syd and I, together forever, to feel this rapture whenever we kissed, for the rest of our lives.

He had stopped kissing me and seemed to be fumbling with the front of my cardigan sweater.

I fell out of love on the third kiss. Syd had one arm around me and the other hand pushing up under my blouse, and suddenly I felt like Moose's father's old Buick, being driven by a boy who had read all the moves in some manual. It wasn't me he was after; he just wanted to go for a ride. And he might (accidentally?) touch the place where my body and Sheila's were stuck together. Or the scars we pretended we didn't have.

I pushed his hand away and moved back from him as well as I could, being pressed in there between him and my sister. (She and Moose were still going at it. I could feel his long-boned thigh moving between her legs and pushing at mine; she was breathing normally as far as I could tell, but Moose was making little whimpery noises.)

"What's the matter?" Syd murmured.

"Don't do that," I whispered back.

"Don't do what?"

"What you were doing. With your hand."

"Why not?"

94

I shrugged as well as I could within his hammy grip. "I just don't like it, that's all."

"I only wanted to touch you."

"Well, it was like you read about it someplace—the Next Move. It didn't feel spontaneous."

"Oh, it was, it was! It was very spontaneous."

"Do you like me, Syd?"

"Huh? Well, sure I do." He said it as if he meant: What's that got to do with anything? Girls sure are dippy.

We sat there for a minute or two listening to Moose's hard breathing, and I was starting to wonder if She was ever going to move a muscle, wishing I could turn and watch to see how it was done. Then Syd got impatient and said loudly, "Come on, Moose, let's get out of here. It's getting late. I got basketball practice tomorrow."

I struggled to sit up, but She and I were sort of squashed down at an angle, neck bones almost resting on the seat. I suddenly realized how uncomfortable I was, how I hated Syd Finkelstein, and wondered that I ever seriously considered loving anyone with pimples and such a Jewish name.

"Come on, Sheila, let's go, for God's sake," I said. I reached around and poked at her.

"Hey, she's got her thing off," Syd whispered right in my ear.

"What thing?"

"Her bra." He snickered aloud. Bra was a dirty word.

"OFF?" I said out loud. That couldn't be possible without my knowing about it—could it?

Sheila and Moose quit what they were doing, and we sat up. "I do not!" she snarled loudly. "You just take that back, jerk."

Syd just guffawed and reached for the door. He opened it and was about to get out.

"Tell him, Moose! You just goddamn tell him the truth!" She screamed, not caring if the kids parked nearby in Alan

Orloff's father's car heard her. I thought I heard them laughing.

"Oh shut up, Sheila," I growled. "Who cares? Let's go home."

"I care!" She insisted, with her I'm-on-the-verge voice threatening us with an all-out shrieker if we didn't give in. "I don't want people saying what isn't true about me!"

"She didn't have it off, Syd. Don't be a jerk," Moose said obediently. He was fumbling now, maybe tucking his shirt in. Or zipping his fly? I tried to see, but he was way over on She's side, half turned away from me. After a minute, he opened the door on his side and got behind the wheel.

"Well, that's a fine thing, leaving us alone back here!" She grumped. At least she was no longer tantrummy. What had I gotten so upset about, anyway? If I hadn't shied away like that, we'd still be going at it, probably. All of us. Well, now I knew what it felt like. Nice. And scary—a person could lose control over herself. Although I didn't think I gave a damn for my reputation or even my virginity, I couldn't risk losing control, not ever.

I wondered how far She had gone with Moose. I could swear she never twitched. And I, on the other hand, must have been trembling like a willow tree in a twister. She must have felt me doing that; how mortifying.

What would happen to me if I ever really did fall in love?

Despair, the old familiar, terrible weight of it, caved in on me abruptly, as it always did, without warning. My life was a nightmare and there was no one to tell it to, no one who would come running and turn on the light and sit with me until it got better. I couldn't even console myself, not even in a whisper, because I would be overheard and mocked. My worst enemy knew every moment of my life, awake or asleep, every last detail of what passed for reality in this endless misery. To be so lonely and never alone, to be young and face the prospect of a punitive world and everlasting humiliation—what had I done to deserve this? What fearful struggle took place in that reluctant womb to earn such hellish retribution?

I stared at the back of Syd's head, hating him for what he had stirred up in me. Then he half turned and leaned against the car door, facing Moose, and slung his left arm over the seat to touch my knee with his hand. When I put my hand down on top of his, he clutched me as if my hand meant something to him, and I melted into love all over again.

Moose pulled the Buick up in front of our house. They walked us up to the porch steps and they kissed us good night. Moose said, "Want to go to the movies Friday night?" and Syd said, "See ya."

As soon as we got inside and up the stairs to our room and shut the door, I wanted to talk, the way sisters do when they've been out on a double date. At least Deanna Durbin and her sisters in *Three Smart Girls* did, and Rosemary and Priscilla and Lola Lane and probably Patty, Maxine, and Laverne Andrews. What about Eppie and Popo Friedman, who weren't even conjoined but had a double wedding anyway? They must have had plenty of sisterly chats about that. (And anyway, how did they just happen to fall in love and find willing husbands at the exact same time? Billie had sighed a lot and said it was the most romantic thing that had ever happened, so perfect and wonderful, all because they really loved each other, as sisters should. But I figured that somebody had to be faking it. Four people just didn't fall in love all at the same time, all of them simultaneously craving to get married in a mass rite. I had sat there in a pew in Shaare Zion Synagogue and watched the two brides come down the aisle, one on each side of their father, and saw all the rose petals and white gauzy veils and handsome grooms and everybody crying [why? why?] and all I thought was, I wonder which ones of them are doing it for show.)

But still, they must have had an awful lot of sisterly talks.

They got to be very famous columnists later, and how do you think they learned so much wisdom? How do you think they got rich telling other people what to do? Why, with all those frank and cozy sisterly talks, that's how.

"Moose really likes you," I said, going for genuine warmth and friendly enthusiasm. I knew if I started with "Do you think Syd really likes me?" I'd get nowhere, although of course that was really what I wanted to chat about.

"I know it," She said, throwing her clothes onto the chair, already piled up with our week's accumulation of sweaters and skirts and blouses and underwear. We hung things up, reluctantly, on Saturdays.

"I guess you're going steady, huh?"

"He wants me to, but I haven't given him my answer yet." She deigned to confide this, but with a tone of voice that was infinitely weary of me and my questions and all the adulation she had to suffer from everybody all the time.

"I know you didn't take off your bra," I told her, trying to sound loyal.

She didn't answer. She was brushing her hair. We had a dressing table with a long mirror hinged on both sides so you could almost close yourself in with an infinity of images of you in every direction. I tried to lose myself in there a couple of times, shutting her out, not that it ever quite worked. She liked to sit on the bench and admire herself in the mirrors while she brushed her thick mop of curls, and usually I bitched about how long it took, but tonight I wanted information from her, so I let her lead me over to the bench and I sat obligingly while she brushed and brushed herself and preened as if looking pretty was the same as accomplishing something.

"That was the first time I ever really got kissed," I said, feeling shy and embarrassed but determined to get to the sisterly level, if there was one. She just snorted, kind of. "I mean with tongues and all. And . . . well, I was surprised at old Syd. Made me feel—well, funny."

She didn't answer. She was counting strokes. The magazines told her she had to brush her hair one hundred strokes every night before going to bed. I just sat quietly watching hundreds of her in all the angles of the triple mirrors while she worked the brush over and over and over through her shining black curls. I had tried this a few times but my arms got tired and I couldn't see any immediate improvement and, anyway, I'd rather read a book.

"So—uh—how far do you think it's okay to go?" I asked and found myself blushing so furiously I looked away from my ugly image in the mirror. She didn't answer. She was counting, moving her lips.

"I know you talk about things like that with Bubbles and Edie, only I never listen because I know you don't want me to and, anyway, I was never that interested before, only now—"

"Goddammit, you made me lose count! Will you just shut up, dammit!"

I am irretrievably joined to my nemesis, the person I hate most in the world, the one who wants to destroy me. Think of your worst enemy, and wonder for a minute how you'd like it.

My mother says that Sheila always has to have the last word, it's her failing. My failing, according to Billie, is that I am "generous to a fault." She thought I gave my favorite blouse and my good leather belt (after She broke hers) and most of my money to Sheila out of generosity, when all I was ever trying to do was to bribe her, buying back a bit of time she owed me anyway or a little temporary neutrality. It generally worked, but even if it had been otherwise, how was it possible to be too generous? Wasn't generosity a good thing? If my mother read my bribery as generosity, well, in me even that was a fault, a flaw.

I began to understand that I'd never do anything right in this duck pond. I began to obsess about getting away. I had read Darwin, and I knew if you can't adapt, you have to find another environment or die. But where would that be? Wherever I went, people would stare, find me disgusting to look at, tremble and shake and get nauseous at the sight of me. They paid money in circuses to see people like me—not in the main ring, either, but in the sideshow, a tacky tent off by itself. In Germany they were pushing around people like me—freaks *and* Jews. In a conformist town in the Midwest of the United States of America, they only went for your spirit.

On Pearl Harbor day, it snowed too heavily to take the car out, so my dad stayed home and we all just sat around reading the Sunday papers all day. Nobody called and we didn't talk much to each other; just before it was going to get dark, She and I put on galoshes and wool hats and gloves and went down to Vandervelt's Pharmacy for some licorice. I saw stacks of newspapers with EXTRA written on them and big headlines about some harbor getting bombed. We walked back home kicking at snowdrifts, eating our licorice, bored. In the evening, Daddy turned on Jack Benny, but the radio was only giving news that night. Daddy got very excited. When he explained what it meant, I felt so dumb I wanted to die. I could have been the one to bring the news. My father would have been impressed with my intelligence and been proud of me for rushing to tell him the momentous tidings—if only I had.

I thought it was just another battle in a war that had been going on for a long time and didn't concern anybody we knew. When the next day in school there was a special assembly and they brought in a radio so we could listen to President Roosevelt say it was a date that would live in infamy, I figured it sure would for me, because it was the day I realized I was not so smart after all. Even at fourteen, I should have had a little more awareness of things outside myself, a little more connection to the world. All I knew about world affairs was that as long as Roosevelt was in the

White House, everything was okay; when I got to be twenty-one I'd vote for him just like my parents did, so what was there to worry about? I had heard of Hitler, of course. He was bad for the Jews.

An Army Air Force base was quickly built just south of town. Handsome strangers appeared on our streets wearing sexy uniforms. Thunderous formations of four-engine bombers roared over our heads daily, reminding us that there were places in the world where planes meant run for your life. (Here, it only scared the chickens, and we almost had an egg-production crisis.) Patriotism was at a constant boil in our breasts, but the real war was, like everything else of interest, going on somewhere else.

She and I took our turn selling war stamps in the lobby of the Orpheum, sitting importantly in the flag-draped booth in the huge red-carpeted lobby, between the goldfish fountain and the marble statue of Thespis in a toga. We collected newspapers and aluminum pots for the war effort, although I couldn't figure out what good they would do anyone. We shook our heads over the evil of some people rumored to be hoarding sugar and tires in their basements. Twice a week, when we didn't have band practice (I played the alto saxophone; She faked the clarinet), we'd go downtown after school to the Jewish Community Center to play hostess to real honest-to-God soldiers.

Most of the Jewish families in town chipped in to rent the whole top (second) floor of a building downtown above a photographer's studio and a fur store. You went up a narrow flight of stairs between photos of triumphant brides and dead animals and came out on a big, airy loft that served as Hebrew school, library, ballroom, Ping Pong room, and movie theater with a screen on a rickety stand for showing 8-millimeter films about planting trees in Palestine. There was a minuscule kitchen with a hot plate and coffeepot and two complete sets of dishes and silverware, to satisfy the kosher laws. There was a general lounge area in one corner, with Mrs. Dorfman's old leather couch and a few sprung, donated armchairs. There was a phonograph and plenty of room to dance.

Our job was to serve coffee and sweet rolls and make conversation with the soldiers. I felt very, very grown-up, and sometimes kind of scared, because it really was just like in the movies, although not quite the Hollywood Canteen. Our base was an overseas training unit. Young men came there straight from radio schools, bombardier schools, navigating and piloting and maintenance schools, and they trained as crews in their own B-17s (later, B-24s) for ninety days and then shipped out to England to go on bombing raids over Germany. This wasn't high school stuff. This was real, and thrillingly romantic.

Just in time, She and I had somehow developed actual figures, slim and high-breasted, with good legs, and we became what were known as "peachy dancers," especially on the fast jitterbug stuff. With the help of our local boys and a few eager young soldiers from sophisticated places like Chicago and Philadelphia and New York, we worked out a lot of intricate, savvy steps with the two of us in the middle, facing out partners and bobbing wildly, for once in our lives in synch with each other. When the boys swung us around or lifted us off our feet or dipped us down at the end of a number so low our heads touched the floor and then swooped us up into their arms again for the final chord, it was all a matter of coordination, which was what jitterbugging was all about anyway, in our case, four instead of two bodies moving to that lindy beat. Our partners felt double clever; lots of times other dancers would stop and stand around watching us, applauding when the number was finished the way crowds of extras did for Astaire and Rogers.

American high school girls during the war led a bizarre, complex existence. We juggled Central High and World War

102

Two with the same innate schizophrenia that characterized everything else in our lives. Double standards were mother's milk to us. Mash notes passed in history class held just as much dramatic potential as V-mail forwarded from an atoll somewhere in the Pacific. Saturday night meant a movie and the Green Gables (where all the Jews went because it was owned by the Rosenblooms) and then parking at War Eagle's grave, or it meant cocktails and dinner and dancing with ardent strangers who might soon be dead. We wore bobby socks and saddle shoes or we put on four-inch heels and turned our stockings inside out so the seams would make the rayon look as sheer as nylon, which we'd never worn but only heard of.

We were good girls and we did bad things that we never, never, never talked about. You could find us at the illicit bars in town (Iowa was a dry state, but suddenly there were night-clubs and bars and saloons and crap games behind every other downtown door, and since the law said nobody could drink, it didn't matter how old you were) or out at the officers' club dances, swaying in a circle with all the other intoxicated, morbidly sentimental couples at around 3 A.M., singing, "We live in fame or go down in flame, nothing can stop the army air corps." How many times did I vomit in parking lots before I learned that two rum-and-Cokes was my absolute limit?

It was only a matter of weeks after my very first kiss from Syd Finkelstein that I was regularly getting fingerfucked by the copilot of a B-17 or a fledgling mechanic on my family's front porch. We were chameleons, acting the way the boys and men expected us to, anticipating what was wanted exactly the same way that we whirled from partner to partner on the dance floor, adjusting rhythm and body to their whims without effort or thought.

Billie was relieved that we were popular. It was all that mattered. Besides, we were patriotic.

I was considered very funny, and She was beautiful and knew how to flirt. She could charm and cajole and lie to a boy until he would do anything for her. At fifteen, we never missed a dance, a party, or a Saturday night date. I was amazed at my success as a woman. Suddenly now my bitter comments on life and everyone in it were considered high wit. I managed to get almost as many dates as She. When I didn't have one of my own, I'd go along with her and her date as *leitmotif*, the good sport, the kid sister you could always count on for a laugh.

I fell in love at least once a week, with soldiers and Boy Scouts indiscriminately. I fell in love with a tail gunner who was twenty-three and had a premonition of death. My second letter to him came back rubber-stamped MISSING IN ACTION. In orchestra practice, I fell in love with a seventeen-year-old half-Sioux boy who played the French horn so sweetly it brought tears to my eyes. There was a redheaded sergeant who worked on ground-crew maintenance and wrote me letters wondering what the hell he was doing on an island called Tinian in the summer of 1945. I fell in love with James Stewart, the movie star, who was stationed at our base and whom I once glimpsed across the dance floor of the officers' club.

The war brought Sioux City a once-in-a-millennium chance to touch life, the real thing, with all its dangers and possibilities. I think everybody was in love, all senses taut and vibrating, for the whole three and a half years.

For the most part, the soldiers treated us quite nicely. Maybe it was because of the war and the danger of being physically damaged themselves. Of course, we had to ignore plenty of staring and pointing and loud, rude remarks and sniggers. Well, we knew by now that we weren't exactly ordinary, and people who'd never seen us before sometimes took a while to get used to the idea. We were very understanding in the case of soldiers. After all, they were going overseas to fight Hitler and might be killed. Since being killed was considered, by most people, worse than being conjoined to your sibling, I remembered most of the time not to get my feelings hurt. Anyway, after a while the soldiers generally came to regard us as just what we were: two small-town high school girls, good company, good dancers, eager to show them a good time as long as we could keep our virginity.

Once a couple of fellows did take us out just to win a bet. A lieutenant told us afterward we should be careful who we went out with because he heard that those guys collected twenty dollars from their buddy. He had bet that there was no such thing as Siamese twins in Sioux City, Iowa, and when we showed up at the Blue Mill roadhouse, our dates took us over to meet this sergeant sitting alone in a booth. He acted drunker than he was and started poking at us, trying to feel under our dresses, saying it was a dumb trick and who did we think we were fooling? She started to holler at her date for doing this to her and I started to cry and it was a holy mess. The only way we could get out of there was to call Daddy, which She did, and we waited outside on that dirt road forever until he finally pulled up and got out of the car. I thought he would kill us, but he just sat there with his mouth all screwed up tight until we had crawled into the backseat. We weren't even supposed to go to roadhouses at all, and the Blue Mill was on the South Dakota side of the river, which was truly cruddy. Daddy shouted at us on the way home and then he got real quiet when he turned onto our street and he said, "Not a word to your mother about any of this, understand? No point in upsetting her, too. I just hope you'll know better from now on than to go to road-houses."

But most of the time it was okay. We invited Jewish soldiers home for dinner. They all loved Billie. Sheila and I were really proud of our young and energetic mom. After dinner the soldiers would take us dancing, or else we'd just hang around, stroll down to Birdsall's for ice cream and bring it back to share with Billie. When Daddy came home from the office or his lodge meeting, they'd tuck in for the night and we'd sit out on the porch necking with the soldiers.

They almost never tried to persuade us to Go All the Way. I guess there were enough other girls and older women who did that. With girls from nice families, they seemed mostly content to take your hand and show you what to do so they could come in their olive-drab hankies. Sometimes I'd have an orgasm, too, shuddering silently there on the glider and holding his hand between my legs tightly so he wouldn't take it away too soon. It seemed a very mature way to behave, compared to the boys our own age, who kept pushing their hard-ons at us all the time, in school and at parties and in cars and movies, urging us to Go All the Way and snickering about the girls who reportedly did.

We were sure of one thing—that nobody we knew personally would Do It, although there were rumors about some of the girls who lived on the west side. Bobby Ferguson and Merilee Potter were steadies all through high school, and when he left to join the navy, he gave her a huge wooden phallus that he had carved in shop when Mr. Hoffer wasn't looking. Said he used himself as a model, and Moose Wasserman told me it was true. Bobby used to sit in assembly with his hand very high up on Merilee's thigh, and she never pushed it away. Merilee smiled glowingly all the time. She was known for her glowing smile. The sign of a satisfied woman, I figured. Other people thought differently; Sheila and Bubbles said Merilee was flushed from embarrassment all the time because everybody knew she and Bobby Did It.

She gossiped avidly with her pals about the other girls and how far they maybe let guys get, but we never, never talked about what we were doing ourselves. Sometimes during the day, sitting in an overheated classroom, I would wonder seriously if what we did at night really happened or whether it was all in my notorious imagination and I was in fact crazy. Maybe I was caged up in the asylum at Cherokee right now, only imagining that I was sitting at a desk behind Iggy Apolitis and listening to Miss Mousie Brown talk about Julius Caesar.

The rules of sexual behavior were very strict, although vague and undefined. Try to get some information and our mother would make a wisecrack and laugh in a certain smutty way, with you as the great dumb-dumb. "Always let your conscience be your guide," she would chirp like Jiminy Cricket, and that was all we ever got from her. Nobody ever appreciated a dirty joke more than Billie, but when it came to information, asking a question was asking to be made the butt of ridicule. And then she'd quote you over the Mah-jongg table to high laughter from a bunch of stupid women parasites with nothing better to do while boys were risking their lives every day to preserve our way of life.

Funny, I don't remember any of the names or faces of the seductive, passionate young men in uniform who had their fingers in my snatch, but my first kiss, before any of them arrived in town, stays with me forever. It was in fact rather sordid and a lot less sentimental than a soldier's kiss and it was only dumb old Syd Finkelstein, so why should it be stuck there in my memory like a wad of gum I can't seem to spit out?

I learned everything there was to know about kissing and petting and mutual masturbation without ever reading a book or having a conversation about it. And at my side, my sister was doing the same. We were very, very popular.

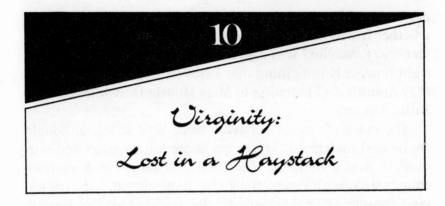

10

Virginity: Lost in a Haystack

Our sweet sixteen party was looming. We had been to two or three already and they were always the same: the Warrior Hotel party room, a sit-down dinner for the same dozen people, the same menu (steak and french fries, with ice cream done up in some bizarre way with colored sauce or something flammable on top), and then dancing. You had to have a new formal dress for each party. If your father couldn't afford to buy that many tulle and taffeta gowns, it was just barely okay for your mother to make them for you, but she had to be very good at it or the others girls would titter behind your back about crooked seams and tacky material. It was all so painful that the prospect made me desperate enough to attempt a revolution.

"We'd better call the Warrior pretty soon and book the party room for a Saturday night before I have to go away for my hay fever," Billie said one afternoon. We had just come home from school and were drinking Cokes at the kitchen table, inhaling her glorious brisket that simmered in the oven smothered in onions and chili sauce and beer.

My heart started to pound, but I had been waiting for this opening and I jumped right in. "I think it's wrong to spend all that money when there's a war on," I said in my disguise as Miss Righteous American Patriot. Clearly an argument with no reasonable rebuttal.

"Why, it's what our boys are fighting for, the right of sweet sixteen-year-old girls to go on bravely with normal life. Anyhow, your daddy doesn't mind spending the money. He wants his girls to remember their sweet sixteen party all their lives."

"Well, how can anybody remember anything that's exactly like everybody else's? If you remember five sweet sixteen parties and they're all exactly the same, how can you be sure you're remembering your own and not Edie's or Bubbles's or Marilyn's?" I was being brilliant, logical, and articulate, but none of these things was valued in our family.

"Edie's was pink-and-silver, and ours will be red-and-white," She said, as if that were some kind of answer.

"Red's your color, not mine," I retorted, losing it. How quickly the forces of stubborn unreason could bring me down to their level. But my crybaby days were mostly behind me and I was determined to win this one—partly just to see if I could ever win anything in this life. "Anyway, wouldn't it be fun to do something special, and diff—I mean, something that everyone will remember, something that's really fun?"

"There's nothing better or more fun than a formal dinner dance," Sheila announced as if she were the women's-page editor of the Sioux City *Journal* with a hot news flash for all the little people who had been awaiting the Word.

"Why do you always have to be different, anyway?" Sheila added. Billie nodded. Brownie points for Sheila.

I was tempted to just shut up and grab a book and let

them do whatever damn thing they wanted to, suffering my rage until it was forceful enough to propel me out of town and away from them—Billie, anyway—forever. Then I thought about getting dressed up in a ridiculous long gown with matching shoes that blistered, and having to sit in the beauty parlor for hours on a summer afternoon getting my hair "done." I thought of having to tell my date what color my dress was going to be and pretending surprise when he brought me a gardenia dyed and already dying. I always felt sorry for the gardenia. It worked so hard putting out that heavy perfume, it deserved a better fate. Gardenias seem to exist only for high school proms and sweet sixteen parties; I've never seen them before or since on any other occasion. A soldier once sent me a dozen roses. There wouldn't be any soldiers at our party. A sweet sixteen party was Sioux City's equivalent of a coming-out ball, a debut into a very exclusive society: all the north side Jews of Sioux City, Iowa, between the ages of fifteen and seventeen, with the occasional addition of someone's cousin from Omaha. By the time a girl "came out" into their company, she already knew the measure of every one of their cocks, having them all butted up against her during one slow dance or another.

I had a truly original idea for our party. This was not a good thing. Originality was encouraged only in variations on a theme: the shape of the nut cups at your dinner party, the wording of the invitations. Truly original was suspect; what'dja want to rock the boat for anyhow? But I thought I'd try, maybe just to see if I could get anywhere with the brains I was supposed to have in lieu of beauty.

Some movie or book had left me with the delusion that the idyllic life was to be found down on the farm. I knew from personal experience that this was absolutely not the case, but here I claim genetic license—why should I have to be the only family member to deal with reality? Helen had broken the news about us to her father and sometimes took us to his farm near Otoe when our parents went away for a Shriners' convention or the World's Fair. The farm had no electricity, only kerosene lamps (President Roosevelt had brought in Rural Electrification, but Helen's father wasn't having any part of That Man and his Gol-danged Socialism) and there was no plumbing, indoors or out. There was a little pump by the kitchen sink and you washed in cold water caught in a basin. Fifty yards from the house there was a ferociously stinking privy. It had a wooden plank seat with two holes, but they were too far apart for She and me to use simultaneously and there was no room for us to pee in our usual way, so we had to use a chamber pot, which was kept right under our bed. It was very strange peeing right in the bedroom. We didn't shit at all when we were there. Everybody had chores to do, and one of ours was to feed the chickens. We'd go out in the yard with bags of feed in our hands and the chickens would get all excited and gather around us and—would you believe it?—start pecking at our shins and ankles with their sharp little beaks. I got to hating chickens so much it's still a pleasure to eat them. I feel sorry about eating other animals, but not chickens.

But in some book I had read, life on the farm was sunny and joyous, with people caring about each other and helping each other and working together and having lots of fun with taffy pulls and hayrides and quilting bees. The girl in my book loved sliding down haystacks. It sounded so jolly that one summer when we were about twelve, I was able to talk Sheila into trying it and down we went. She screeched and didn't stop crying and whining for a day and a half after the last sharp sticks of hay and stickle burrs had finally been plucked out of us with Helen's tweezers.

I hoped she had forgotten the haystack, because I was about to propose another bucolic pleasure involving the same substance: a hayride for our sixteenth birthday.

"A hayride, oh God, Mother, make her stop! That's hor-

111

rible! Everybody else gets to have a formal dinner dance and no, my sister says let's have a hayride! It's childish and disgusting, Sandy. For God's sake."

That was the reaction I had expected. I was prepared for that. I was going to stay calm and clever. I was going to summon up images of romance and moonlight and the peaceful clopping of horses' hooves down a country lane at night. A wagonload of good friends, in twos. It was more Hollywood's idea than mine, of course.

What I didn't expect was the way my mother looked at me, as if she were almost actually seeing me. Me, singular. It was odd, and therefore uncomfortable, to look straight into her eyes and I remember noticing that they were green; looked straight into, they were clearly green rather than the indeterminate greenish-brown-flecked color I had thought they were.

Now I would call it the shock of recognition: My mother perceived something in me that she had denied or not ever seen before. Naturally, it turned out to be herself. "We used to go on hayrides when I was your age," she said slowly, and then her eyes let me off the discomfiting hook and she became sentimental, seeing not me but something that happened before I was born.

"And in the winter, we'd go sleigh riding," she said dreamily, wishing she were back there. We listened. I felt sad and guilty, listening to Bella talk of the old days, meaning the days before we came to destroy her life. Our mother's days of innocence were precious to her, every memory crystalline and pure. Since our birth, it had all turned ugly and burdensome. People stared and toilets overflowed and pipes froze and nobody danced the tango anymore; Billie's waist was thickening and her real family—Grandpa and Aunt Rose and Uncle Freddy—were three hundred miles away. None of these things would have happened if it weren't for us.

"The man next door had the wagon, and the horse was a

runty old nag, but it was strong. That horse could pull anything. Ugly as sin, but in the moonlight it didn't matter. We'd all pile into the wagon and my brother Freddy would take the reins—everybody knew how to drive a rig in those days, even in Minneapolis—and we'd go bouncing on the smelly old wooden floor of the wagon, a whole load of us kids, my sisters and their beaux and me and my friends. I was the youngest, and all the neighborhood kids would pile in, and Freddy would drive us all the way out to Mr. Yensen's farm. That's what we called him, well, that's what he called himself, all the Scandihoovians, you know, never say their *J*'s. We'd all jump out and the boys would help Mr. Yensen pile in some hay and then we'd spread blankets out over it and climb way up on top and off we'd go. I suppose those old dirt roads are mostly paved over now. But it was so much fun then."

"It's for farmers," She said after a silent moment of respect for our mother's holy past. The word *farmer* was second only to *greenhorn* on Billie's list of the lowest objects of derision. Then She added the magic words that were almost always the final clincher: "It was okay in those days, Billie, but this is now, and the *people we know don't do that*."

I was ready for that one. The battle was now on more familiar ground.

"I'd like to do something just the way Billie did it when she was our age," I said shamelessly.

"My brother Freddy had a beautiful tenor voice, just like an Irishman," Bella remembered. "He knew all the old ballads, and he'd give them the lilt, you know, just like the micks do. There were plenty of them in our neighborhood, so he picked up the accent. Oh, how I loved to hear him sing. And the stars out . . ."

"Gosh, it sounds romantic!" I sighed loudly.

I imagined I could feel the blood in She's body start pumping with possibilities.

"I was only a kid," our mother said sharply. "I never went on a hayride with your father."

Okay, so it wasn't romantic, it was only good clean fun. My mistake. But a seed had been planted in She's tiny brain and finally began to show signs of life.

"It would be something different, all right," she said cautiously.

(Different was not usually good; different was to be avoided. Look at us.)

Billie turned her thoughts to the present. "I'll bet if we did that, everybody in town would wish they'd thought of it first. It would be very original. We could—let me see— decorate the house, sort of like a barn, well the basement anyway, and we could serve hot dogs and corn on the cob first and then hire a farmer with a wagon to come and pick you kids up . . ."

I felt She shudder. *Farmer* was the wrong word to use just then. "Everybody would talk about it for a whole year, I'll bet," I said quickly. "They'd all be jealous."

With Billie on my side—for once!—She finally gave in and pretty soon started to think it was her own idea. Who cared? With much more excitement than necessary, the plans were made; a farmer with a hay wagon found (at an exorbitant price, Billie thought), cleverly rhymed invitations written by me and penned by all of us and mailed out, pretty gingham-checked dresses bought and fitted to us. Really getting into the spirit of things, Billie got a whole keg of root beer someplace and bought hot dogs from a wholesale butcher out at the stockyards.

We just hoped the newspaper reporters and photographers would keep away; since the war started, they had let up on us. Two-headed babies were pretty much out; little tales of bravery and sacrifice sold more papers. Ernie Pyle's G.I. Joe was a lot more popular than Robert Ripley's Believe It or Not.

114

Billie decided we'd start the party with a square dance in the basement, now supposed to look like a barn, with yellow crepe paper wound around the big overhead pipes and photos of sheep and cows Scotch-taped to the grungy walls and red ears of corn and stalks of hay stuck here and there. She and I had cleaned out as many washtubs, sleds, ladders, rakes, ice skates, and broken lawn furniture as we could fit into the coal bin, but our cellar wasn't a rec room and never would be. For one thing, we had removed the basket that always stood in the middle of the floor under an open chute that originated in the bathroom. During the party, Daddy absentmindedly chucked down a pair of shorts and a sleeveless undershirt, just missing Marilyn Pickel's head. The party got off to a bleak start down there in the basement. Kids who had known each other all their lives stood around like embarrassed strangers, dressed in hayseed farmer clothes, starched overalls, and hick dresses and wide straw hats feeling stupid. Eating the hot dogs helped, but the square dancing never came off, despite Billie's moving the phonograph down there and having sent away to New York for a special record of fiddling and calls. It was a relief when it got to be nine o'clock and almost dark outside and we all went upstairs and out onto the front yard to wait for the wagon.

Hanging around in the sweet summer air under the early stars, sitting on the grass that had been newly cut for the birthday party, surrounded by our friends, we all started to relax. Syd Finkelstein put his arm around Sheila and gave me a friendly half shove-half pat on the shoulder.

Although I had made it clear to Alan Orloff that he was my date, he paid no attention to me, not at first. He was over there walking on the fence that separated our yard from the sidewalk. You had to be a good balancer—excellent, in fact—to walk that fence, but now was not the time. I felt abandoned, publicly unwanted.

One of the hallmarks of a sweet sixteen party was that we

115

were all now in pairs, male and female. Marilyn Pickel's fourteen-year-old brother Dilly (not even he knew what his real name had once been) had to be invited to make it come out even; Bubbles drew him as her date and at first she was furious about it, but later in the evening she seemed to find him irresistibly sexy. I just sat and glowered at Alan for showing off with a stupid balancing act anybody could do if they weren't joined at the hip to their goddamn sister.

Then the wagon came rattling down Grandview Boulevard and we all leaped up to see. There were two broad-beamed, almost-prancing young horses and they were wearing little bells that jingled faintly, like the noise the stars might make as they twinkle. I experienced an instant of pleasure so acute I thought I might faint, or die, but it was quickly over.

The wagon pulled up at the curb and the farmer got down to go in the house for his money and final instructions. All the neighbors were out on their porches and front yards to see what was going on; the only horses that ever came on Grandview Boulevard anymore belonged to an occasional farmer selling vegetables and eggs directly to the housewives or to some Amish folks lost in the big city. So there were all our neighbors, lined up like they were auditioning for the Most Unforgettable Character I Ever Met in the *Reader's Digest* competition. They just stared and we just ignored them.

Each of the girls had been told to bring a blanket (mindful of the stinging summer of the haystack slide). The boys climbed aboard first and leaned down to grab the blankets. With some dickering for place, they soon staked out the territory up there while we girls stood below and giggled.

Moose Wasserman leaped down from the top of the wagon, earning an admiring gasp. He then gallantly took Edie's arm and led her over to the rear of the wagon. He showed her how to put her foot on the wheel's axle, and as she did so, he grabbed hold of her rear and scooped her right up, probably looking up her dress as she clambered for a foothold on the slippery hay. Once up there, Edie laughed loudly and falsely and shouted down to us that it was easy.

Alan reached down his hand for me and I took it, but we waited for Syd to maneuver himself over to the same spot and take She's hand; in one alley-oop they pulled the two of us up and almost into their arms. We had two blankets, red plaid and blue plaid. Alan and Syd spread them out so they overlapped. We sat down and wiggled our bottoms into little round nests in the hay. All the boys put their arms around all the girls. Mr. Wilson came out of the house and so did my parents. They waved and smiled self-consciously, shouting, "Have fun! Be good! Sweet sixteen and never been kissed!" and Billie laughed too loudly for the sake of the neighbors and then with one soft cluck of his tongue, Mr. Wilson gee'd the horses and we started off, along Grandview to 27th Street and down the hill that 27th makes until it runs right into Broken Kettle Road, where the cornfields start. In no time at all we were out of town and the hayride had begun.

We were pretty quiet at first, everyone looking up at the sky. There was something to see no matter what your angle: in the west, long streaks of fading amber and rose; out toward Minnesota, you could see the long whitish fingers of the Northern Lights; or you could look straight up into an ocean, a universe, a dizzying limbo of darkening nothingness with stars lighting up, first magnitude, second, until you could swear you saw the third-magnitude stars, the ones too far away to be named, tricking the eye because they'd disappear when you tried to stare straight at them. Even a gang of teenagers could be awed into silence for a little while by that August sky.

Everyone lay down, the better to see the stars. She and I were on our sides, cuddled up to our dates, ignoring each other as much as possible. Whispering in Alan's ear with what I hoped was a sexy, throaty, thrilling June Allyson

117

voice, I pointed out the two dippers, and Cassiopeia and Orion. I was about to tell him how to find Arcturus when Bobby Dorfman started humming the opening riff to "String of Pearls." It was an instrumental, no lyrics, but this bunch knew every note in every side Glenn Miller ever cut, and without anybody actually leading, we all took different parts—brass, reeds, someone taking the trombone solo, someone else doing drums. We went from there to all the records we lived by: Harry James, both Dorseys, Woody Herman, Benny Goodman, and others I've forgotten now. Bobby Dorfman had a nice croony voice, and the girls would take turns being Helen O'Connell with those cool and limpid green eyes, or Marian Hutton or the Modernaires.

Our records, 78 revolutions per minute, were our link to the world. The two radio stations we could get in Sioux City played hillbilly music between reports on hog belly futures. The big song that summer was "With the Bible on the Table and the Flag upon the Wall." I also remember having to listen to a lot of "I'm Gonna Hop on into my Pickup Truck and Truck on Down and Pick My Baby Up." It would be thirty years before hillbilly music was renamed country-and-western and became stylish. Except for a couple of after-school serials, Sunday night comedians, and the absolutely required "Your Hit Parade," which managed to squirm all the way through the network to reach us, we scorned the radio and lived by our phonograph records, which we bought at Schlosser's Music Store as soon as they came in. Sometimes Mr. Schlosser didn't order enough and someone would be too late to buy one and would have to borrow. Borrowing records was an honorable pursuit, if a treacherous one. Woe to the borrower whose younger sibling put sticky stuff on the record, whose father sat on one, or who left it too close to the radiator.

So there we were, as promised. Moonlight and starlight, the soft clip-clop of the horses, everyone nestled in each other's arms on the hay, and our own singing to top it off. Bobby's voice was enough to make the girls fantasize Sinatra, and I guess everyone got to feeling very amorous.

The amount of energy pent up in the back of that hay wagon was like rocket fuel compared to the two-horsepower that was pulling us. Teenagers are always right on the brink anyway, gonads and hormones being what they are. Stars and a sense of being nothing much under the infinite sky only made the blood run hotter; and there was a war on, people getting killed, what are you saving it for ... the thrilling nearness of a boy's newly shaved face, his eyes pleading with you, singling you out from all the other billions of girls in the universe, wanting to make love to you. What a misnomer, love. Yet that was exactly what we were doing: making love. Maybe not to each other, but to life and the astonishing concept of male and female. It was a rush to know a boy wanted you; it made you feel excited all the way through your body and especially in the secret parts, the parts he wanted so devoutly to touch. They were dying to be touched, forbidden fruit pulsing because its nature was to seduce. You felt hot and moist and trembling inside you and then he knew and he took your hand ever so gently and slowly and put it on the swollen bulge in his pants.

After a while even Bobby stopped singing. Everyone was concentrating on sex by then. Mr. Wilson either didn't know or didn't want to know what was going on behind him and his team. He just looked straight ahead and kept the horses walking at a nice slow pace. I remember hearing their bells faintly jingling as though from very far away. When we passed by a farm of his acquaintance, we heard someone call out across the barnyard, from a dark screened porch, "Hiya, Harry, what kinda load you got there?"

And our charioteer answers, "I got me a bunch of Jews hyar. Havin' a hayride!"

"Jews on a hayride! Well, ain't that a hoot'n holler!" The

chuckle echoed on the summer night air, but then it was behind us and faded into nothing. We clung to each other, but if a shadow had passed over us, a remembrance of grand-parents, a connection to other caravans, all such thoughts were gone quickly and we had heard nothing to spoil our fun. We were young and safe and it was a party. This was America. Swing your partner in a do-si-do and on we go.

The muffled little moans we heard from all around us made us more passionate; well, everything and anything made us more passionate. I felt dizzy and didn't care; I could feel She writhing and jerking around, but with Alan's arms around me and his urgent need for me (me!), his closeness covering me like welcoming darkness to shut out everything else, everyone else . . . I could only give in to it. I wanted to.

Alan and Syd must have exchanged some kind of signal; they moved at the same time to slide under She and me, a little awkward what with the blankets and the hay and all, and other people's legs, but there we were. Alan was holding me from behind, on our sides, spoon-fashion, nice. I could feel his erection between my legs, huge and straining. He took my hand and moved it behind me to hold him, and then he slowly slipped his zipper down, and I was holding the real thing. It was so warm and so hard and suddenly all I wanted was to feel it against my softest flesh, my thigh, up close, closer, to the vortex of my body, not inside, not that, no, no, but just in between my lips, all along from behind to front, lying there stiff and pulsating, now thrusting a little, just a little, not serious, just nice, nice. And then he was rubbing and slipping along in the moisture and gently, slowly (where did a kid named Alan Irving Orloff learn such wonderful things in Sioux City, Iowa?) inserting it inside me.

I was going all the way but it didn't matter, nothing mattered. Being attached to Sheila didn't matter—for the moment, I wasn't! I forgot about her, about disgracing my parents, about injustice and getting VD or pregnant and being ashamed of myself. I didn't care if the horses turned up 27th Street again and took us right down Pierce Street all the way to Fourth for the whole town to see Alan Orloff's penis inside me. I didn't care if everybody on that wagon stopped what they were doing to point at me and laugh. What I was feeling was overpowering and I never wanted it to stop. I responded to Alan's thrusts and slow, gentle in-and-out movements with my own instinctive rhythm. I wanted to turn around so he could kiss me, but instead I grabbed his hand and sucked on his fingers; I felt him shudder with plea-sure and he moaned and then he was throbbing wildly inside me and spurting and with his other hand he reached down to hold himself inside of me and when his fingers touched me I came, too.

After a while, I started to hear the horses' bells again and their hooves and the stirrings and murmurings of the other kids. Alan slid out of me, all soft and sweet now. I gave him one last caress and then he moved out from under me and I started to look for my underpants. When they had come off and where the hell they could be I had no idea. I started to giggle, remembering when Mary O'Brien's huge bra was found way up on top of the lilac bush in the O'Briens' front yard one Sunday morning after a Knights of Columbus dance; she and Tom Flanagan had had to get married be-cause of that. I felt a deep female kinship with Mary, whom I didn't even know personally. I was a fallen woman, too, and now I realized how awful it must be for her—would always be—to be thought of as a smutty joke by the whole town. I wondered if Alan might marry me. I wouldn't mind. I'd even work in his dad's auto-parts store every day alongside him if it meant spending the whole night with him in the same bed every night of my life.

Yeah, me and Sheila.

She and Syd weren't finished yet. I couldn't squirm around too much or even turn toward Alan for a little afterglow kiss. I had to lie there groping in the scratchy hay with my foot, trying to snag my panties. I could hear Syd groaning and panting, but as far as I could tell, She wasn't doing much of anything; she was just lying there.

"Hurry up, Sheila," I whispered. Why did I think that was funny? I started to giggle.

Alan was sitting up, turned away from me, lighting a cigarette.

Sheila kicked me. My panties were wrapped around her foot. Or maybe they were her panties. I thought of putting them on, and decided not to. I'd have a delicious, dangerous secret: no underwear. I wanted to keep that sexy, illicit feeling going forever. But in the same instant it now occurred to me to hope I wasn't pregnant.

Girls who got pregnant dropped out of school with mysterious ailments for a whole semester or more and their mothers went with them to Arizona or California for their health or to visit relatives, but everybody knew.

"Don't come inside her, Syd," I whispered to him, giggling uncontrollably but still thinking I'd rather marry Alan than have her marry Syd Finkelstein.

Alan leaned over and gave me a puff of his cigarette. "Thanks," I said, letting the smoke out slowly, like Ida Lupino.

"Come on, Syd, for God's sake, we're heading back to town," I said.

"You shut up," Sheila snarled.

Syd must have figured it was now or never. I think the whole wagonload heard him start to huff and puff and utter little sounds like "Uh-uh-uh-uh-uh-UUUUUHHHHH!" and damned if a couple of the boys on the other side of the wagon didn't actually laugh out loud and even cheer. "Yeah, Syd, way to go!" and stuff like that.

I looked over and saw that Syd had jerked himself off. He was wiping himself with his handkerchief. Sheila just lay there. She still had her pants on, so those had to be mine twined around her foot. I reached down and grabbed them and pulled them on quickly. I was all sticky.

"Gimme a cigarette," Syd grunted to Alan.

"You'll set the whole haystack on fire," Sheila protested sharply. We sat up, and I was glad we couldn't look each other in the face. "Don't anybody smoke!" She called out loudly, with an imperious edge. "This hay could go up in a second and kill us all."

" 'They said someday you'll find, all who love are blind, when your heart's on fire, you must realize, smoke gets in your eyes,' " sang Bobby in a rare display of wit, and everyone laughed and settled down again, boys' arms around girls. You could take a photograph of the whole scene and show it to anyone: a bunch of nice, wholesome kids on a bucolic Midwest hayride, corny but sweet; it's Andy Hardy time.

That night, lying awake listening to She's postnasal drip, I had a terrible attack of guilt—not about my lost virginity, good riddance—but about the war. I turned on my flashlight and wrote a poem in my private code in the notebook I kept under my pillow. The poem was deeply ironic and spoke of "that great Ogre, Sex, appeased at last, Like Hitler with the Munich Pact." My conscience felt much better after that, and I slept very well.

11

We Are Sent Out
into the World

"*I'm so humiliated.* How could you act that way? How could you do that to me? You're nothing but a cheap tramp!"

"You were doing the same thing. Everybody was."

"No they weren't! Nobody else was doing anything except you! Tramp! How can I hold my head up in this town after this? I'm ashamed to admit you're my sister. You Went All the Way, didn't you? I'll bet you did! Ick, don't tell me! God, I don't want to know, so shut up!"

"I didn't say anything."

"Everybody's going to know about you. I just hope Billie doesn't find out because it would just break her heart, it would just kill her, that's all. Why can't you learn how to act like a respectable person? There's a word for girls like you."

"Slut?" I offered sullenly.

"Yes. That's what you are. A slut. I don't know how I can hold my head up in this town anymore. And the way you

124

talked! Saying out loud what you said to Syd, and he wasn't doing a thing! Not because he didn't try, but I never let him. I'd never let any boy do that to me because I have pride and self-respect!"

"All I said was—"

"Don't say it again! Just shut up. Nobody wants to hear your foul mouth. Oh God, my own sister. How am I ever going to live this down? You're just a—a slut."

"Go to hell, hypocrite."

"I hate you. I wish you were dead. Everybody wishes you were dead. You're nothing but a disgrace and an embarrassment to the whole family. If it weren't for you, everything would be just perfect. You spoil everything for everybody."

I shut my ears to her. I thought about picking up a hammer and knocking her on the head until blood poured out and her brains fell out onto the floor. All of her brains together would probably only make a spot you could wipe up with a Q-Tip.

"What are you two fighting about now?" my mother called out from the hall outside our door.

"Nothing," we sang out in unison.

"Well, I hope not," Billie said, going away. "Why can't you love each other like sisters should? You'll be the death of me yet." Her voice trailed down the stairs while the old refrain echoed up to us.

"Why can't you love each other?" I mimicked meanly.

"Slut," Sheila said, by the way of having the last word. You had to let her have the last word if you ever wanted the subject dropped.

For reasons having nothing to do with my sister's opinion, I never Did It again with Alan—although he seemed to think I would. For the rest of our time in high school I tried to avoid him, and if I had to sit next to him in school or at a party or even if I danced with him, I tried to be as aloof as Marlene Dietrich. Alan couldn't figure out what was wrong, but the fact was I now found him slightly repulsive. Once in civics class I couldn't take my eyes off a big red and yellow boil on his neck, even though it made me queasy. I never wanted to get into a situation like the hayride again, where I just said yes to everything someone else wanted. If I gave up control of my life for even one instant, someone else would grab the reins and run with them. I had all I could do to hang on against my own family; I sure as hell wasn't going to hand over the works to Alan Irving Orloff. Once during our senior year when we were all at Edie's house, dancing with the lights out, Alan grabbed my breast as if he had a right to it and I kneed him in his balls. He bent over and groaned, but he wouldn't tell anybody what was wrong. Avoiding him was easy after that.

All the seniors had to fill out questionnaires for the yearbook: what is your nickname (Melody); what extracurricular activities are you in (band, orchestra, English Lit. Club); your favorite band leader (Glenn Miller); secret crush (Frank Sinatra); pet peeve (my sister); secret ambition (to go out on a date with my dad).

Miss Brown, the faculty adviser for the yearbook, called me in to her room and showed me my filled-out questionnaire. "You can't say this," she said gently.

"Oh. Well, it's true I just made up that nickname. I'll erase that. I'll put Sandy." I leaned over her desk with my gum eraser ready, but she touched the back of my hand to stop me.

"It's not that," she said. We called her Mousie, but she was just a very nice, sweet elderly lady with a great love for William Shakespeare, which I had clandestinely caught from her. She was my favorite teacher, but I could never let her know that.

"It's this—your secret ambition . . ."

I looked down at what I had written and I felt myself blushing. "Oh gosh, how did that get there? Gosh, I sure didn't mean to write that!" I erased it furiously.

126

"What'd she write?" my sister wanted to know, straining to peer over at the paper.

"Never mind," Miss Brown said. "Now, Sandra, what would you like to put there instead?"

"Let's see . . . I'll have to think. Secret ambition . . . I don't know," I said miserably. I didn't really want to *date* my dad, not in any sexy way or anything Freudian, for God's sake. It was just that I'd never thought about a secret ambition before, and when I thought about it I thought, Well, I'd really like to have a conversation with old Henry, just the two of us, maybe over a root-beer float or something. That's all. No big deal. But they didn't really mean for us to reveal our secrets. It was just another asinine student thing—one more booby trap, and I was the booby. I erased furiously.

"I thought you wanted to become a writer?" Miss Brown prompted.

"Yes, that's right. I guess I didn't understand when they said secret. That's the part that confused me."

"Oh boy," my sister muttered in disgust.

"I can see how that would confuse anybody. You're absolutely right, it shouldn't be a secret ambition at all. Thank you, Sandra."

"Thank you," I mumbled.

When we got out of the room, She was all curiosity. "What did you put down? What did she make you change? You'd better tell me."

"I put . . . I wrote . . . I said my secret ambition was to be a fireman."

"Oh God! No wonder she stopped you! You would have been the laughingstock of the whole town. A great big grown-up girl wanting to be a fireman! Oh, spare me!"

"You're spared," I said glumly. Why couldn't I ever remember the rules: honesty-is-the-best-policy was the biggest lie there was. Truth was a trap, honesty got you laughed at, reality was a mirage. Stick to fiction, kid; everybody else does.

I stopped in my tracks and told She I had to see Miss Brown again for a minute, it was urgent. Her reputation as well as mine depended on it, I lied. We worked our way back through the crowded, noisy hall to the quiet of Miss Brown's room, where she was still poring over the questionnaires.

"May I change that answer again, please?" I asked breathlessly.

Miss Brown pulled my paper from the stack; it was still on top. "Why, yes, Sandra. What do you want to say?"

"I want to be a fiction writer. Not just a writer, a fiction writer. It's important. I'm sorry to bother you," I said all in one breath.

I loved the way she looked then. Her tired old eyes lit up and her face crinkled in a shy, rare smile. "Yes," she said. There was real pleasure in her voice. "Yes, you're right. You've discovered something, haven't you, Sandy?"

"Have I?" I asked, bewildered.

"Well, maybe you haven't put it into words for yourself yet. But I think," she said as she herself wrote in a caret and inserted the word *fiction* in my answer, "I think what you've discovered is that fiction may be the only way to tell the truth. I believe you really might become a writer someday, Sandra."

I found myself staring directly into a teacher's eyes, and she was looking straight back at me, with—wonder of wonders!—thoughtfulness and even a kind of respect. It was the best moment of my entire life. I felt an impulse to kiss her dry cheek, but of course that would have probably been an expellable offense. I let Sheila lead me out of Miss Brown's room; I was Alice stepping back through the looking glass into the mundane hallway to be greeted by Bubbles Bernstein's hyperthyroid giggles as my sister told her what I had done. Well, at least I'd lied about that, thank God.

And finally it was time to graduate! The war in Europe ended that May and victory over Japan could not be far behind and we were the class of '45, who would step out to greet the peace. What glorious timing! All the soldiers would be coming back—to college, a lot of them, and there we'd be.

People always said to seniors, "Well, enjoy your last fling while you can, you'll be facing the real world soon enough." They made the future sound dire and all prospects grim; I gathered from this that they hated their lives and wished us the same. The speaker at our commencement talked of the challenges that lay waiting just on the other side of the threshold where we stood. *(Fifteenth and Douglas?* I'm sure some graduates decided right then and there never to cross it, and they never did.) He hinted in a gloomy, stentorian voice about the sad need to leave childhood joys behind for-ever. Who was he? Someone running for public office, an Elk or a Moose or a Lion or an Eagle, a Legionnaire or a Mason or a Shriner, a Rotarian or Oddfellow or Knight of Colum-bus, a big duck in that little pond because of his oratorical powers or his money. He rolled out the rhetoric in rumbling vibrato that shook the halls of the old auditorium. He trem-bled and gestured to punctuate his vague clichés of the great weight of the future whose burden we were about to shoul-der, the herculean task of carving out a better world than the one they had tried to leave us (the Augean stables, with thirty years' accumulation of horseshit, came graphically to my mind), the unknown pitfalls of life ready to attack us from all sides unless somehow we attacked first.

We all squirmed in our seats, waiting for his speech to end so we could go home to dress for the prom. All I could think of was getting out of that town, where we had misspent our entire lives trying to be just like everybody else. Why? We were not like other people, dammit. I needed to know the outer boundaries of that, what it could lead to in the world. Sheila looked forward to making personal conquests, and so did I. Hers were of the social variety; mine would be . . . I didn't know yet—something no one else could do as well as I. My preference for novels and movies over real life hardly

129

seemed a vocation, despite Miss Mousie Brown's encouragement.

The commencement speaker talked about separation from the Ties That Bind. I snickered aloud, embarrassing Sheila. She kicked me with her high heel. I took out the safety pin that was holding my black robe closed and stuck it in her thigh until she yelled, "Ouch!" and everybody turned to look at us. We both slunk down in our seats and hoped Billie and Daddy, sitting in the back of the auditorium, hadn't seen.

We wore matching dresses for the prom. She's was pale pink and mine was pale blue. Our dates—Moose Wasserman for She, Bobby Dorfman for me this time around—brought us tinted gardenias the color of our dresses. Our shoes had been dyed to match, too. One of the few things we agreed on was that we loathed being dressed alike, but Billie got all sentimental right there in Martin's department store, talking to the saleswoman.

"My girls are growing up and about to fly right out of the cozy little nest I've made for them. Wouldn't you think they'd do just this one thing to please me—it's not as if I ever ask for anything for myself. Is it so terrible for a mother to want her girls to shine? Nobody knows what I've been through for them, giving up everything just so they can have all the advantages I never had. I was practically a baby myself when they were born, you know, and I'll be forty soon, can you imagine that? I can't! Oh, thank you, everybody says that, but I don't know . . . pretty soon they won't need me any more at all—so just this once wouldn't you think they'd wear what I want them to? Is my taste so bad? It's such a little thing, but it would make my heart so happy."

It was such a little thing to do to please her, playing Tweedle-dum and Tweedle-dee just one last time. The dresses would be tulle, which is a kind of stiff gauze that makes you feel like you're wearing a barbed wire fence.

So here they are again: the petite curly-haired beauty with the delicate complexion and the flashing lively eyes, and the other one, with glasses and blackheads, lousy posture and self-conscious laugh, joking around like Goofy. There couldn't be two more different types, physically and in every other way, so why do they want to dress alike and stand so close together all the time? Why does everyone always say they are "identical?"

The dance was in the ballroom of the Warrior Hotel. By the time we arrived, the gentiles were already whirling around the floor and laughing and they looked golden and innocent and there was an illusion of spotlights following them wherever they went, highlighting their shiny hair and radiant features. My old friend Louise Hansen looked particularly beautiful, I thought. Her braids had turned to a bright twirled cascade of precious metals, and she wore a blue homemade taffeta dress exactly the color of her eyes. I was glad to see that she was popular, even though she still turned the other way when she saw me coming.

The Jewish kids stayed in a clutch together for the most part, near the punchbowl and potato chips, except for Jerry Fein, who was class valedictorian and planned to run for mayor when he finished college and law school. He danced with Betty Lou Larsen and even Nancy Teller, who was homecoming queen. Jerry's date, Marilyn Pickel, just stood on the sidelines and watched him proudly, as if his dancing with gentile girls were her own idea. Maybe it was. She called him Jay. She wanted to marry him so she could be the mayor's wife someday, never mind his buck teeth. He went to Yale law school and married a girl from Racine, Wisconsin. Marilyn Pickel married a Jewish farmer with two hundred acres near Centerville and competed every year of her life in the strawberry-rhubarb-pie division of the State Fair and never won any kind of ribbon (my mother said it was because she was Jewish; everyone knew all those farmers

131

hated Jews, and what was a Jew doing on a farm anyhow?).

Except for Jerry (who did become Sioux City's first Jewish mayor, but so what?—the town changed to a city-manager system right after his term), the rest of us danced with our own kind. Oh, there was the traditional moment when we all got into a big circle and held hands and sang the school song. I felt a special sense of belonging, privileged to be allowed into the same circle as Nancy Teller and Tom Moran and all the luminous people.

After the dance we went to the Gables for hamburgers and curly french fries and then made our way up to War Eagle's grave. But it was so crowded with other cars that there was no more room; some kids didn't even bother to eat first; they went to park directly from the prom. She and Moose and Bobby and I ended up way out in a cornfield someplace in South Dakota. It was dark all around and we weren't sure that we hadn't driven right onto some newly planted corn, and we felt kind of nervous about that and generally excited about being graduated at last, so mostly we just sat and talked.

Then Bobby drove us home but when we got to our house nobody moved to get out of the car. Bobby turned around to face the three of us, put his chin down on his folded arms, and sighed dramatically.

"Listen, I want to wish you guys the best. I know that sounds corny, but I mean it sincerely and I just wanted to say it."

We were all deeply touched. "Well, we wish you the very best too, Bobby," I said softly.

"Oh well, I'll probably get sent right to the Pacific," he said bravely.

"Well, you're not going till October. Your birthday's not till October," Moose pointed out. "The war could be over by then. Maybe you won't have to go at all." There was nothing romantic about Moose Wasserman.

"We're all going out into the world," Sheila said. "We may never see each other again."

"Well, nobody's going anywhere for the whole summer," I had to point out. "We'll see each other all summer."

"God, leave it to her to put a damper on everything!"

But Moose knew what I meant. "Want to go to the movies tomorrow night?" he asked Sheila, with a brusque laugh.

"Well, all right. I guess so."

"Let's all go," Bobby offered.

"Okay."

"Okay."

"And anyway, in the meantime, I meant what I said. I wish you all just really good lives, you know what I mean?"

We knew what Bobby meant and we all shook on it, solemnly, and got out of the car and shook hands all around again and wished each other happiness and success in whatever life had in store. The next night we all went to the movies and the Green Gables and War Eagle's grave, just like old times.

12

A Ring for Sheila

"*What kind of name* is Moritz?" Billie asked Roger point-blank. We were having dinner in the dining room, the first time Sheila brought him home.

"It's Swiss, Mother," Sheila said grandly.

"Well actually, my grandparents were citizens of Luxembourg," Roger explained. I don't think any of us had ever heard of Luxembourg, certainly not as a country. Maybe as a cheese.

"I mean is it a Jewish name," Billie said, with a little laugh in case the lieutenant had made a joke. The laugh served two purposes; it was also supposed to take the rude edge off the question. Like taking the edge off a hacksaw by running it across someone's finger.

"I don't know," was Roger's interesting answer. "It certainly could be, I suppose."

"Oh, then you are Jewish," my mother said, visibly relieved.

134

"Oh, Mother, that's so old-fashioned!" Sheila said prettily.

"What's the diff, they're not going to church," I said, drawing frowns.

"And what does your father do, Roger?" asked the undaunted inquisitor.

"He's a sculptor," Roger said. He was so at ease with this that he went right on eating pot roast and didn't seem to notice that we had all stopped chewing to stare at him.

"Oh, that's nice," Billie said vaguely. "You must have lots of nice statues around the house."

"What does he do for a living?" Daddy asked, his attention finally piqued.

"Well actually, he inherited quite a bit, so he doesn't really have to worry about—uh, I mean—yes, ah, he inherited quite a bit."

"Enough to live on?" Billie asked, all pretense down the drain. Her mouth was actually open, and you could see the half-chewed meat and carrots in there.

Roger nodded and blushed furiously and Billie shot a look of pure triumph over at Daddy, and then she reached for the platter and held it up as an offering to Roger's father's money. "Have some more pot roast," she said reverently. "I made it myself. It's my own recipe. And cooking's not my only talent! Did Sheila tell you I used to be a dancer?"

Roger and Sheila had met out at the base in early spring, one Saturday night at an officers' club dance. This sweet-faced second looey with sandy hair cut in on her and neither of them danced with anybody else after that. Her date was furious and called her a goddamn freak anyway and stomped out into the slushy April snow, never to be seen by us again. When the dance was over, Roger came with She and me and my date. We all climbed into Daddy's Chrysler (with fluid drive, the last model before they stopped making cars for the duration of the war). I was driving. I always drove, since I was on the left side. Sheila's date usually sat next to her on the front seat and mine had to sit all alone in the back. Sometimes we'd end up at the diner down the road from the air base, or the Green Gables if the soldiers were presentable enough to be introduced to practically the whole goddamn Jewish population of the county. But the night we met Roger, I was feeling a little crampy—maybe I was getting the curse or maybe it was just from the two of them sighing and gazing at each other so icky-gooey. Believe me, I wasn't jealous. It was just that if it had been a movie, I'd have walked out on it.

I drove straight home, and our dates had to walk the whole fourteen blocks back downtown, because there were no streetcars after ten o'clock. The army bus shuttled from the airbase to 4th and Pierce every hour or so all night long; they could go inside the temporary shelter and have coffee while they waited. The bus stop was also known as a pro station, which meant condoms were dispensed there, although we weren't supposed to know that.

Roger was such a gentleman he didn't even try to kiss Sheila that night, so my lieutenant got tangle-footed and didn't kiss me, either. We said good night and then I was in for hours and days of listening to her maundering to Bubbles and Edie in person and on the phone about True Love. Roger Moritz was the man of her dreams, and she had already decided to say yes when he asked her to marry him. "You just know these things," She said. To my fury, it all turned out—for quite a while—exactly as she had planned it.

I can't account for it. Roger seemed perfectly normal to me. Not only that, but he was in the Intelligence branch of the Army Air Force. They don't call the air force part of the army anymore, and if they've got any brains at all, they don't call what Roger did intelligence, either. I was relieved to learn that in fact he just typed other people's reports. He was nice—I liked old Roger well enough—I just never thought of him as intelligent. For the first year or so that he knew us, he thought She and I were only joking about hating each other.

Billie started calling Roger "my son" and giving out lots of advice on how to hold a man's interest. It all centered around making him desperate with desire for you in every way you could but never letting him go too far, because if he got everything he wanted free, why should he pay the price by marrying you? And you'd be damaged goods for the next customer.

I listened to this thoughtfully. Was I damaged goods? My virginity was in the same never-never land as the shadowy time long ago when I'd tried to separate us with a razor. Certain events in our lives were simply not ever mentioned; they lurked only as dark and terrible shadows impossible to confront, despite the scars we carried.

For a couple of months, even if I didn't have a date of my own, I was schlepped to the movies, to the officers' club for dinner and dancing, to the base fence to whisper good night after taps. Some nights I was laid out on a blanket in Grandview Park or up near War Eagle on the river bluffs. I'd lie there trying to identify all the stars and planets and signs of the zodiac while She and Roger petted and cooed and did everything except It. I got so I hardly even noticed as my pelvis was pulled this way and that.

Why would a nice, rich normal Harvard law student fall in love with a girl from Iowa who was grotesquely attached to her sister in a way sure to bring unpleasant attention? All I can tell you is that Sheila knew everything about roping in a randy young ram. And we had mastered the knack of appearing more attractive than not, most of the time. Could it be that in us Roger saw the answer to boring monogamy? He and I became pretty good friends; he found me someone to talk to, someone who was on his side in all the quarrels and misunderstandings to come. That was later, though. In the beginning, during their mushy phase, I stayed as much out of it as I possibly could.

College would be my Swan Lake, where I would be discovered by my own species. I ached to be in an atmosphere where brains were an asset rather than a liability and conversation was witty and people knew how to behave in libraries. Professors would stimulate my mind and marvel at my brilliance, handsome young veterans home from the war would intuit my true worth from across a classroom. I would learn Latin and Greek and music and philosophy, read all the good books that had ever been written, and write fiction that would make everyone laugh and cry and understand just a little more about life. My high school teachers had already predicted that I would do very well in college. I had been looking forward to college ever since I gave up on Oz.

But by summer Sheila was in love, and now she didn't think she wanted to go to college after all. This time I knew for certain I would really kill her. But, lucky for everyone, Roger had to go occupy Germany. (I thought this was very brave of him, being Jewish, but he said what did that have to do with it and I decided he was either heroic beyond measure or the most dull-witted person I had ever met. But of course he didn't think of himself as Jewish and never had. His parents were so rich they didn't have to be Jewish if they didn't want to.)

She wanted to get married before he went overseas, but Roger thought they'd better wait to see if he came back. A touch melodramatic, I thought, considering that the war was over by the time he went. Roger was twenty-two, but She was not even eighteen yet and if it was true love, it would still be there after "the duration plus six months," which was when everybody would get out of military service. So, much to my relief, we proceeded with our plans to go to college.

Billie had been making loud jokes about finally getting us out of her hair, but at the same time, I think she feared for the reception we might get in a strange place, where people were sure to think us—well, different. Our parents had both been convinced that no one would ever take us off their hands, so Daddy thought after a year or two of college, we should learn to work in his office and maybe someday even become his partners; not that either of us had any aptitude or interest in accounting. But Roger Moritz and the Great Romance changed everything. Our folks looked at us with new respect. An incredibly desirable potential son-in-law actually wanted to marry one of us.

Edie said, "What are you going to do about Sandy?"

My sister just shrugged. "I don't have to do anything about Sandy," she sniffed. "Nobody'll ever want to marry *her*. She can just come along with me and keep her goddamn mouth shut, that's what."

Edie giggled and her hair leaped around her head like the salvos from a Fourth-of-July sparkler. "Well, I mean in bed, at night," she snickered. "It's gonna be kind of crowded, isn't it?" Edie and Bubbles both broke up at this and you could just tell they had laughed about it together before. She got so mad they had a fight and she lost both her best friends for a couple of weeks.

In the meantime, it was agreed that She would be a better wife for a Harvard man if she grabbed a little education. We said goodbye to Roger with three or four sickeningly sentimental evenings. He gave She a diamond ring that had been his grandmother's. His father sent it from New York. She said once the old-fashioned setting was changed it would probably be just fine, although she had sort of had her heart set on a heart-shaped diamond. He promised her one for their tenth anniversary, and she said, "How about for the first baby instead?" and they giggled and kissed and She spent the rest of the evening turning her hand this way and that way so the light would catch the diamond.

Finally, Roger actually flew away. Having pledged eternal fidelity, never even to look at another man, She's life suddenly sucked itself up and there was nothing left. Without boys, guys, men, what on earth was there to think about or talk about or *do*? We might as well go to college.

Girls chose which school to attend on the basis of which sorority they had the best chance of getting into. For us, the choice was considerably narrowed down, not because we were conjoined but because we were Jewish. Most schools had quotas, and there were only two Jewish sororities in the whole United States and on some campuses, only one.

If you didn't get into a sorority, the rest of your life would be ruined. Nice boys would not date you and you wouldn't get to meet people who would be important contacts (professional for boys, social for girls) for your future. Anyone ever meeting you for the rest of your life would know you hadn't made it when it counted. A girl who had been turned down by a sorority was low-class, unworthy, ugly, and without social graces. What you studied meant nothing; what sorority you pledged was all. Oh well, it was true you had to maintain a C average to stay active in any sorority—university rules—but your sisters were there to help pull you through.

And so the thing to do was to select a college where someone you knew was already a member of a sorority and could be counted on to get you in. For some reason, Sioux City girls were expected to be loyal to other Sioux City girls whether they liked them or not. Ducky Fein and Fran Goldman were already members of Sigma Delta Tau at the State University of Iowa, and our mother played canasta with their mothers.

One day that summer two girls we didn't know came to look us over. One was from Omaha and the other from Dubuque, and they belonged to SDT's Iowa chapter. One of them wrote on stationery that had the Greek letters engraved at the top, to ask if they could come meet us. Billie got all aflutter and wrote back yes, and they came for tea at four o'clock one afternoon. It was the first and last time Billie ever entertained at tea in her life, although she tried to act like she did it every day. Helen polished the silver tray and made her special almond cake—and they were only snotty girls a year or two older than we were! They stayed for exactly one hour and said not one word the whole time that was of any interest to me at all. They showed real animation only when admiring Sheila's diamond ring. I despaired. College was going to be exactly like the rest of my life so far.

After they left, Billie said they had beautiful manners and she thought it went well—meaning maybe they wouldn't think we were too peculiar to be pledged to their sorority. We knew for sure when we got thank-you notes from them (same Greek letters on same weight but shorter pieces of blue paper) saying they looked forward to seeing us again at rush week in Iowa City should we decide to go to school there, which they hoped we would.

So we did.

I studied the catalog and found hope. There was a writers' workshop for me and a theater department for She, who had decided she wanted to be an actress. (I have to admit I loved the idea and would gladly have encouraged her if she had asked my opinion, because I figured such a bizarre course could only lead to hilarity. Even if some deranged playwright wrote parts for Siamese-twin sisters, there was no way anybody was ever going to get me on a stage.) There were history and lit courses and social studies and art appreciation and Latin and Greek and poetry and drama and political science and just literally millions of things I couldn't wait to learn.

We celebrated V-J Day on our eighteenth birthday, August 15th, 1945, and now the war was really over. We packed our sweaters and skirts and socks and saddle shoes and party dresses and blouses and new slips and panties and bras and fake pearls and basic-black dresses and accessories and formal evening gowns with matching pumps and long white gloves in our identically initialed sets of matched luggage (hers red, mine blue) and finally we were away, carrying our square makeup cases and new fur coats over our arms.

At last we were on the train to Iowa City, more than halfway across the state. Off into the great unknown, which just had to be better than the known—didn't it? College would open our minds, even Sheila's. We would meet fascinating new people and we would never go home again. I think of us now, the two of us dressed in new tweed suits and little round hats, wearing high-heeled imitation-alligator shoes, clutching our imitation-alligator purses, sitting on the train facing east, watching cornfields and telephone poles go by, each thinking our very different thoughts. She was thinking about the sorority and hoping I wouldn't spoil her chances. I was dreaming of impossible freedoms.

Rush week took place before the "independents"—rejects, loners, intellectuals, and other oddballs who were not good enough to join the elite—arrived on campus for registration. The prospective sorority and fraternity recruits were housed in dormitories, and rush week was devoted exclusively to parties. The sororities would send invitations to carefully culled lists, which became shorter each day. Girls ran all over the dorm shrieking with excitement as invitations arrived; the ones who didn't get them did their weeping behind closed doors. One girl slashed her wrists when she didn't get invited to a Kappa Kappa Gamma do. She bled all over the third-floor bathroom and then her folks came and took her back to Des Moines. Our invitations came only from Sigma Delta Tau, of course. Gentile girls had ten or twelve houses to choose from; we had one, and the choice was not ours.

The first party was tea, at which the housemother poured. She was an elderly woman who lived there as chaperon. I could tell she was drunk, although she held it pretty well. Aunt Sil, they called her. She poured the tea from a huge silver pot into translucent cups that rattled in her hand. The house had a grandiose living room, a large dining room, a sun porch, and a so-called library on the first floor, all heavily garnished with shining silver candy dishes, bud vases, picture frames, a spectacular samovar, and the ornate tea-and-coffee set on its giant silver tray. A great deal of money had been spent here by the daddies of the SDT's. The members all had identical little gold pins over their hearts and paper badges with their names: HI, I'M GLORIA! We were given paper badges to write our names on. She wrote: HI, I'M SHEILA! I wrote: "The Hon. Sandra Lazarus."

"Hey, that's funny!" said a member labelled HI, I'M BARBARA!, plumping herself down on the couch next to me.

"Do you think so? I wondered if anybody would think so. Sometimes I go too far," I confessed. She was a tall girl with pale skin, thin brown hair forced into waves, and a calm, quiet voice that I liked. She said she was from Dubuque and majoring in business administration and starting her junior year. She looked straight at me as if she actually saw my face. She seemed interested in talking to me even though she'd probably drawn my name in a lottery for this segment of the tea party.

"What's 'the hon' stand for?" she asked, pronouncing it like the first syllable in *honey*.

I couldn't stop myself in time; I pronounced it the same way. "Honorable?" All was lost. My voice quavered. Maybe I shouldn't have imitated her articulation quite so precisely; she'd think I was making fun of her, acting superior. I'd probably blown all our chances by being a smart ass again . . .

Barbara burst out in quiet and refined but very honest laughter. "I like you," she said. "You've got my vote."

"Really?"

"Sure."

"I like you too, Barbara. Thanks."

"So. What's it like being a Siamese twin?" she asked,

helping herself to a single candy-covered mint and popping it into her mouth. Barbara was not the type to need more than one piece of candy or let it smear her fingers.

"Sticky," I said, watching her and thinking what would happen if I tried to take just one candy.

She laughed again and so did I, because I started to believe she really did like me. My sister, who was carrying on a very formal and apparently strained conversation on the other side of the couch with a tall young woman wearing rhinestone-studded glasses, spun around to see what was going on. She was absolutely sure I had ruined everything.

"She said she liked me and she's going to vote for us," I reassured Sheila on the way back to the dormitory, but she couldn't believe it.

"She was laughing at you. People always laugh at you."

"We were both laughing. Because I said something funny. Honest. It's okay."

"How would you know?"

There were several teas and coffee hours and buffet luncheons and sit-down luncheons and sherry parties and an evening soiree; each time, the terrible tension of waiting to be invited, each time, the relief at someone else's expense, each party with fewer guests and more intense concentration on you . . . and then, the big day, the one that you either got invited to or you were permanently OUT: the formal announcement luncheon. Nobody slept the night before. She was so nervous she vomited up her breakfast. Her retching twisted my ribs and made me feel sick, too. Invitations were hand-delivered to the dormitory all morning long, from Theta Beta this and Alpha Omicron that, and finally from Sigma Delta Tau. Sheila got one. I got one, too.

"They had to invite you because of me," She pointed out. Maybe it was true—after all, Barbara was just one vote, and I had spent the rest of the week talking with an endless lineup of dressmakers' dummies. I was apprehensive and miserable as we packed our things for the move into the house. "I can't believe they actually took you," She said. "They must have really wanted me real bad."

"Badly," I said.

"Bad enough to let you come, too."

"It's not as if they had a goddamn choice, Sheila!" I exploded.

"Well, *I* certainly wouldn't have voted for you," she said.

I wondered whether, if I banged my head against the wall real hard, really very, *very* hard, someone might pay attention, ask me what was wrong, even listen to my troubles and—and nothing. There was nothing anyone could do.

13

Sorority

The house was sunny, and our new sisters-to-be—just what I needed, more sisters—were lined up at the door to greet us as we arrived. They sang a welcome-to-our-house song on the front porch and then each member stepped forward to take one of the lucky new girls under her wing. They ushered us inside the house, which was decorated with yellow bunting and fresh flowers in rooms full of elegant containers. (As a pledge, I would spend many hours polishing all that silver.) My pledge mother was Barbara Goldfine. She was the one who liked me because I made her laugh on that first visit; I wondered if she might even have asked especially for me. She put her arm around my shoulders and said, "I'm going to be your special friend, and I hope you'll always come to me with any problems or questions you have about sorority life or school or anything."

"Sure," I said gratefully. "Sure, Barbara, thanks a million, I will. I'll be your friend, too."

"Well, of course!" she laughed. I thought maybe I'd said the wrong thing again.

She's rabbi was a large, jolly fat girl with oily skin who had worn cashmere sweaters over real silk dresses (a different one for each occasion) for the entire week. Her name was Joanne and you could tell she was thrilled at the chance to be special pal to a strange person. She was overexcited and gushed like a firehose while Sheila gulped it down as if she had trained for this all her life. Barbara and Joanne led us into the dining room with the other pledge mothers and their thrilled adoptees.

"I'm so glad you're in," Joanne raved. She was having trouble figuring out whether to speak only to Sheila or include me, and her thin, dark pageboy whipped across her face as she yammered and turned from one to the other of us, her face reddening with the effort. Barbara and I just went along quietly, listening to Joanne's manic monologue: "You know, I was one of the ones who fought for you. We had to take it to national! We're actually setting a precedent here! National doesn't like it when a chapter does something out of line, and you got to admit, you two are really something different, right? But I wanted you in right from the beginning, and I'm the one who pointed out that even if we get in the newspapers, all they can say is how broad-minded we are, right? National was scared to death we'd get in the newspapers. I guess you guys get in the newspapers a lot, huh? Well, you've got your sorority sisters to protect you now. Golly, imagine being a sister to Siamese twins. And you're engaged! Oh God, that's so exciting! Let me see your ring again. Priceless. Lucky you. Personally, I'm thrilled, and I hope you'll love us as much as we already love you, right?"

And all the time She kept nodding her head like a Punch and Judy puppet, saying, "Uh-huh, uh-huh, uh-huh."

The luncheon proceeded, and after the chicken salad, the lights in the basement dining room went out and the president came in carrying a cake that had WELCOME CLASS OF '49

PLEDGES and the Greek symbols for sigma, delta, and tau in raised blue frosting. Then we all stood up and the members sang their most sacred song, the one that you're not allowed to sing until you're initiated. The lights went on and the president called out our names, and one by one, except for the Lazarus twins, we stood up and our pledge mothers came around the table to pin little blue-and-gold pledge pins on our left breasts and kiss our cheeks and after it was all done they sang a welcome-to-our-hearts song and then we ate the cake.

After lunch, Barbara and Joanne took us upstairs—the other pledges were getting the same treatment—and showed us their tiny individual bedrooms, where we would be keeping our clothes.

"Here's my room, isn't it a mess? I tried to clean it up for today, but you know, I never made a bed in my life before I came here. So I don't know how, and I really don't see the point in learning, I mean once you know how to do something then you're expected to do it all the time, and back home we've got tons of servants. And while you're pledges, why, you'll be making my bed for me. Sorry about the closets. Here's where you'll hang your stuff. I'll try to make a little more room for you, but honestly, I don't see how I can. Back home I have a whole wall of closets just to myself, with mirrors on the doors. Gee, I never thought I'd be talking like this with Siamese twins, just regular and ordinary like it was nothing special. You don't mind me calling you that, do you? Siamese twins, I mean?"

"Well, I don't let anyone else call us that ordinarily," Sheila told Joanne, "but since you're my pledge mother, well, *you* can if you want to."

Barbara hardly talked at all, but smiled almost shyly at me and made me feel okay. She had conscientiously divided her closet space exactly in half, and my space even had a couple of scented hangers in it. I would have died before telling her that perfume made me cough.

The pledges slept in an attic loft in double-decker bunks (except for us; we had two cots pushed together, the most uncomfortable two hundred and three nights I've ever spent in my life). The only good thing about it was a girl from St. Louis, who had a lovely singing voice and knew all the words to all the verses of "I Wanna Get Married." She sang it for us every night, just about. At least once or twice a week, the lights in our attic dorm would suddenly be blasted on at some horrid hour and the members would roust us out of bed to go down to the living room and be read a dossier of our crimes, then punished on the spot with humiliating tasks: polishing someone's shoes with our own toothbrushes, crawling all the way back up to the third floor on our knees, reciting the Greek alphabet (the closest thing to an intellectual pursuit that ever came out of the house), or having to go, the next day, into the college pharmacy and purchase condoms. Minor hazing, just to see if you could "take it" and still keep up a big C average in your—oh, yeah, I remember—classes.

The sorority got in the way of everything I wanted to do. There were people on the campus I yearned to know: self-confident kids from New York, a brilliant and terribly handsome assistant professor who had published a novel, a girl from India who wore a jewel in her nose, and a boy in my workshop who had been a fighter pilot and worshiped Ernest Hemingway's work. I gravitated toward exactly the people my sister wouldn't be caught dead with; bohemian types, she called them, in a tone exactly like Billie's when she talked about greenhorns and Scandihoovians and shvartzes. I sighed after the art majors with paint stains on their clothes, actors who posed themselves in the student-union cafeteria, talking and gesturing self-confidently, musicians who carried scores and instruments with them and vanished into the listening room, where my sorority sisters had forbidden me to go because just sitting and listening to classical music was a waste of time.

I began to obsess on the need to be alone. I guess you always want what you can't have. But it was making me nuts; not just my sister but swarms of other girls constantly with us, always talking and never saying anything. I couldn't read or study or think a clear thought. I had to have a little space of my own, somehow, or all the pressure building up in me would explode all over everyone, in hideous, splattering wrath.

A sorority was a closed unit. There was something suspect about wanting to mix with anyone outside your own group. When not in class, we were ordered to be in the main library, where members took turns keeping track of us. In the evenings, all twenty pledges were required to "study" en masse at the dining room table, with a member proctoring to make sure we didn't whisper or move from our assigned places. It was maddening. Someone was always cracking gum or blowing cigarette smoke my way, and there was so much rustling and whispering and giggling that concentration was impossible. I begged to be allowed to study elsewhere, just She and I on our own, but the members were not inclined to stretch a rule and it was the last thing my sister wanted.

I managed to get my pledge mother more or less alone in her room after a particularly frustrating day.

"Barbara?"

"Yes, pledge."

"I can't get any studying done here."

"Sure you can. Everybody else does."

"Barb?"

"What?"

"There are a lot of interesting people in this school."

"Sure thing."

"That's what college is all about."

"That's right, Sandy. There are a lot of interesting people right here in this house, once you get to know them."

"There's this very bright girl in my journalism class. She lives in Currier Hall and—"

"Better stick with your own kind, Sandy."

"Why?"

"It's just wiser in the long run, that's all."

"Barb?"

"Yeah, kiddo?"

"Sometimes I think I'm not a happy person. I'm not happy here. I hate it. I really hate every minute of my life, and I don't know whether it's because of—you know—"

"Shut up, I'm trying to read," Sheila put in.

"I'm talking to my pledge mother, so you shut up."

"Try not to listen," Barbara suggested gently, over my shoulder, to She, who started twisting and shrugging to annoy me.

"Anyway, I'm just miserable. I think I'd be happier as an independent, I really do."

"Now, now, you don't want people to think you can't take the hazing, do you?"

"It's not—no, I guess not."

"Well, you've got to have the bitter with the sweet."

"Yeah."

"And now it's time to get down to the study hall. My goodness, you're late already. Here, I'd better give you a note to the proctor. Don't want you getting any more demerits, do we?"

Barbara's kindly advice was benignly meant. Conformity was paramount to her; she felt lucky to be in the sorority at all. It was common knowledge that her father was dead and her mother had a job. It had been another example of generosity and compassion for the SDTs to take her in as a scholarship sister, meaning she didn't pay quite as much in dues as the others all did. She didn't have a single cashmere sweater, but it didn't seem to bother her. She was always calm, with a permanent half smile, like the Mona Lisa.

151

(Could the Mona Lisa have been trying to cover up braces?) Barbara was my friend. I looked up to her and tried to make my voice quiet and serene, like hers.

Not only had the girls taken her in, they had voted her treasurer. One day, one of the other pledges told us that something terrible had happened; hadn't we noticed all the members going around glum and whispering in corners? It had something to do with my pledge mother. A scandal. Fifty dollars was missing from the treasury, and some of the sisters thought Barbara had taken it.

"Who said that? That's a terrible thing to say!" my sister retorted, to her credit.

The girl who had whispered it to us in the bathroom was Helene Berman. She was from Chicago and probably used to that sort of thing. She just shrugged and kept on combing her long black hairs into the sink. "That's what I heard," she said. "Well, everybody knows she needs the money, and she's the one who had access to it."

"I don't believe it!" She said indignantly. "And neither does Vivvy, do you, Viv?"

Aviva Gottlieb was my sister's new best friend, a fellow pledge. She had expensive clothes and psoriasis all over her hands and arms, and sometimes her face and neck. She slept all wrapped up in gauze-covered salve, a real mess. But she was a merry girl and everybody liked her. You just didn't want to touch her where the rash was, that's all.

Aviva thought about Barbara and the treasury and then she shook her head. She had natural brown curls cut very short all over her head. "I don't think old Barb would steal," she said thoughtfully. "I like Barbara." To me that was a non sequitur, but Aviva apparently thought it made sense and She nodded vehemently in agreement.

I was silent. I really liked Barbara, too. I thought maybe she had taken the money. There was terrific pressure on all of us all the time to buy things: new clothes; jewelry, with or without the Greek letters on it; an extra hamburger between meals with your pals; stuffed animals to prop up on your bed; get your hair done for the dance at the ZBT house; buy gifts for everyone's birthday. It was assumed that your folks picked up the tab at the bookstore and your room and board and tuition and sorority dues and that they sent you plenty of allowance for the extras, but nobody ever stayed within that allowance, and the richer girls had checking accounts they didn't even bother to keep a running balance on. Daddies just poured it in at one end and it gushed out the other. Most of us never thought about how much we were spending or where it was coming from, but Barbara didn't have a father. Her mother had a job! That was shameful enough, but she was only a clerk in a dry-goods store in Dubuque and probably made very little salary. Barbara probably felt terrible having to ask her mother for money to keep up with the rest of us. I sympathized achingly with her. It seemed clear to me that we should all stand by her no matter what she had done. It was vile of her "sisters" to whisper about it behind her back.

"What do you think, Sandy? Do you think Barbara would . . . *steal?*" a girl I hated, named Fran, asked me. We were still at the sinks, and she was so titillated with the gossip that she was delaying her trip into one of the booths and wriggling around anxiously.

"Anyone would steal if the pressure was on them the way it's dumped on around here," I snapped.

"My God! You're her pledge daughter, and you think she did it?"

"I'm her friend and I don't care if she did it or not," I tried to explain.

Sheila was bristling. "My sister doesn't understand anything. She's so stupid. Listen, dummy, no self-respecting SDT would steal! It's just not possible. If the sorority ever caught any of its members stealing, she'd be *depinned,* for God's sake! Don't you even know that much?"

Fran dashed into the booth and we heard the dam burst.

Aviva was absentmindedly twirling one of the tiny short curls around an index finger. I wanted to shout at her, "Stop! You're going to spread the heartbreak of psoriasis into your scalp!" But I looked away. "SDT would never have a thief as a member," she said. "It couldn't be Barbara. But where do you suppose the money went?"

The girls puzzled over that for quite a while. I was more and more disgusted as the rumor grew and spread. Within a few days, it was impossible to have a conversation about anything else; all the members were whispering in tight little knots of two or three, and they'd stop melodramatically when a pledge came near. Our attic was so abuzz at night nobody slept. We couldn't help noticing that the other members had started to treat Barbara coolly. Study hour tensed with speculation, and I observed a curious thing: The proctor pretended not to see that we were all whispering and passing notes.

I was dismayed but not much surprised when it turned out that I was the only one who thought Barbara might have taken the money. For someone who could never be really alone, I sure was a natural-born loner.

One day I went into Barbara's room to change my clothes and found her lying face down on her bed, weeping. Sheila tried to back away into the hall, but I pulled her over to the bed and forced her to sit with me on the edge while I put a tentative hand on my pledge mother's shaking shoulder.

"Barb?" I said hesitantly. "Barb, I'm sorry. I know what you're crying about, and I just want to tell you that I'm on your side completely."

She turned and looked at me. There were no tears on her face, but she looked infinitely sad. "You don't believe what they're saying, do you?"

I touched her cheek and looked at her with all the friendship I had been saving up since Lulu. Barbara and I had a real bond, more than the phony pledge-mother thing. We were alone against the philistine hordes. "Barb, I just want to tell you that I really am your friend. If you took the money, it's okay with me, because I can understand why you might have felt you had to do it. I'll help you. Maybe I can lend you enough to pay it back, a little at a time. I just want you to know I'm one friend you can count on, okay?"

Her eyes opened wide and she stared at me. "You think I did it!"

"No, hey, Barbara! What I'm saying is it doesn't matter to me. I'm your friend either way, whatever you did or didn't do. I just wanted you to know that." I was making a mess of it. Sheila was clucking her disgust with the whole business, and Barbara kept on staring at me—accusingly.

"You think I stole the money," she said flatly. She yanked her shoulder away from my loathsome touch.

Sheila and I stood up. "I'm sorry, Barb. I—I just wanted you to know—well, see . . . I'm on your side, don't you see that?" I mumbled. We backed out of the room and shut the door.

"Now you've done it," She hissed. "God, you're mean."

Late that night they woke us to come downstairs and sit in a circle and be told that what we had been through was a loyalty test. With Barbara's full cooperation, the members had started the rumor and let it rage for a week or so, until all the pledges had had a chance to react. The purpose was to see which pledges were loyal to the spirit of Sigma Delta Tau. All those who refused to believe that Barbara had stolen the money passed the test.

I stared across the room at her, basking in the good graces of her sisters, who thought she was the best sport in the world. I couldn't catch her eye. She was avoiding me. I hoped it was because she couldn't bear the weight of having rejected the only offer of genuine friendship she was ever likely to get for the approval of forty spoiled girls in training for lives of smug hypocrisy.

If I hadn't been attached to my goddamn sister I would have walked right out of the house that night, that very moment. In my pajamas and robe and slippers, I would have braved the undergraduate girls' curfew and the deserted streets of Iowa City in the middle of the night; and somewhere, somehow, I would have found a way to set that fucking house on fire and kill them all and melt their goddamn silver, too.

That was when I knew I had to get out. I would wait to be initiated so they couldn't claim that I was a bad sport. And it was all so important to my stupid sister. So I waited, not saying a word to anyone, but dreaming about the independent life to come. One night in May they woke us and led us to the basement. Informal initiation: blindfolds and touching wet spaghetti and raw liver, being told these were the entrails of girls who had gone before us but erred by not keeping the sacred secrets. We swore and were sworn. Then the formal initiation—off with blindfolds, each pledge mother wrapping her charge in a hunk of blue material cut like a cloak, some secret words said and candles lit and tears shed as the pledges received their little gold pins and were allowed to sing the holiest song. Barbara pulled the cloak around me, pinned her own little double pin with its slender gold chain on my breast, all without looking into my eyes. I hoped she could feel the withering heat of my scorn.

The new members spent the rest of the night talking loudly and excitedly up in the attic dorm. No attempt at quiet now; we were no longer mere pledges but real human beings, and we could make all the noise we wanted to. I told Sheila quietly that I didn't want their goddamn pin or anything else to do with any of them and was resolved next year to live independently in a dormitory.

I might as well have said I planned to move to a trailer camp on the outskirts of Wahoo, Nebraska. "Oh no, you're not! You've always tried to ruin my life, but you're not going to do it! These girls are more sisters to me than you ever were or ever will be!"

"Hey, She, what's the matter?" Aviva, rewrapping herself in gauze, was one of the few people who ever dared involve herself in our familial spats.

"None of your goddamn business!" She whipped out at her sister (not me; her truer one). She shut up then, but kicked me so hard she wrenched both our backs.

Turned out you couldn't depin. They had to vote to depin you. I said fine, do it. I don't give a damn what you do. I'm through with it. Stupid bitches. She cried and screamed and kicked. In her glorious egoism, she thought I was doing it solely for the purpose of hurting her. I didn't want to hurt anybody, not even She. I had no choice; I couldn't live in that house anymore. The solution would have been the old half life: six months in and six months out. The sorority (national actually had a meeting about it) made it clear that they would allow me to live with them and share their secrets only because of Sheila's being a much loved member in good standing. But they were pursuing a legal course of action (legal services donated by some member's father) to have me swear before a judge that I would never reveal any secrets to anyone. I just laughed and figured if it ever really got that far, what the hell, I'd swear. I didn't intend to know any people in my entire future life who would be the slightest bit interested in hearing the secrets of Sigma Delta Tau.

Obviously, they were sorry they had ever gotten involved with us. I'll bet the Iowa chapter took a hell of a scolding from national. This sorority would never make the mistake of taking on anybody so *odd* ever again, you could be absolutely sure of that. I was making it tough for all the Jewish Siamese twins of the future.

At home, the news went over like a turd in a punch bowl. Billie cried and yelled at me and got Daddy to yell at me, too. But somehow that didn't have the weight it used to. Billie told me I had ruined her socially, she couldn't hold her head up anymore. After a while she just sighed aloud and shook her head whenever she looked at me, which wasn't often, because she and She kept huddling together, trying to figure out how to cope with the tragedy. Daddy could hardly stand to be in the same room with me. It was so unrelenting that I even started to feel sorry for Sheila, whose life they all assured me I had demolished.

"Even if you really don't care for your own sake, how can you do this to your sister?" Billie would wail, setting Sheila off in a howl of self-pity.

But, as always in any good-girl/bad-girl story, virtue was rewarded by the appearance of Mister Right. Just in the nick of time to save the beauty with a kiss, Second Lieutenant Roger Moritz was honorably discharged from the U.S. Army Air Corps and would soon come charging across oceans and mountains and plains to claim his bride.

14

In the Castle of the Prince

We came home in June to discover that peacetime had dropped over the old hometown like a shroud. Where squadrons of four-engine bombers had filled the sky with thundering formations, there was nothing now but blue tedium, an occasional cloud and, once a day, the drone of the U.S. Mail plane passing us by on its way from Chicago to Denver. Our base was being turned into a municipal airport, some of the runways being converted back to cornfields. No more officers' club, no more blue-eyed strangers in break-your-heart uniforms. The special soldiers' bus stop had disappeared off the face of Pierce Street, and all the bars were closed. The high school boys were now younger than we were. Stripped of adventure, Sioux City was flat and dull and stank with the wind coming upriver from the stockyards. Nothing was left of romance except Roger's twice-weekly V-mail letters to my sister.

He never missed a deadline, Old Faithful, all through their long-distance engagement: the nine months of our gestation as pledges and the long, slow summer that followed. Every time a letter came—usually on Tuesdays and Saturdays—She would read and reread it and then carry it around with her in her purse with the blue V-mail paper sticking out so no one would miss it. She wouldn't let me see the letters, but she couldn't resist reading parts out loud to anyone who might be envious, and so I learned of my future.

Forget college; in the fall, Roger would return and they would get married. Nobody ever asked me what role I would like to play in this ménage. They both seemed to think their plans affected only themselves. I didn't want to spoil it for them, honestly I didn't. It wasn't my idea to turn the happy couple into three's-a-crowd, but of course I felt guilty. Anybody would, horning in like that. It didn't occur to me until years later that they might have said something like, "We're not a couple, we're a trio, so let's figure out a way to be a happy trio. Let's include Sandy in our plans and then we'll all work together to figure out how to be happy." Well, it's dumb to expect that. What two people in love ever stopped to include a third, even one they couldn't avoid?

It meant dropping out of school, but Roger himself wrote to me to promise that it would only be for a year, while he finished law school in New York. Then, when he landed a job somewhere, I could go back to college if I still wanted to. (Girls who actually went to college for four whole years were only admitting they couldn't get a husband, and it was fervently hoped by all concerned—myself included—that I wouldn't have to stay in school *that* long.)

While She played Blondie-does-the-housework for a year, I'd have time to write some stories and poems. And we'd be in New York! I was grateful to She for that. After all, she could just as easily have fallen in love with somebody from St. Paul, Minnesota, or Dry Hump, Arizona: It wouldn't have made any difference to her; Sheila was well adjusted. But I dreamed of cocktail parties and lunches in restaurants with white tablecloths, and witty conversations with people familiar with *The New Yorker* magazine and sidewalks crowded with people all rushing to do very important things, too busy and interesting to give a damn about what I wore and what I said and whether I happened to fit their standards of what was normal.

"Sure," I said when Roger's letter to me had been read and passed around to everyone in the family for judgment. "It's okay with me. I'll really be glad to live in New York and it's only for a year, and then I can transfer to a school wherever Roger and She decide to settle." By now I had heard of the Ivy League.

"It's not Sheila's decision; you mustn't blame her," my mother said. "A woman always has to go where her husband's work is."

I wondered if that was a law or just another one of Billie's perplexing rules. "But I'm not blaming anybody. I'm really excited about it. I *want* to live in New York," I said.

"You're just jealous," She said.

"What can you possibly get in New York that you don't have right here in Sioux City?" Billie snapped.

"You want to go away from me! I'll be the only mother in town who doesn't have her daughters nearby. I won't be able to watch my grandchildren grow up. Your lives will just go on without me. You'll never think about me again until it's time to throw me into an old ladies' home and forget about me." We had to promise this could never, never happen.

Our friends had changed while we were gone. Syd Finkelstein was angry about the war's ending before he had a chance to get into it. He had decided not to go to college and was working for his dad in the insurance business. Edie Rosen and Marilyn Pickel had gone to the University of Illinois and become Alpha Epsilon Phis—members of the other Jewish sorority and therefore Sigma Delta Tau's archrivals. This created a strain on She's friendship with Edie. I guess they were afraid they might reveal some sacred secrets if they talked to each other too much.

The boys all had summer jobs, generally working for their fathers, and dating only took place on Saturday nights, without energy. Where was there to go? A movie and the Gables. She wouldn't go up to War Eagle's grave because she was engaged, and no one was particularly urging me to go. We didn't even go to Leif Ericson pool anymore, because people stared at us more since we had stopped being kids, and anyway, two-piece bathing suits were in fashion and we couldn't get away with that.

We spent the endless summer shopping for She's trousseau. For each outfit she chose, I had to be fitted out with something that would blend in without being noticeable. Our college wardrobes, bought the summer before, were pronounced by She and Billie to be absolutely and totally inappropriate for the life we would be leading in New York City as the wife and a half of a rich, young soon-to-be-lawyer. After all, Daddy didn't want Billie to be ashamed of us, did he?

I inherited, under bitter protest, She's entire collection of pajamas while she stocked up on ridiculous nightgowns that had to be hand-washed and would surely bunch up uncomfortably under her, and maybe me too, when we slept.

The summer moved along at about the pace of the Paleolithic Age, and I watched from my mental cave as we shopped and drank gallons of iced tea and then shopped some more. Roger's letters arrived with the regularity of a dripping faucet. The only topics of conversation in the world were clothes and plans for the wedding. If they noticed me at all, it was to remind me (Billie perfecting her sigh) of the shame I'd brought on the family by washing out of the sorority.

After all these years, I've forgotten what the plans were,

since they didn't happen the way they were supposed to. I think Roger was going to go directly to New York from Germany and we were to join him and his family there, to meet everyone and have some formal engagement parties and showers in order to get as many gifts as possible. Then back to Sioux City for more parties and a big wedding, with his family all coming to us. But what happened instead was that Roger's mother threw a snit when she heard he was planning to marry a Jewish girl from Sioux City, Iowa. When they brought her around, they thought they'd better give it to her all at once (Roger's sister told me later), so they also mentioned that by the way, this girl had this sort of handicap. Margaretha Moritz booked herself onto the *Mauritania*, heading for a sanatorium in Switzerland (in St. Moritz, which she probably liked to think was named after her husband's family, when in fact the family name had derived from something closer to Morishnivitz than Saint anything) to recover from the awful shock.

Roger was so sweetly dumb I'm sure he didn't realize his mother's illness had anything to do with his plans to marry. It seemed pretty clear to me that she was holding out for him to call off the whole bizarre thing, but dear Roger was in love. The world's biggest yes, dear chump had met up with the cosmic do-what-I-say champ.

That was the appeal. Our being caprices of nature had nothing to do with it. Listen, it's even possible that Roger hadn't noticed. Certainly, he didn't mean to smash any social codes—that was the last thing old Roger would ever do on purpose.

I had naturally assumed that he, like any other normal man, regarded us as something of a break from tradition— you might even say a full-scale revolt: Anybody who would take us home to his mother had to have some seriously important parts missing if he didn't intend to upset her. I found out later what they were. Sweet Roger didn't have a rebellious cell in his body. Sheila had told him he was in love and they should get married and he had grinned and agreed. It was as simple as that. If I have to describe Roger's will and determination, the word *marshmallow* comes to mind.

For the time being, his mother had no idea she had suffered a temporary setback in the 1946 Toughest Bitch Takes All stakes.

Roger's background was a lot more proud and rigid than ours. Both of his parents' families had been early immigrants and could talk about great-grandfathers, whereas any claim we had to gentility and breeding had been invented entirely by our mother. The Moritzes were snobs and they lived in a world where the rules had been written in runes. So Margaretha took to the Alps waiting for her son to come to his senses, and Roger, worried about his mother's health but too dumb to know he was being blackmailed, came back to Sioux City to put his head in the noose.

He was wearing the first Brooks Brothers suit I ever saw and he was the only ex-officer I ever saw who actually looked better in civilian clothes. Our folks threw a formal dinner-dance at the Warrior to announce the engagement to everybody who knew all about it already. Billie was on the verge of orgasm all evening, introducing "my son to be." She was thrilled to be able to say *Switzerland* a lot; her chin went up and her lips pursed as if she were tasting her favorite sour cherries dipped in chocolate.

"No date for the wedding yet because Roger's mother is unfortunately ailing and she's getting a cure in *Switzerland*." The more often Billie repeated this, the prouder she sounded. I wondered if I should try to let her know that the phrase was "taking the cure," but I was wise enough to keep my mouth shut and turned up at the corners. Billie was radiant and fully as much in the spotlight as She and Roger. People congratulated her, and me ("And it's your turn next, Sandy!"), as if I had something to do with it, and then they told She to

be happy and congratulated Roger on getting such a wonderful bride—the most popular girl in town—and then Billie
picked up the floral centerpiece to take home and the party
was over.

Roger had to get back to law school and couldn't bear to
be separated (as they say, but what do they know) from his
love, so She and I got to fly to New York and live in his
family's house, all very proper, to await the news that Mrs.
Moritz was recovered enough to come home and we could all
get on with the wedding.

Turned out they lived in a genuine mansion, across the
road from Arturo Toscanini, in Riverdale, New York. You
could never see anything but trees and hedges and a big iron
gate, but they said it was Toscanini's house and I believed
them—why not? Toscanini had to live somewhere. The
Moritzes' house had a circular driveway with a fountain in
the center that had ivy growing all around its base and water
pouring into it from a pot held by a naked stone lady. It was
from Italy, and Roger's sister, Mindy, told me it was unique,
one of a kind, a work of art. Things like that were important
to the Moritz family—not that they considered Roger's
choice of a wife something to cheer about, even though she
was unique.

I had never seen a house like that outside of the movies;
neither had She, of course, but she was damned if she'd let
on that she was impressed. After all, it was only what she
deserved. But my mouth hung open and I gawked plenty as
Roger and Mindy showed us around. On the vast second
floor, there was no such thing as just a bedroom; everybody
had a suite, with a sitting room on one side and a huge
bathroom on the other side (shared with the next room; but
one had to make some sacrifices). The bedrooms all had
built-in bookcases and fireplaces that worked and window
seats where you could curl up to read and look out over the
grassy lawn and immaculately kept flower gardens.

The house had three floors; the stairs leading to the top floor were enclosed and meant only for servants and children. There was actually a "nursery" up there: a big cozy room with a fireplace and a piano and shelves for toys and books lining all the walls, and a bedroom off each end of it with more toys, just like in an English storybook. These rooms had a view over treetops to the river (and a smudge that could have been Toscanini's roof), but the rooms on the other side of the hall looked out over distant apartment buildings and a highway. Those rooms were for nannies and cooks and maids and for storage: whole rooms filled with linens, cases of toilet paper, cedar chests for out-of-season clothes, and I'll bet during the war they kept other stuff there, too.

Roger's father had a studio somewhere on the grounds (I never saw it, nor any of his sculptures, but I figured whatever he did there was his business). He was absentminded—deliberately, I think. It is an excellent way to get through life without letting it touch you; observing how it worked for him made me wish I could perfect my own version. He had a pleasant, vacant smile, preoccupied eyes that never looked straight at you, a calm that could not be dislodged. He wore stiff collars, which gave him a nice, old-fashioned look that was cozily compatible with the out-to-lunch sign on his face.

Mindy was a year younger than we were, and I liked her. She showed a healthy, straightforward interest in us and whispered to me that she was delighted to have a little fresh blood brought into the family. She said she hadn't thought her brother had the guts to do anything so nervy as to marry a Siamese twin.

"Conjoined," I said.

"Oh good. Conjoined. Thanks," Mindy murmured softly.

"What do you mean, guts? Are you implying it takes guts to marry me?" She snapped. The long engagement was making her basic personality disorders break out like hives.

"She didn't imply it," I pointed out. Why do I say troublemaking things like that? It just slipped out before I thought. I had hoped Mindy would like me, but there I went sounding as bitchy as the person on my right.

"You shut up," She snarled. "I'm talking to my sister-in-law-to-be."

"I'm sorry," Mindy whispered.

I thought Mindy had a speech defect until one day when we went to the city with her and it turned out she could talk in a regular voice after all. It was only in the house that she whispered.

She took us to the Museum of Modern Art. Sheila was bored with the paintings and even more bored with the movie we saw there, which was surrealistic and had a scene where a razor cut across an eyeball. Afterward, She said she felt sick so we went out into the garden of the museum, where there were benches and winding paths through white gravel, some sculptures, and a hot dog stand.

A well-dressed man at least in his thirties came over to the bench where we were sitting and bowed slightly to Mindy and then to me and to Sheila.

"Excuse me," he said politely. "May I ask you a question? You certainly don't have to answer it if you choose not to, but it would set this gentleman's mind at ease and be a true contribution to the intellectual, uh . . . body of information in the world." He trailed off and stood there looking rather sheepish but earnest.

"Sure," I said.

Sheila giggled and Mindy tensed up silently beside me. Too late I remembered that in New York you're not supposed to talk to strangers. But what could possibly happen to us on a sunny afternoon in such a respectable place?

"What do you want to know?" I asked him.

"You sure you don't mind?" He looked at us, She and then me, back and forth, one and then the other.

167

"Yeah, go ahead, it's okay," I said.

"You sure?"

"What is it?" Sheila put in impatiently.

"Well, okay, what I want to know is, when you fuck do you need two guys or would just one do, because I've got a cock that would satisfy both of you and your friend here as well and I—"

Mindy was already up and pulling at us, and we got off the bench fast and ran back inside the museum. Mindy went to tell the guard, but the guy had disappeared by then. It wasn't the first time we'd met up with a sex-crazed lunatic—after all, we'd been through the war—and it wouldn't be the last, but having this happen at the Museum of Modern Art in the middle of a sunny day made it the smarmiest.

We went back to Riverdale still shaky, but agreed not to tell anyone about it. Why upset Roger and his dad? They couldn't do anything about it, and besides, it was embarrassing. We couldn't possibly repeat what he had said to us. Had we been sitting with our legs too far apart or talking too loudly? What had we done to provoke that geek? Best to forget it as quickly as possible. It was too creepy to think about. Think about something else we saw at the museum. Think about *Guernica*.

We waited, some of us more patient than others, for Margaretha to get well and come home so the wedding could take place. Letters from Switzerland on pale cream stationery (her own, from Tiffany's; she would never be crass enough to use hotel stationery) hinted broadly that she hoped to return soon to better news than that which had sent her into a decline. I didn't think she was at all subtle, but she was way over her family's collective head. Her letters were read aloud at meals by Roger's father, and then they'd all three smile and reassure each other that her tone or her news was very encouraging. Her husband with the absent mind, her daughter too terrified to speak up in her own house, her

168

son with the ring through his nose for anyone to catch hold of—all smiled and said, "Oh, it really sounds like she's getting better. She'll be home soon." And one or all of them would write back to Margaretha, but never with the all-clear signal she was waiting for.

Roger went to bed in his own suite every night but then tiptoed across the hall and crawled in with us after the house was dark and silent. For the first few weeks, it was agony for me; hours of snuggling and whispering sticky glop from B-movie soundtracks ("Are you my honeydew?" "Oh, honey, do!" Giggle giggle. "I lovums." "Wuv you too." "Can I bite that little ear?" "I'll bite you back!" "Pwomise?" Giggle giggle. The world will little note nor long remember with what self-sacrificing, silent strength I managed to hold back barfing noises) and kisses and more kisses and Roger pleading to put it in just half an inch and She murmuring or sighing (faking it, I think) and saying no they mustn't, not till they were married.

I couldn't believe how long Roger let her get away with that, but I ground my teeth as quietly as I could, going along with the game called Let's Pretend Sandy Isn't Here. It wasn't a new game for me, God knows, but damn difficult when it was twenty-four or -five nights out of every month, hours of it, and me with no beau of my own or ever likely to find one.

Some of Roger's pals from Harvard and Columbia Law were very nice to me, and one or two tried a little funny stuff, but I could tell right away they were put off by Sheila. Anyway, I figured I was piling up time in the bank for in case it ever did happen to me, and I was as polite about ignoring them as anyone could possibly have been under the circumstances. Sometimes Roger would touch my leg instead of She's and it made me shiver and tremble because of my natural frustration, and I'd yank my leg out of his way as if I'd gotten an electric shock. Sometimes I'd clench my fists so hard the stubs of my bitten nails would leave dark stigmata on my palms for days.

I was relieved when She finally let him in. It only took him a couple of seconds to come and then it was over. He seemed embarrassed by it all and eager to be away from there then, so I finally got most of a night's sleep. He kept on getting into our bed every night, but I guess he figured they had done enough foreplay to last them the rest of their lives, so it was generally pretty quick and routine and so to sleep. Sometimes She would start a fight, I think maybe just to keep him there a while.

When She missed a period, we both went down with hysterics. I was angrier at her than I had ever been. How dare she bring a baby into our lives when we hadn't even started to live yet? Her tears were aimed at maneuvering Roger into position. His mother was still in Switzerland, but the wedding would proceed.

15

Honeymoon in Haiti

Mindy's and Roger's uncle Maudie made all the arrangements, choosing the place for the wedding and reception (no synagogue, not even a reform temple; in New York you could get married right in a restaurant). There were some engraved invitations and a lot more engraved announcements ordered from Tiffany's, and silver and crystal patterns were duly chosen; thank God there was a certain urgency about it all or She'd still be trying to decide on patterns for dishes and glasses and forks and spoons. Uncle Maudie was Mr. Moritz's brother, a terribly nice, genial man who dressed in smart designer gowns made to order, wore stiletto-heeled pumps that were hand-made for him in Italy, and had a full-time live-in valet who did his makeup. Uncle Maudie had had an unhappy marriage to a woman and a messy divorce, which cost a lot of money and embarrassed the family, but all that was long in the past and the family now ignored Uncle

Maudie's little idiosyncrasies, along with his string of handsome live-in boyfriends. You couldn't help loving Uncle Maudie, or anyway I couldn't, for his dippy name as well as his generous and loving nature. He absolutely adored us; especially me, and kept staring at Roger with what he said was a new respect. At first, it was just the idea of us that he found delicious, but when he came to know us as individuals, I think he really liked me. He and I talked about books and writers, some of whom he knew personally.

Uncle Maudie rented the roof-garden restaurant of an elegant hotel on Madison Avenue for the wedding. It was square, with glass walls on all four sides; you could sit at a table and look out on whichever view of Manhattan, the Bronx, Queens, or New Jersey you preferred. (It did not in the least remind me of a certain bluff on the Missouri River from which you could see three states. For one thing, this view had lights. Light is what God supposedly created first, and believe me, God knew what made all the difference.) A wide terrace wrapped around three sides of the restaurant. There were tables and chairs out there in the nice weather; otherwise you could still step out just to appreciate the view. My sister's wedding took place in the winter, so most of the guests stayed inside.

I thought it was interesting that they hired a rabbi none of them had ever seen before to come to a restaurant and perform the ceremony without a *chuppah* or any of the traditional things we were used to. The rabbi got the pronunciation of Moritz wrong; he put the accent on the first syllable, making it sound Jewish. The ceremony was performed on the dance floor of the restaurant, with all the guests standing around drinking their cocktails.

The rabbi reminded me of Larry Parks in *The Jolson Story*, melodramatic and at the same time bored, doing his number with a singsong rhetoric that made you think about more pressing matters and wonder how long it was going to take. It was pretty brief, actually, and then he was telling Roger to kiss the bride. I swung around to enable Roger to oblige, accidentally clipping the rabbi with my elbow.

I guess he hadn't noticed our affliction, probably thought I was just standing real close to my sister because I loved her so much. He reeled back from my jab and then politely touched my shoulder to indicate I should get out of the way. I shrugged him off, but he dug his fingers into my upper arm and yanked at me.

"No, no," he growled. I was interfering with the solemn ritual of the first officially sanctioned kiss. I was insinuating myself between the rabbi and the blessed couple. I thought he was going to have a convulsion. His stage whisper developed a little whinny under it. I tried to ignore him.

"What are you doing, where are you going, stop that!" The rabbi seemed to be losing control. He was behind me now. Roger and Sheila were finished with the Kiss and we started to head back up the improvised aisle that the guests were opening up for them. I saw Uncle Maudie with mascara-rimmed tears streaming down his face. Several glasses, mostly empty now, were lifted to the happy couple.

We left the rabbi behind, and I think he must have gone directly to the bar because next time I saw him, he was stewed to his tortoiseshell spectacles. Eventually, he passed out and had to be taken home and there was a big flurry because nobody could remember his name or what temple they had gotten him from. Uncle Maudie kept shrieking, "The Yellow Pages! I found him through the Yellow Pages!" and then he would collapse against somebody in a fit of hilariously contagious giggles.

I had a nice time at the wedding, although I felt a mite sorry for myself, drank too much champagne, and had to throw up. Sheila was furious. She never got sick on booze no matter how much she tossed down, and it wasn't her idea of fun to spend her wedding reception hunkered over next to a toilet seat watching me toss my caviar.

We spent the night in that same hotel, in a huge, elegant

suite with a living room and my dream kitchen: sink, fridge, and no stove, just a phone with a direct line to room service. We ate chicken sandwiches and drank more champagne, and by the time we rolled into bed, Roger couldn't get it up one little smidgin. She was furious and they had their first married fight. She said he shouldn't have drunk so much if that was what it was going to do to him. He said he'd never had this experience before and how was he supposed to know this would happen and couldn't she be a little nicer about it, after all they had their whole lives ahead of them and she said fuck their whole lives, they only had one wedding night and she would remember it the rest of her life as a big nothing. Roger begged and begged her to forgive him, and finally she did and finally we got to sleep, but it was daylight by then. We got up after about two hours. I hadn't said a word all night, but no one appreciated it. We took a taxi to Idlewild Airport and then we flew to the island of Haiti.

We stayed at a famous little hotel run by a man who reportedly remembered first, last, and nicknames of everyone who was ever there. You were supposed to feel like his personal friend. He invited all the guests for cocktails every night and so you got to know them all whether you wanted to or not. We were the hit of the week; people who'd never seen conjoined siblings before stared and asked extremely rude questions. They were all buzzed on banana daiquiris all the time, starting at breakfast. I tried very hard to keep my mouth very tightly shut—after all, this was my sister's honeymoon—but my misery showed and I spoiled everything.

"You are such a goddamn wet blanket! Why do you have to spoil everything for me? You and your long face make me sick!" she screamed at me one morning when Roger had gone for a swim before breakfast.

"I'm sorry, I can't help it. I'll try to help it. I mean, I'll try not to have a long face, I don't want to spoil your honeymoon, honestly I don't. But—well, you have Roger and he has you and I just feel like such a tagalong. I hate it."

"Well, I certainly didn't invite you!"

That was true enough. "I'm sorry," I repeated again and again, more miserable than before. "But, well . . . everybody stares at us all the time." I was trying to define my melancholia. Why couldn't I ever have a good time?

"Well, of course they do. It's because they know Roger and I are honeymooners. People always stare at honeymooners. It's because we're so happy. I guess we give off a kind of glow."

I had had a faint hope that with Roger in our lives, I might have someone to talk with when things got bad. Without another human being to tell me I was sane, I sometimes felt in real danger of slipping over the edge. With my mother and sister in league against what I perceived as reality, I had longed for a confidant, someone who would actually listen and converse and maybe even sympathize with me from time to time. But Roger wasn't going to be any help. His mission in life now was to keep his wife happy at any cost.

The beach had no secluded area, so we mostly stayed in the room or down in the bar, with the big ceiling fan going around and around like the one in *To Have and Have Not*. A couple of times we went into Port-au-Prince to walk around and eat in a restaurant and see what there was to buy. I got so depressed by the poverty in town and the drunks at the hotel that I couldn't help crying a lot of the time.

"There she goes again, goddamn her!"

"Sandy, hey, what is it this time, pal?"

"I'm sorry. It's that woman over there sitting on the ground with the baby in her arms. Look how dirty they are, and sad. Come on, I want to give her some money—"

"Don't you dare drag us over there! They just do that for tourists, don't you know that much? She's probably got a Cadillac waiting around the corner. Come on, let's go to the straw market! Oh shut up. God, I can't stand your sniveling all the time. You're ruining my whole honeymoon! You're ruining my life! Roger, make her stop!"

I looked at Roger and he looked at me and then he quickly broke away from us and bobbed some coins into the sad woman's lap. He quick-stepped back to us, as if his largess embarrassed him.

"Well, I hope that satisfies you," She said, yanking me down the narrow sidewalk, with Roger coming up behind us.

But on the next corner there was a dog lying in the middle of the sidewalk with scrawny ribs sticking through his thin scabby coat and his big brown eyes mutely crying out for help and I dissolved in sobs all over again.

Thinking back on Haiti, it seems to me now that crying all through my sister's honeymoon was the way for me to loosen the pressure valve—and a damn good thing, too. Held back, it might have erupted violently years earlier than it did.

16

Happy

After the longest week of my life, we left the enchanted honeymoon isle and headed back to Riverdale. Roger moved his clothes and books into our suite of rooms. He went back to school and **She** and I went into New York City nearly every day. It wasn't that people didn't ogle us there, but they didn't stop in their tracks, they kept on going. We were just one more thing to gawk at in a raree-show of wonders on all sides; we stared as much as we were stared at.

She ordered monogrammed stationery from Tiffany's exactly like Margaretha's and wrote to everyone she had ever known about the fabulous wedding and thrilling honeymoon she and Roger had had. She did a lot of shopping until Roger, much to my relief, sat her down and explained that they were going to live on his income, not his projected inheritance. (His income fell into their bank account automatically every month from a trust fund and it wasn't exactly life on the dole.) She pouted for a week and only forgave him when he gave her some damn gift or other with her new monogram on it.

She played her pregnancy for all it was worth in backrubs and whimsical demands. Nothing in her body twinged or twitched or ached or bubbled without everyone she encountered for the next two days getting regaled with every lurid, boring detail. As she got front heavy, my back started to feel the strain, but I never said anything about it. Her doctor was an obstetrician, so he was hardly interested in me at all. And frankly, I was afraid that if we both complained all the time, the Moritz clan would send us back home. I mean, I knew they wouldn't, but still I was afraid they might.

If I couldn't be alone, and it looked like I never would, I was just as happy to keep on living in their big house. I liked Mindy and wished I could think of a way to get through her wall of fear. I liked Roger's father and I liked the cook and the gardeners and the housekeeper and the maids, although it made me nervous to be waited on, and I shrank with dismay when She snapped orders at them. Once Roger said, "You take so easily to having servants. You know just how to handle them. Where did you learn that?"

And She made a joke. "I've had four in help all my life," She said. "My mother, my father, my sister, and Helen."

Ho, ho, ho, we both laughed. We always encouraged any little ray of sunshine, no matter how dim. She was not a happy person anymore. The dream had been achieved and now there was nothing more to look forward to except, of course, the baby. We started shopping for layettes.

Roger and Mindy and Mr. Moritz often talked a kind of family shorthand, making references to things we had no clue to. A line or just a word or a place name would send them into polite little tittles of laughter or, in Mr. Moritz's case, a vague fond smile. This could make you feel very much the intruder. For a while, Sheila would ask politely (and later, demand angrily) to be let in on the joke. But I was always sorry she had asked, because when they did explain, it would turn out to be a long, complicated, stiflingly boring story with a dull, obscure point. Sheila wanted to be part of all the family jokes and traditions and private references, and until Mrs. Moritz came home the others in the family were amiable enough in trying to put us in the picture. After all, She was Roger's wife. Until Mrs. M. glided in like an alpine glacier, covering everything in her path with a millennium of ice.

If my sister's marriage ever had a chance, it was no contest once her mother-in-law descended from the mountain. I knew the first time I saw Margaretha Moritz's eyes looking us over that there wasn't any room for us in that family. For Sheila, I mean. I was just along for the ride.

I thought I knew what embarrassment was. I had, after all, just come through a childhood and adolescence in which self-consciousness and shy longings to belong were totally appropriate. Our environment had allowed us, sometimes, the illusion that we were normal. We were even"popular," thereby pleasing our mother, but I always knew (although She never did) that being popular in Sioux City wasn't exactly a run for the roses. Once I saw Roger Moritz's mother and the way she looked at us, I knew my sister's wedding was her last win in that league.

To Margaretha Moritz, we were never merely two young women from a decent family trying hard to please and to overcome being Jewish, Midwestern, and medical anomalies. She saw us as trying to insinuate ourselves into her life, and no sin could be greater than that, no trespass more violating. Even if Sheila were normal, even if she were intelligent, there was no way Roger's mother would accept her. She must have had her own plans for Roger, as she did for Mindy (Margaretha, Jr.; does that tell you anything? Jews are supposed to name their offspring after the dead).

A few weeks after she got home, Roger's mother threw a dinner party. (Life must go on.) It was in honor of Alexander Franken, the semifamous artist, who had just had a painting bought by the Metropolitan Museum or the Museum of Modern Art, one of those.

Well, that's what the dinner party was really about, but out of her own pitiful need, Sheila got it turned around slightly in her mind so that the evening was actually in honor of herself, the new daughter-in-law. The famous artist, She decided, was being invited along with a few other dignified and rich people for the purpose of meeting the bride. It was sweet (if only to be expected) of Roger's mother to do this for her. In this scenario, I was the beloved sister in town on a little visit.

Nothing we had bought back in SC was good enough to wear in NY after all. We spent three or four grueling days shopping at the fanciest stores on Fifth Avenue. The number of hours She owed me was getting right up there next to the national debt, although she had it figured out this was more for my benefit than hers. After all, she already had a man, so I was the one who really needed the plumage. We fought about that until we weren't speaking. She finally picked out three dresses for herself and two for me, figuring she'd decide which seemed best on the night.

We spent most of the day of the party in a beauty hole, getting shampooed and cut and curled and puffed and brushed and fried and manicured, enduring the humility of whispers and glances, employees and clients of the establishment finding excuses to poke their heads through the pink curtain of our stall to grab a gawk at the Siamese twins getting snipped and pawed by two smirking gentlemen. She loved the attention, would have paid extra for it. I wanted to kill. There was the usual long interval during which She joined the others in looking critically at my limp mop in the mirrors, wondering if anything could be done to make it have the body and bounce that hers did.

"We're not the same," I said. "We're different. We've got two different kinds of hair. Leave me alone."

"But you could be identical if you just let me give you a boost of this super treatment—"

"No! I don't want to look like her!"

Everybody thought this was a richly funny line, and my reputation for ready wit was reinforced even unto the hairdressers here assembled. If tears rolled down my face as they twisted and sprayed and teased my hair, nobody noticed.

Roger was going to be late getting home; his mother had (inadvertently?) scheduled the dinner party for a night when he had a late class. She and I came home on the New York Central commuter train, a fifteen-minute ride that took a half hour to prepare for—getting to the station, buying the tickets, waiting on the platform. (You could also get to Riverdale by subway, but She would never do that, because it was tacky.) We soaked in a hot tub until our skins were shrinky. She doused unbelievably expensive perfume all over herself, giving me a coughing fit. We were pulling on real nylon stockings when the little phone on the wall next to the bed made its funny hiccup sound. It was the house phone; someone inside the house was calling us. I was near it, so I answered. "Hello?"

"Hello, dear, it's Margaretha." Roger's mother did not want She to call her Mother, and Mrs. Moritz was what she had always called her own mother-in-law, so she had settled on the familiar as the least offensive form of address for us. Two out of two mothers of Siamese twins prefer being called anything but Mother, Mom, or variations thereof.

I didn't know whether she thought I was She or not; they tell us we sound quite alike on the telephone. She was busily inspecting her toenail polish for imperfections, so I just went on with the conversation myself.

"Hi," says I.

"Darling, I have a big, big favor to ask you. I know you're going to think I'm awful, and it's true, I just don't know where my head is these days, but—well, I've done something terrible and I need your help to get it all straightened out?"

It was put in the form of a question to which there could be only one answer.

"Sure, what is it?"

Sheila perked up, interested. In the mirror, she mouthed at me, "Who is it?" but I pretended not to see. Some deep instinct told me that letting Sheila talk directly with her mother-in-law just now might be a very bad move. Something icky was happening here, I just knew it.

"Well, silly me, I invited too many people to the party tonight. I don't know where my head was. I know our dining table seats only eighteen comfortably and I've gone and invited twenty!"

She seemed to expect me to leap in and say something. Sheila probably assumed I was talking to Mindy, and her attention had wandered back to herself in the mirror. She leaned forward for a closer look, I obliged, and that was how I happened to be in a position that precluded my falling over backward in a dead faint when I heard what Mrs. Moritz was asking us to do.

". . . so I've got to disinvite someone, don't you see? It's so terribly awkward, and all because of my giddiness with all the excitement, and of course there's no one on the list who isn't a truly close friend of Alex's . . . except you two girls, don't you see . . ."

I saw, but I didn't say anything. Why let her off the hook?

"Dear? Are you still there?"

"Yes." Too bad, Margaretha. I'm still here.

"Well . . . you do see, don't you?"

"You're disinviting us."

"Well, yes, that's right. I knew you'd understand."

"Oh sure. As a matter of fact, I'm thrilled at not having to come."

"What?" I heard her say as Sheila grabbed the telephone away from me.

"Hello? Who is this?" She asked querulously.

Mrs. M. must have identified herself and then realized she had been talking to the weird sister and had to go into the whole thing all over again. If she had my vantage point, she would have stopped her spiel about a third of the way into it, because in the mirror I was watching my sister turn into the Wicked Witch of the West. Her skin reddened and then purpled as her temper rose. Her perfectly curled hair bristled against its newly applied lacquer; I felt her body trembling with the furies that were gathering. I could only hear Margaretha's voice, puny and metallic over the house phone and at a distance, and I couldn't make out the words, although I knew what they were.

And then came the explosion, the eruption, the lava spew, the earthquake, and the fire: the wrath of Sheila Miriam Lazarus Moritz.

To know She was to fear her temper. Everyone, from parents and teachers to bus drivers, gave in to her rather than suffer one of her unrelenting screamers. She never never *never* gave in. Giving in was not part of her religion, which was the theology of SHE WINS. I never heard her apologize, never heard her back down. She could cry (loud was the only volume she had, no point in crying softly to oneself; she told me once I was wasting my tears since no one even knew I was crying) for days and days and days. Weeks, if necessary; She could carry a grudge like Mao on the long march. She could hold her breath until her face literally turned red, white, and then blue, and maybe longer; nobody ever waited to find out. She was unrelenting in her fury, could remain livid and call on an infinite store of energy to fuel the tears, the screams, the kicking feet, the flailing arms—however long it took to get her way. As Billie put it, "Sheila always has to have the last word."

Roger had learned it the first time he crossed her. We had been living in the Riverdale house for about a week, and one morning at breakfast he asked her please would she use the marmalade spoon to dip into the marmalade dish rather than her knife with butter and crumbs on it from her toast. It seemed like a reasonable request to me and addressed part of the mystery of all that extra silverware on the table. One of the spoons was for the marmalade. Okay. Except that Sheila took it as a personal attack on the way she was reared and her table manners and her mother's inferior background as the daughter of immigrants and a slur on the whole country west of Riverdale, New York, because they didn't know which spoon to use, and what he was really saying was that she was not good enough to be his wife. She was screaming so loudly that the door to the pantryway recoiled inward on its hinges; the servants must have been bunched up on the other side to listen. I checked out mentally while Roger shrank back into his green silk chair, visibly cringing, trying, I think, not to cry. He looked like a little kid seeing Godzilla for the very first time.

Margaretha had her first glimpse into the belly of the beast the night she tried to disinvite us to her dinner party. I don't think that properly brought up lady had ever been shrieked at like that before.

My sister had a marvelous time at the party. She was really thrilled and excited to meet a famous person, not that she'd ever heard of him. She carried on exactly as if the party were in her honor. She put her arm through Margaretha's to form a pretty picture of mother- and daughter-in-law love.

I was so furious at having to be there I wanted to spit in the *oeufs à la neige.*

184

17

My Life on Hold

One Sunday morning Mindy came downstairs in dazzling white shorts, white cotton shirt, white gym shoes, and white socks, with a white sweater thrown across her shoulders, sleeves knotted across her chest. She was carrying a tennis racquet and even I could guess where she was going. But "Gee, you look cute. Where you going?" asked my sister.

"Uh . . . club," Mindy mumbled. It was pretty obvious she was trying to get out the door and into the waiting car (I pictured Ollie, the chauffeur, out in the circular driveway holding open the door of the Lincoln Continental for her) as quickly as she could.

But no one was fast enough to elude Sheila Moritz, worldly young society matron.

"What club?" she asked sweetly.

Poor Mindy was caught, presumably doing something she had been told not to. "Uh . . . just an old club we go to," she whispered.

"We who?" She asked, still nice-nice.

"Uh . . . oh, just me and—uh, Mother and Papa."

"Not Roger?"

"Oh yes, Roger. Sure, Roger belon—uh, used to belong. I don't think he goes there since he got out of the army, though. Probably not a member anymore. Well, I've got to be going. See you later." Mindy tried to walk past us, but She took her arm. The three of us strolled toward the front hall, and in the big oval mirror with the elaborate gold frame I saw She's big phony smile.

"What's the name of the club?" She wanted to know.

"Uh . . . I forget . . ." Sheila didn't let go. "The—uh—Riverdale Yacht Club," Mindy whispered, clearly terrified. She dashed for the front door. "I'm late, see you later!" she gasped, and vanished.

"That's what I thought," said my sister the OSS agent. "It's that place we went to that time, remember, and looked through the fence like two goddamn orphans, and all the time this whole family belongs to it!"

I remembered then. The two of us had been driving along the Hudson River and we stopped to look through the fence of a waterfront property almost as big as Toscanini's. We guessed it was a club, not just another mansion. We couldn't see much except perfect grass and big old shade trees, but we heard the bounce of tennis balls and kids laughing discreetly from what was surely a pool. There was an ivy-encrusted iron gate but no sign with any name on it.

After Mindy squeaked out the door, we went into the library and Sheila made a pitcher of martinis and put it on a tray with two glasses and a bucket of ice. Then we walked up the stairs and into our bedroom. She opened the bathroom door without knocking and I was prepared to be mortified, but Roger was only shaving. He had on his maroon-and-gold silk bathrobe. Harvard colors.

"What's this shit about the Riverdale Yacht Club?" She demanded. "Have a martini."

Roger shook his head at us in the mirror, but She put the tray down on the wide corner of the sink, where he was standing. We sat down on the side of the bathtub. It was an old-fashioned tub, set into a wooden frame and not uncomfortable at all to sit on.

Roger looked almost as scared as Mindy had a couple of minutes before. He had just put his custom-blended shaving cream all over his face with the special brush made out of animal hairs you could only get at Brooks Brothers. He had a special cup for it, in fact several. The razor was also supposed to be special; he didn't know that She shaved her legs with it.

"Huh, oh, the club, well, it's really nothing, I mean it's very old, and run-down. You'd hate it. Same old people who've belonged forever. Boring. Really. I haven't been there in years. Used to go when we were little kids, you know, tennis lessons and swimming meets and boring supper dances . . . it's nothing special, believe me."

"How come you never even mentioned it to me? Maybe I would like to go there and sit by the pool to cool off, and maybe I would like to meet some of your old friends, and maybe you're ashamed of me and that's why you never even once mentioned that you even belonged to a club. How do you think it makes me feel when I see my sister-in-law sneaking off to play tennis as if I wasn't supposed to know the whole family even belonged to a club!"

"Well, see, darling, that's just it. We only still belong for Mindy's sake, so she can meet nice young men and have properly supervised dates there. That's all, really."

"What else?" She persisted, letting the martini slide down her throat and pouring herself another.

"Nothing else, sweetie, honest. It's just an old clubhouse. They have really boring dinner dances every Saturday night in the spring and summer and fall, same people all the time. There aren't any yachts! Don't you think that's funny? It's called the Yacht Club, but there aren't any yachts! Just a swimming pool . . . well, two, counting the one for kids, and six or eight tennis courts. That's about it. Oh, and of course, the squash courts."

When I heard that, I thought the club was doing something worthy with its prime real estate. I envisioned courtyards bursting with a harvest of zucchinis, pumpkins, acorns, and butternuts, but squash courts turned out to be echoing cement cells down below the locker rooms, smelling faintly like Leif Ericson pool, giving me a surprising nip of nostalgia for that fungus-ridden place in the sun where rich people and poor people, knowing no better, climbed down together to have a look at what swam under the surface.

"You're ashamed of me. That's why you won't take me to the Yacht Club!" She said when he'd finished telling her about it and she'd finished two martinis, or "tee martoonies" as she joked when in her better moods. This was not one of her better moods. I reached for Roger's half-finished glass, took a swig myself, and set it back on the corner of the sink. He nodded at me absentmindedly in the mirror and nicked himself in the chin.

"Ashamed? No, no, I'm proud of you, don't you know that yet? Don't ever say that, darling, no, no, no! Okay?" He was dabbing at himself with a towel and one of those styptic pencils, but he couldn't seem to make the bleeding stop. She didn't make a move to help him.

"Well, if you're not ashamed of me, what the hell is going on? Why can't we go swimming and play tennis with the rest of the family?"

"Well, gosh—" Roger actually said "gosh," which nobody in Sioux City ever did, and I doubt that he picked it up at Harvard; he was just a gosh kind of guy. "I knew you couldn't play tennis, uh, in your condition, I mean, and anyway, aren't you tired of being with the family all the time? We should strike out on our own more. I know what! Let's go to the beach!"

Sounded good to me.

But She was hugely uncomfortable, and the idea of the long ride back from Jones Beach, sunburnt with sand in her crotch, didn't appeal to her. We had been there the week before. Roger was always trying to think up swell things to do on weekends; I think now it was in order to keep us away from the club—on his mother's orders, I'd bet the farm—so we wouldn't wonder where Margaretha and Mr. Moritz and Mindy were going in their tennis whites and gauzy ball gowns. He tried manfully, but organizing social outings was not his strong suit. His imagination extended to visiting old Harvard pals, having dinner in town, taking in a show. When did he study? Not on weekends. She made it very clear to him that he was a married man and his weekends, at the very least, belonged to her. Sitting home bored out of her skull while he studied on weeknights was enough of a sacrifice for her to make.

In the matter of the club, Roger was once again caught between the Furies. Margaretha must have made it blazingly clear to her son that he was never to bring his wife and her sister there. It dawned on me later that being invited to join that club had been a major triumph of Margaretha's life, better than giving birth to a son, since practically anybody could do that. But the Moritzes were the first—whisper it, please—*Jews* ever to be asked to join the club, and they were still the only members who could be traced to that background. They were tokens, white Jews, non-practicing, educated beyond their breeding, and rich enough to be counted upon for huge guilt/gelt contributions without even having to be asked. Membership in the no-yacht yacht club (that was the great club joke—it broke members up every time they repeated it, which they did a lot) was sacrosanct, handed down from father to son, and even then the son had to be voted on, although as yet no legitimate heir had ever been rejected, despite spectacular Commandment-busting performances such as passing out on the dance floor, vomiting into the kiddie pool, coveting and having one's neighbor's wife, fiddling client funds down on the Street, lying, cock-sucking, taking the name of the Lord in vain, all those things.

When we went that Sunday afternoon, I took my camera, thinking I'd record the look on Margaretha's face when she looked up to see us walking into her club, but at the last minute I got too shy to use it and left it in the dressing-room locker. Driving down there, Roger was sweating a lot more than the temperature accounted for. Poor Roger. You could really feel sorry for him. One lousy mistake, one lapse in judgment, and his whole life was wobbling on its hitherto solid-gold, rock-set foundations. HARVARD BOY MARRIED TO SIAMESE TWIN DESTROYS MOTHER SOCIALLY, RUINS SISTER'S CHANCES FOR A GOOD MARRIAGE, FEARS ENTERING HIS OWN CLUB.

She was determined to walk in there and win everybody's instant admiration. What an exquisite, well-bred, and truly charming wife dear but dull Roger has found! Why, Roger, where have you been hiding this treasure? Come, Sheila, sit here with us and tell us all about yourself. Waiter, a glass of champagne for this lovely creature, that bottle the club's been saving for a really special toast. We're so lucky, so grateful to you for joining us, Sheila dear. Won't you come to the opera with me next week and sit in the royal box?

I really think she expected something like that. Instead, we got shocked eyeballs. Until that minute, people hadn't really been able to believe that someone they knew personally, an actual member of their own club, had done this extraordinary and disgusting thing. Married two sisters physically joined together! Yes, yes—Siamese twins, it's true, do you believe it? And of all people, that Roger Moritz— you know the fellow, sandy hair, on the short side, pleasant enough but—well, you know, you do know, don't you? I mean, very nice family, quite like the rest of us in many

190

ways. But he's done the damnedest thing. Makes you wonder about the rest of his race, you know. What's he up to? Trying to sabotage this club? I said when I blackballed them that letting even one in would lead to our ruination, and now look. We've got honest-to-God freaks walking around here as if they owned the place. If you ask me, Hitler had the right idea.

Well, we did look odd that summer. Lopsided, with Sheila far gone into the most enormous pregnancy, and me, taller and having to bend to the left to try to balance her load. We were the original traveling curiosity shop. Sheila wore a kimono, down to the ground and flowing, in bright purple and blue. I wore a bathing suit, artfully sewn to the side of her kimono, by me. My bathing suit was navy blue, one-piece, and as innocuous as possible. But I have to say my figure was still slender and great. I was self-conscious about everybody looking at my incredibly terrific figure. For that first second I actually forgot that my other half was still there, but then I quickly cottoned on that it was She they were gawking at. A couple of the elite laughed out loud, the rudest, most bestial sound I've ever heard. No, I take it back. Beasts would never hurt each other like that.

She ignored them, as she knew how to do so well. She led me over near the pool, and we sat down carefully on a white wrought-iron couch covered with faded flowery cushions. Roger, a step behind us, had turned firehouse-red. His eyes locked in on his wife as if there were some salvation to be found in her, a way out. Maybe he just wanted some acknowledgment that they were in this together. But She was smiling at everyone but him; she was enjoying the lovely day and the lovely yacht club and looking around for her lovely in-laws.

Margaretha must have seen us first, because she was nowhere in sight. She must have dragged Mindy off with her, but Mr. Moritz, bless him, came off the tennis court just then, perspiration rolling down his forehead, all flushed from the exertion. He saw us and broke into a nice big welcoming smile, ingenuous and innocent. As he came toward us, hands outstretched to clasp ours, you could hear the murmurs of "Didn't I tell you" and "How can we get rid of them" fluttering around the place like bats in heat.

Even though I loathed those people for all the right reasons, I was humiliated and wanted to die on the spot. Only my sister and Mr. Out-of-it Moritz were immune to the slings and arrows of outrageous bubbleheads. I wanted to be above it, wanted desperately not to care what these people thought or did. In my fantasies, they came groveling and apologizing to me in Stockholm just as I finished accepting the Nobel Prize in Literature with a speech more memorable than the Gettysburg Address. In reality, they reduced me to blushes and mortification and tears, rage and anger that had no place to go. But my sister stood as I wished I could stand, head high and smiling down on the multitude. She thought they were praising her, adoring her, accepting her. Sheila made the world do and say what she wanted it to. Her fantasies just sauntered in and took over. She thought these people loved her.

I felt a twinge of pity for her as she took the salute. But mostly I hated her for putting me through this, and I wanted to die. Maybe she'd die, too, before we could be cut apart; that's what happened to Chang and Eng. I'd gladly go with her life on my conscience if I could be certain we'd separate in hell. I often thought about ways of doing it. Not so easy to sneak in a suicide when there's someone who knows every goddamn little move you make every minute of your life.

Somehow we managed to get through that terrible day, winding up with a buffet supper: ham and headcheese and mayonnaise salads set on a long table inside the clubhouse; paper lanterns stuck around in the grass, where people took their plates out to settle in little clusters of chairs and couches. Nobody sat with us. Roger's father had gone home shortly after his tennis match, needing a rest. Sheila was happy, happy, happy, chattering away to Roger and me about how darling everything was, why on earth didn't we find the time to come long before this, she couldn't wait to bring the baby here, had we noticed the little wading pool for toddlers? She was just sure she was going to have very close personal friends, lots of them, among all the nice-looking people she'd met today.

It was true, we'd been introduced to a lot of thin, blond women and smiling young men already going to paunch. Everyone had drinks in their hands all day. She had had four martinis by the time we plowed into the cold cuts. Chatter, chatter. She loved it all. Roger was glad she was so happy. He was a little worried about the baby; should She really have that other drink? Yes, she snapped.

Finally, we got home and to bed. Sheila had started snoring since her pregnancy prevented her from sleeping on her stomach. Her pregnancy also prevented me from sleeping on my stomach, and her snoring prevented me from sleeping at all. On the other side of her, Roger slept the quiet doze of one temporarily released from tension. I felt that I was in prison, but after the nine months were up and then another two, I'd be out of it. It would be my turn. Roger had a job in Boston starting in September, at a small but awfully, awfully prestigious law firm, while he studied for the bar. I had already enrolled at Wellesley College, and Daddy had paid my tuition in advance. It was all going to work out fine. She could take the baby with her to my classes, or leave it home tied up in a gunnysack, I didn't care.

Roger graduated in June. She had a darling baby in August (a girl, named Margaret Millicent Moritz, to be called Millie), a week after we turned twenty, and in September we moved to Boston. Of all these events, I will say only one thing: It is not easy to be joined at the hip to a woman who is giving birth. She screamed and demanded things: massages, cold cloths on her forehead, Roger's hand to hold, a sedative, a painkiller, flowers, special food brought in, the food taken away, a drink. I lay beside her trying not to cry or cry out. I have had excruciating backaches ever since. I don't blame anyone; I'm glad to be Millie's Aunt Sandy. But a little attention to me wouldn't have cost anyone anything.

Of course, I loved Millie the minute I saw her and never regretted for a minute what we went through to get her (although it's not true that you forget the pain). But all my thoughts were looking forward to Boston, an apartment of our own, and Wellesley College. It was finally going to be my turn.

18

Tea for Three

I could do a book on the different ways people stare in different places. In Boston, you get yahoos who can stop in their tracks and turn around and stand there just gawking at you as if you were the next thing on the Freedom Trail after the Old North Church. But guess what? It's only the tourists. People who live in Boston can't be bothered; they're much too preoccupied with something mental. The ones who aren't writing books in their heads are working on symphonies or fission research.

We—excuse me, they—found an apartment in a little semisuburb between Wellesley and the Back Bay section of Boston, where Roger's office was. They were lucky to get it because there was a fierce shortage of places to live. It was really a garage attached to the back of someone's house and you could still smell the grease, but they had cleaned out all the junk and laid linoleum over the cement floor and put in some windows and walls and all the modern conveniences so that it was a tiny but decent place to live. Sheila wanted to live right in the middle of the city, in a townhouse on Beacon Street or one of the little hilly streets going upward from the Public Gardens.

"I don't want to live in a goddamn garage," She bitched, "in a goddamn suburb."

"Hey, look, it'll be very convenient for Sandy's classes at Wellesley; the train runs right by here—" Roger bumbled.

"Oh, convenient for Sandy! How nice. What about me? Don't you think it's unbelievably selfish for her to make me go back to school with her? I'm a mother now, with responsibilities. I have to put little Millie's best interests above my own, and that means Sandy should, too. Just 'cause she wants to meet arty-farty people with no morals and go to parties and talk about books all the time, I'm supposed to abandon my little baby. It's not fair! It's not right!"

Was I being selfish? Was it the social contacts I wanted, the beer parties and bull sessions, the chance to make friends? Was it unfair to ask baby Millie to come along in her carriage, comfortable or not, while I wrote stories and read them, hands and voice shaking, aloud to a writers' workshop class? What if I didn't have any talent at all, or half the brains I thought I did? Did I have the right to pull my sister away from hearth and home, husband and child, to follow my own clouded destiny when maybe all I really wanted was to have fun?

Daddy decided for me. He never talked to me about it, but he paid the tuition and sent me a letter from his office about what I could count on for allowance and books, and he filled out the forms that parents fill out. And so it was done. I was enrolled. And for our birthday, he bought us a car. A new, postwar Buick, with tail fins and shiny chrome, so we could travel back and forth from Sheila's life to mine in the most comfortable way possible.

I had paid my dues, and with very little complaining. She owed me a whole year, and we both knew it. So, under duress, complaining every minute of the day, she accompanied me to my classes and lectures and seminars and to the library for studying. Roger's parents paid for a sitter to take care of Millie every day.

One day I was writing in the library when I suddenly became aware that my sister was shaking all over, crying silently. Not to herself; she never wasted tears on that. Just silently.

"All right, what's the matter?" I whispered fiercely.

"My poor baby!" she blubbered. "I miss my baby, and it's time for her feeding and she's going to get it from a stranger and it's so unnatural I—"

"SHHHHH!" several people around us muttered.

"Oh, shush yourself!" She snapped out loud. Then she went back to her litany in a weepy whisper. "Millie doesn't have a chance in hell of growing up normal, and I never should have had her, on account of you. If it weren't for you, I'd be home with her right now, and—"

"Girls, I'm afraid you'll have to stop talking if you want to stay in the library." A lean, mean librarian was standing behind us and she wasn't saying maybe. We got up and left.

After that, I tried to arrange to do my studying at home. It was more like the horrors of study hall at the SDT house than I cared to remember. She needed constant music and voices around her. The radio was on all the time, and we were one of the first families in our part of Boston to get a television set.

Maybe I shouldn't blame my sister entirely for my failures as a student. Sex had a lot to do with it, too.

Wellesley was an all-girls school, but Boston was a seething swamp of male students leering or smiling at you from all directions. Coffeehouses and beer halls, saloons and hamburger stands, candy stores and drive-ins, bookstores and

co-ops, gas stations and park benches, movies and restaurants, Durgin Park and Filene's basement; all were exten-
sions of the campus to the thousands of postwar students
who filled Boston and its many colleges to the bursting point.
It was hard not to meet someone every time you ventured
out. Boys—young men, veterans—were initially curious
about the two of us, then attracted to She, and when she
turned out to be married and the two of us turned out to be
not so strange as we looked, I sometimes ended up with the
fellow. I was ecstatic, in love with love again and a different
guy every three or four days.

Nothing delighted me more than sitting in a coffeehouse
for hours, talking about philosophy and politics and literature with earnest, handsome young men who admired my
mind and hoped to get to my body as well. When She got
fitted for a diaphragm six weeks after Millie was born, I
figured I might as well, too, since there I was in the doctor's
office lying on an examining table pushed up next to hers. I
told the doctor it would just save me the trouble later, if I
ever got married. Not that I got much chance to use it—none,
in fact, until the time I'm going to tell you about in a
minute—but I thought about it a lot and it was exciting to
feel ready for anything.

Sheila thought my choices of men were all worthless
(they were always poor, for one thing) and disgusting (they
used words just beginning to be allowed into the country in
books with redeeming social value, books that were not being sold in Boston). I yearned for sex. I knew it could be
better, *had* to be better, than the inarticulate conjugal quick-
ies that went on in my bed once a week.

There was a terrifically attractive MIT graduate student
who had been a captain in the army who wanted to sneak me
up to his dormitory room, and I was ready to go—dying to
go—but She said she'd scream in the lobby and elevator and
all the way down the hall if we tried it.

"You're the one who's not fair!" I barked at her. "You owe me a whole year, but you poison every second of it. Why can't you stay out of my life like I did for you? Why can't you stop whining and bitching all the time about what *you* want! When is it ever going to be my—"

She interrupted me. The ex-captain was looking from one to the other of us, across the tiny table in the Coffee Bean. He seemed amused, and I could sense him backing off and away, which only made me more furious at She, who was clearly determined to spoil any chance I ever had at fun, let alone romance.

"What I want! What I want!" She shouted. Everybody stared over at us. "It's not what I want! My baby needs me! How can you be so mean?"

"Baby? Baby?" the fellow said. He pushed himself away from the table in a gesture so subtle it could have meant anything or nothing.

"I'm married and I have a baby and I should be home with her right now and I would be if my sister weren't so selfish!"

To his credit, he looked at me sympathetically, with his head cocked to one side and a rueful it-could-have-been smile playing across his lower lip, and then he picked up the check, stood up slowly while we both looked at him in silence. He left some change on the table, shrugged his shoulders, gave me that look again, and left the coffeehouse.

I started to cry; I couldn't help it.

"Oh well, if you're going to make a scene, let's get out of here," She said.

"When does my life start?" I asked sullenly. I refused to budge. "Never mind the whole year I've been devoting to you and your boring marriage. What about the six hours out of every twelve that are supposed to be for me right now?"

She was pulling at me, trying to get up, but I dug in. I planted my feet firmly on the floor and crossed my arms and sat down hard on my tailbone and just stared into the space where my chance at romance had been.

"He only wanted you for the freakiness of it," She said.

"Bitch."

"Calling me names won't change anything. It's too bad you'll never understand the mother instinct, but I thought you cared about poor little Millie. She's probably screaming her lungs out right now wondering where I am, and me hanging around here in this crummy place full of communists. For God's sake, Sandy, there's no point in hanging around here, is there? Except to punish me and my helpless little baby?"

"Mrs. Simpson takes better care of Millie than you do," I shot back.

"Take that back."

"It's true."

We sat there glumly, at one of our impasses again. Then She had an idea.

"I'm willing to compromise," she announced, as if she were the queen giving away Africa to the wogs. "Let's just get out of this dump and we can go someplace else. We don't have to go home just yet. Mrs. Simpson probably gave Millie her lunch already anyhow. I'll tell you what, let's go have a little drinkie. Isn't that a good idea? You'd feel a lot better with a martini or two in you. Might actually help your lousy disposition. Come on."

"I don't want a goddamn drink."

"Well, I do."

"Oh, that's no surprise. You're turning into a goddamn alcoholic, you know that?"

"Sticks and stones. You're just jealous because I've got a husband and a baby and you never will. You ought to be thankful to me for saving you from that jerk's clutches. All he wanted was your body. Or mine, more likely. Probably thought he could get at me through you 'cause you're so frustrated it's obvious."

"You think anybody who wants me is really after you. Boy, that's sick."

"Well, he wouldn't be the first one with delusions of orgies." She pronounced it with a hard *G*.

"Orgies," I corrected automatically. Soft *G*.

"Whatever. He sure lost interest fast. You ought to be grateful I saved you from something really stupid. You can get arrested for going into a man's dormitory."

"I'm not grateful and I'm not thankful and I want to lead my own life!"

"Sure, and go to bed with every man who comes along."

"Yes, if I want to!"

"And get syphilis and go crazy and die!"

"YES, IF I WANT TO!"

"People are staring at us," She whispered.

And so I let her lead me through the afternoon sunshine into a bar, where we sat in the dark and listened to the jukebox. It was still the late '40s and girls didn't go into bars without escorts, especially in Boston. Sitting in that bar in the afternoon made me feel cheap and used and useless and futureless. Sneaking into a man's room at MIT would have been a lark, a dare, a thrilling adventure, but this was depressing. She drank martinis and I drank two brandy alexanders and three Cokes. Men kept coming up to us and wanting to dance or sit with us or just talk dirty. In the semi-dark, they couldn't tell right away that we were conjoined. That was the only good thing about being there.

Somehow, I drove home. I always managed, even with She snoring on my shoulder.

Some nights Roger took us out to dinner. He and She loved to eat lobsters, cracking all the little shells and sucking them dry, wearing paper bibs tied around their necks. But I couldn't get used to the ugliness of the poor things, which had to be dropped *alive* into boiling water, and anyway, I'd kill anybody who tried to put a bib on me, so I generally went for a steak, well done.

One night when I asked for my steak well done and coffee served with the meal, please, the waiter seemed oddly amused. (As soon as I found out the way things were done in New York, believe me, I started eating steak rare [ugh] and went without coffee until after.) Anyway, this waiter grinned at me with what looked like delight. I looked up at him to make sure he wasn't having a laugh at my expense and got what was almost an electric shock.

I just couldn't believe how marvelous-looking he was. Dark brown hair, rich with light, just growing out from a GI haircut, shaggy and defiant of any comb or style. He had dark eyes, sexy and understanding, that looked straight at me as if he liked what he was looking at. I thought his mouth was the most exciting thing I had ever seen and I knew I could never get tired of just looking at it, watching it form words and smiles and wry expressions that made me die to kiss it.

"Where do you come from?" he asked with what seemed genuine interest. He was looking at me as though he saw only me and no one else for that moment. I felt myself leaning into him, mesmerized. His voice was as good as his mouth was. I definitely felt a funny tickle down in the back of my lower body. And down in front, too.

Determined to be fascinating and sophisticated (however had he guessed I wasn't from New York, or Boston for that matter?) I smiled with my super blend of tolerance, gentle patience, and warm promise of possibilities to come. "Oh, I'm from Iowa," I chirped gaily, hoping he would think that interesting rather than as prosaic as it sounded to me.

He looked puzzled, but kind of intrigued, too, in a friendly way. He never took his eyes off me. Roger was making noises, ahem, but the waiter and I were a million miles away. "You've heard of Iowa, haven't you?" I jousted wittily.

"Oh yes." His smile widened. How wonderful! His grin

was a bit crooked, just enough. "But," he said, twinkling his eyes at me, "in the East we pronounce it Ohio."

"Well!" my outraged idiot sister gasped.

But I laughed out loud, for once not inhibited by what She and her friends had forever branded as my horse-laugh. I think it was the very first time I had ever laughed spontaneously at something someone else meant to be funny. I just hadn't ever found anybody funny enough before. But this extraordinary fellow had made me forget myself, and I would have loved him for that alone even if all the rest hadn't happened.

"What's your name?" he asked me, still ignoring Roger's impatient noises and my sister's visible bristling.

"Sandy."

"I'm Thaddeus, and I'll call you tomorrow morning if you give me your number. What time do you get up?" Without transition, he turned to Roger and became the total waiter. "Yes, sir, and would you like to see the wine list?"

I wrote my name and phone number on the inside of the restaurant's matchbook, with "6:00" after it, and then I thought that might seem too eager, so I changed the 6 to an 8. Then I was afraid he would call after I had left for school, so I scratched out the time and wrote "anytime" instead. Let him think whatever he was going to think. This was not going to work at all if we started out playing the Game. I wanted someone I could be totally honest with; it was everything I had ever wanted. But . . . would he vanish if I handled things stupidly? Of course he would. I was scared, suddenly, because I had never paid enough attention to learning how to get what I wanted in this world. And oh, I wanted Thaddeus the waiter to want me.

He did. He called the next morning and he said "Sandy?" in the sexiest voice ever, because it wasn't put on. It was sleepy and that was what made it work so insidiously down in my vitals.

"Yes . . . Thaddeus?"

"Yes. Is it too early?"

I hoped he could tell by my voice that he made me smile. "You read what I scratched out, didn't you? Well, I've been waiting for you to call since six o'clock."

"It's four minutes after."

"I know."

I heard a small, pleasant chuckle, a nice sound, amiable. "What do you do with your days, Sandy?"

"I go to school. At Wellesley."

"But you don't live on campus."

"No."

I wondered: Hadn't he noticed anything when She and I got up to leave the restaurant? Maybe he didn't know. Maybe he would be out of my life like a flash the minute he found out. Should I tell him? No! Definitely not. I'd have to chance it. I had to see him again, even if only once.

"I go to school, too. I'm twenty-three. I was in the army for four years. I'm in school on the G.I. Bill and I work as a waiter and I hope that doesn't put you off. Did you ever date a waiter before?"

"Why should that put me off?"

"Ah, Sandy. I'll bet your mother wouldn't approve, though, back in Iowa."

"What does that matter?"

"Will you go out to a very inexpensive dinner and a long, long talk over coffee with me tomorrow night? It's my night off."

This was where I should play the game and be coy, or reticent, hard to get. Fuck it. "Yes," I answered, and held my breath to see if there would be a change in his tone. Men don't want things (women) if they're too easy to get. Everybody knew that about men.

"Oh, Sandy! I love your directness."

Well, that did it. I was in love. It wasn't the first time, it was the only time. I knew that then and I was right.

"Thaddeus . . ."

"Yes, only everyone else calls me Thad. You can if you want to, or not. Call me anything you like."

"I like Thaddeus. It's a beautiful name."

Next to me, my sister was making gagging noises as a critique of my end of the conversation. I could hear Millie starting to kvetch in her crib, waking up.

"Good," Thaddeus said. He waited for me to say what was on my mind. It took a minute for me to think how to say it.

"Uh . . . Thaddeus . . . do you . . . would you mind if . . . if my sister came along with us?"

"I don't see that we have any alternative, do we? You two are joined together, so I guess your sister's going to be a very good friend of mine. We might as well get acquainted. Okay?"

Okay, Thaddeus. I love you.

"Okay."

"Tell me your address and I'll pick you up at seven."

I spelled out the address. She was making rotten faces while I talked, standing there in the little makeshift hallway with her arms folded over her chest. She might as well have been in China for all I cared.

" 'Bye, Sandy. See you tomorrow."

" 'Bye, Thaddeus."

Then I turned to the mirror over the telephone table and caught She's expression. Looking straight into her eyes, I said slowly, so that she knew without a doubt I meant it, "If you do or try to do anything to break this up, I'll really kill you. I really will, because I won't give a damn for my own life. I mean it."

She believed me. Her eyes widened, but all she said was, "Do you mind telling me what night we have a date for? I've got plans of my own, you know. You could consult me before you make dates for me."

205

"Tomorrow night," I said, hardly believing it myself. We edged our way down the narrow hall. We always had to turn sideways to get through into the little dinette attached to the even smaller kitchen.

"Well, that's too bad because Roger and I are going to have dinner with the Allens tomorrow night. We've had the date for ages, haven't we, hon?"

Roger nodded without looking up from his newspaper. He had gotten Millie up and changed her and he had mixed her warm cereal. She was sitting on the table in one of those mummy rests they strap infants into. She started fretting.

I loved Millie. I loved Roger. I loved cornflakes, coffee, that sticky little kitchen, the crumbs on the butter knife, life itself. I felt interesting and attractive.

"You'll have to cancel the Allens," I said as nicely as I knew how. "I'm sorry, She, but this is terribly important to me."

"Well, the Allens are important to me! Tell her, Roger!"

Millie was catching the spirit and she started to fret. Her doting mother tried shoving some Pablum into the baby's open mouth, but Millie just let the stuff dribble out while she worked up to a good-size scream. We had to raise our voices to be heard.

Roger said, "It's been a long time since Sandy had a date of her own, honey. We can postpone Bill and Janet, they won't mind. It wasn't anything very—"

"GODDAMNIT! What about me? What about my life? What about our marriage? Do you think I want to go out with a goddamn WAITER? And what about you, Mr. Superior? Are you going with us or are you going to stay home and make me be a third wheel? What kind of life is this? I had a lot more fun before I married you!"

"Honey, you're upsetting the baby."

"She, this is important to me."

"TO HELL WITH ALL OF YOU!" And she tried to get up,

to stomp off to the bedroom no doubt, hoping to slam the door, too. I dug in hard and stayed put. She socked me, hard, on the side of my head. Roger stood up quickly.

"Oh my God!" he said, although this wasn't the first time he had witnessed violence in our tight-knit little family. "Stop it! Stop it!"

I didn't hit her back. To hell with her. I found that I could ignore her, really and truly forget that She was there, even while she was attacking me. It didn't matter. What mattered was a phone call, a date to look forward to, a crown of thick brown hair that leaped with life and a mouth I couldn't wait to feel right down on mine. Inside my head I was hearing "Thaddeus, Thaddeus," and its music drowned out my silly sister and her tantrum. I felt—funny to say it—detached.

With Roger and me both against her, She had to give in, not that she had to do it gracefully. It was Roger who called the Allens and arranged for the sitter. He kissed Sheila when he went to work, but she stayed tight-lipped and wouldn't even say goodbye. She sulked all day in my classes and ruined any fun I might have had at lunch in the Coop. When we got home in the afternoon, I tried talking to her.

"C'mon, She, don't be like this. It's only a date. You know you owe me hours and weeks and months. What's the big deal about one date?"

"I don't like your choice of social partners," she said. "And you got the baby all upset this morning."

"I'm not the one who upset the baby this morning!"

"You certainly are, too. Are you going to accuse me of not being a good mother again? That's what you're hinting at, isn't it?"

I tuned out and tried to lose myself in Henry James, not always an easy thing to do. I sat with the book in front of me, but I thought about Thaddeus and I ignored my sister as much as I could. If She was sulking, to hell with her. What should I wear? For the first time in my life, I gave a damn about what I should wear. Were all my clothes too much She's taste and not my own? I didn't want to be dressed up, but I couldn't go out in slacks, either. Did my blue print shirtwaist dress make me look like I was going to teach Sunday School? Was my black sheath too sexy for a first date? If my sister and I had been talking to each other at all, I might have asked her expert advice. And if she were a real sister, she'd lend me her new green cashmere sweater set. Oh well, who needed her? I'd wear the blue print dress and the highest heels I owned.

When Roger got home he kissed She and gave her a box of chocolate turtles, her favorite. Then he made up enough of Millie's formula to last in case we were out late the following night. By the time we went to bed, She was softening, and they made love the way they always did, quickly and without words. I had gotten so I could doze right through it most of the time. I'm afraid She did, too.

19

Thaddeus

Thaddeus rang our bell at seven on the dot. I love promptness in a person. Roger opened the door and there he was, taller than I had thought, handsomer than I had been able to let myself remember, smiling first at Roger and then, miraculously, at me. Roger offered drinks. She started talking fast and it occurred to me she was flirting with Thaddeus. I hoped he wouldn't decide she was too obnoxious to put up with. I wished there were some way to let him know the furniture in this makeshift apartment was not my idea of beautiful.

"What a fascinating job waiting on tables must be! You must meet all kinds of people," She offered up as a socko opening gambit. I watched with interest to see how he would deal with my sister's idea of serious conversation. Would he get down to her level? Would he sneer at her (and by extension, me)? Would he apologize for his lowly station in life, indicating that he got her point but wasn't bright enough to parry it?

"I do it for the money," he said with a little smile, sort of half a grin. "I'm not writing a sociological study of how twentieth-century Americans behave in restaurants, although, you know, it's not a bad idea at that."

She laughed prettily, taking it as a compliment to her giant brain. And I guffawed without meaning to, so delighted that the comely fellow could not only talk but cut through bullshit without the shitter even knowing it. He looked at me and I cupped my hand over my big mouth, mortified because I had forgotten how donkeylike my laugh sounded, hee-haw, hee-haw. But the way Thaddeus looked at me made me feel like I'd been singing Mozart.

"I've got the G.I. Bill, of course," he said, "but a hundred and twenty a month doesn't stretch very far, so I wait on tables. Actually, Sheila's right, it probably would be interesting if I could remember to think about it that way while it was happening."

Roger asked him where he went to school and you could see the relief flood him when Thaddeus said Harvard. I caught Thaddeus's eye and realized instantly he had Roger's number, and Sheila's, too. And what they were wasn't going to make the slightest bit of difference to him and me. We already had a secret language. Our eyes had met. I felt thrilled down to my soul.

I have to try to describe how beautiful Thaddeus looked to me then. There has to be some accounting, something so powerful on the credit side of the ledger that it can explain why later I allowed the debits to pile up as they did. Think of Cary Grant in his prime, but Cary Grant had a roundish, almost moon face. Think of Cary Grant and slim down the face, leaving the generously full mouth and the chin with a hint of a cleft to it. Thaddeus's eyes were large and brown and kind, I thought, intelligent and guarded, quick to catch on to any nuance in the air, probing into my thoughts with real interest; his eyes gave him away, I thought, as that rare man who really cared how someone was feeling. His cheek-bones were high, almost Oriental, giving him a perennially pleasant, even cheerful, aspect; he always waited too long to get a haircut, so that he usually had the shaggy look of a rowdy little boy; looking at the back of his neck could make me weak with pleasure and desire. His skin was taut and had a deep patina, like fine wood after years of thoughtful oil rubs. Not that he ever did anything more to his skin than shave it and wash it in cold water. It just seemed, like the rest of him, healthy and well cared for. The rest of him? Tall, broad, not muscular but firm. Oh yes, firm!

That first evening was fun and easygoing. We all relaxed and had a good time. For me, it was feverishly sexual, too. Thaddeus was the most desirable man I had ever seen in person. When I looked at him, I wondered what it would be like to kiss him there and there and there. What would his eyes look like when he was in the throes of passion, its object ME? What was his chest like, his thighs, his belly . . . I found myself blushing. He was talking easily with Roger and Sheila, and I wondered if I had been staring at him with my mouth hanging open. But then he reached for my hand under the table. I wondered if he could feel how hot it got at his touch.

My thoughts ran simultaneous and headlong into each other:

> I wouldn't mind being mindless and out of
> control with him
>   but
> any man who wants to make love to me has
> something wrong about him.

A torrential wave of despair almost drowned me right there and then. I've never hated my sister so much as I did that evening while I was falling in love.

My brain was on automatic pilot. I was keeping up my end of the conversation and all the time praying that this was more to him than something weird to top all the other guys' stories back at Harvard Yard. And thinking I'd probably be better off if that's what it did turn out to be. And looking at Thaddeus and knowing that if he'd have me, on any terms, I'd be grateful the rest of my life.

We went to a Chinese restaurant called Foo's Garden, which was the quintessential lantern-lit chopstick-and-fortune-cookie kind of place that was featured in movies about big cities, especially the ones with Gene Kelly in them. It was perfect, even to the humorously accented owner and sweet jangly music playing on an old record machine in a room behind the beaded curtain. I felt that somehow this restaurant and his taking me there signified that we were indeed meant for each other, or else how could he have known how much I longed to be taken to a place exactly like this?

She fussed about too much garlic and a lipstick stain on her napkin, but mostly she was cheerful, having shifted automatically into her "good date" mode. Going out on a date—whether hers or mine, apparently—went right to the heart of her basic training: This above all, Be a Good Date. She was being sweet and charming and pretty and amenable, a happy young woman, in her element, swilling down drinkie after drinkie and getting adorably flushed and giggly. Roger was finding her irresistible, and he started touching and caressing her hands, her arms, and her hair. I feared that Thaddeus would see how much cuter and more fun she was than I, but he was only polite to her and when he looked at me I knew, although I couldn't quite believe it, that he liked me better.

We learned about each other—the things we wanted to tell, anyway—that first evening. Thaddeus was an English Lit major and—coincidence of coincidences!—was living in

Roger's old House. He was from New York (the lower East Side) and he had a brother and a sister and a mother and a dad and he liked them all a lot, he said. Well, we said we liked our folks back in Sioux City a lot, too, and Roger said he liked his parents in Riverdale, too. Thaddeus had been in the air corps ("Another co-inkydink," said She) flying P-38 fighter planes. He hated the war even while it was going on and swore he never saw anything glamorous about being a fighter pilot and killing people, even Nazis—they were just people, after all, mostly scared kids who were just doing what they were told, like our own boys when it came down to it.

He was the first pacifist I had ever met, and as I listened to him, I felt all my old blindly accepted notions falling away.

"But we had to stop Hitler, didn't we?" I asked tentatively, totally prepared to abandon that notion should Thaddeus tell me I was misinformed.

"Of course," he said, to my relief. "It was a just war, it had to be fought. It was ugly and terrible, but yes, it had to be done," he said, looking me right in the eye, taking me seriously. I could hardly stand the acute bliss.

"But both sides always say that in every war, don't they? That God and right are on their side? I think men have some kind of need to fight and they justify it—"

"Oh, let's not be so gloomy!" my sister exclaimed, and she was right. She lifted her gin fizz and we all clinked glasses and laughed and let her lead us into a discussion of the couple who were sitting in a booth opposite us. "Look how short her skirt is! I saw them come in. Wait till she gets up and you'll see. Isn't that awful. Doesn't she know about the New Look? Nobody wears their skirts that short anymore."

"He seems to like her anyway," I commented dryly.

"Do you girls dance?" Thaddeus asked us.

"Do we! Sure! I was the best dancer in Sioux City!" She
yelped, bouncing up and down on the hard bench.

"Well, how . . . I mean, how exactly do you manage? I
hope you don't mind my asking."

I did mind, though. A chill ran through me; he was a
freak-fucker after all. I watched him as She bubbled on and
on, but he didn't seem to be listening or making up mental
pictures or anything. Maybe I was wrong.

"Well, first of all . . . honey, can I have another drinkie?
Well, it takes two guys, in the first place!" For some reason,
She found this hilarious and got off giggling so hard and so
infectiously we were soon all laughing with her. Yeah, me
too. Thaddeus had straight white teeth and he threw back
his head when he laughed and his eyes crinkled and he
caught my eye and I decided I trusted him.

He said he wasn't a very good dancer, had never gotten
the hang of it, and we promised to teach him someday. Our
dinner came and we dug into the food with some more hilarity at our handling of the chopsticks. Thaddeus and
Roger taught us how and we did get proficient enough to
get all but the last bits of rice from our little bowls. A lot
of it fell off my lap when I got up, though, but with Thaddeus, that was just something more to laugh about. He
didn't seem to think I was a klutz—he probably wouldn't
even know what the word meant—and for once my sister
didn't say it.

By the time we left the restaurant, I felt light-headed, and
not only from the gin fizzes. It was Thaddeus himself; I
couldn't believe in such perfection.

Roger drove, with Thaddeus beside him; She and I sat in
the backseat. Roger offered to take Thaddeus back to Cambridge, but, "Oh no, I want to take Sandy to her door," he
said. He'd make his way home from there, no problem. He
kissed me good night ever so gently when we got to the
doorstep. I literally got weak in the legs and thought I was

going into an honest-to-God genuine swoon. I had to hold on to Thaddeus to keep my balance and he laughed that nice little chuckle and kissed me again, harder. Then he said good night to She and Roger and shook Roger's hand and we went inside and he went away.

She couldn't pretend she didn't like him, so she raved about him as if he were her discovery. I asked Roger for his male opinion about whether he figured Thaddeus would call me again, and he said yes, he thought so. But then I thought if Thaddeus did the things Roger considered right and appropriate, he'd be as dull as Roger. So I still didn't know, and I stayed awake for hours, replaying the evening and wondering. Millie woke up twice and I was sorry I couldn't get her bottle warmed and feed her all by myself so She could go on sleeping, since I was wide awake anyway.

Just as I fell asleep, or so it seemed, the telephone rang. I tried to leap up and run to the hall, but She was rocklike, immovable. I didn't blame her, but I knew it had to be Thaddeus calling, and my heart started to race and my pulse was beating staccato for fear he'd hang up before old Roger quit yawning and scratching and got his slippers and got himself out of the goddamn bed and over to the phone. It was five after six and still dark outside. And when Roger said, "Oh hi, Thaddeus," I pulled She out of bed as if she had miraculously turned weightless.

"Hi," I murmured into the phone. God bless Alexander Graham Bell. You could make your voice really sexy by hunkering down into the mouthpiece and speaking low into the other person's ear.

"Good morning. Did I wake everybody up?"

"Not at all," I lied. "What are you doing up so early?"

"Waiting until it was time to call you."

Wow. As if that weren't enough, as if he knew how thoroughly he had rendered me paralyzed with pleasure, he added, still in his rumbling, husky intimate morning voice,

"Can your sister hear me? I want to say something for your ear only."

I was dazzled at the thought of having secrets from my sister. In all the years that She had harangued on the telephone with her friends, I had felt excluded, but it had never dawned on me that with an accomplice of my own, the situation could be reversed.

"No. I don't think so. No." I looked at She in the little hall mirror. She was dozing, nodding against the back of the chair we were precariously sharing. There was only a single chair in the little hallway and She had gotten rounder in the bottom lately, so I was sort of perched on the edge, supporting my weight with a foot propped up against the wall. Her eyes were closed and she was more than half asleep. "Tell me," I whispered.

"She must be kind of hard to live with," he said softly.

In my bottomless insecurity, I immediately assumed this to be the end. He was saying he couldn't live with her. That meant he couldn't live with me. He was saying goodbye. Well, decent of him to call. Most guys never bothered to explain.

"Yeah, I understand. Hey, you don't have to spell it out, okay? I appreciate your calling anyhow. And I still had a lovely time last night. 'Bye, Thaddeus."

I hung up before my voice broke. I poked Sheila to wake her and we started back down the little hallway toward the bedroom. The phone rang again. I turned and stared at it. Could it be? Probably a wrong number; nobody else would call anybody this hour of the morning. I answered apprehensively.

"Hello."

"Sandy, don't hang up on me. Why did you do that? Don't hang up, please. Tell me what I said to make you angry. I'm sorry if you thought I was asking you to be disloyal to your sister. Is that it? Sandy? Please answer me."

All I could say was, "Thaddeus?" It wasn't that I didn't know it was he; I just couldn't believe it.

"I'm sorry I said that about your sister. I didn't realize you . . . felt so strongly about her. In fact, I thought . . . well, never mind. Just say you're not mad at me, okay?"

"I thought you were saying . . ." I glanced at the mirror. She was nodding off again. I lowered my voice and cupped my hand around the mouthpiece. "I thought you meant you didn't want to see me anymore on account of her," I whispered fiercely.

"Oh no, baby, no! I was just commiserating with you. I thought you didn't like each other much, and I thought I could empathize with your predicament. But I guess the way you leaped to her defense, I read the whole thing wrong. I'm sorry."

"No, you're right, you're right! It's just—" Groping for an answer, I came up with the Awful Truth. It glittered and shone splendidly as I grabbed for it, seeing it straight on for the first time. "It's just the very first time anyone's ever been on my side," I said, filled with an almost religious awe.

He was silent for a moment. Sheila yawned loudly. I quickly covered the mouthpiece of the phone with the palm of my hand, but probably too late. Only a fart, of which she was also capable, would have more effectively ruined that moment. But if Thaddeus heard her, he didn't let on.

"I'm on your side, Sandy. All the way."

I didn't know precisely what that meant, but it was enough. "Thank you," I said softly.

"I have to work tonight, but can we meet for lunch? Oh no, hell, you're all the way out in Wellesley."

"It's okay, Thaddeus. I'll cut my afternoon class. It's only a lecture anyway. And She'll be glad not to have to sit there for two hours being bored by insights into the metaphors of Thomas Mann." I was pleased that I knew how to pronounce it. "Where shall we meet?"

He named a place and time; I realized I'd have to cut another class to get there, but what the hell, it was only this once. And I was in love. When I hung up the phone, I felt new and reborn; this wasn't me. I didn't know who I was. I had to put my hand down along my right side, to touch the place where I was different from everybody else, to remind myself that I was still tied to this earth, this clay, this sister of mine.

20

One Too Many

Sheila *was as nice* as she could be during most of the time when Thaddeus was courting me. Of course, she got vicarious kicks from his attentions and the fun of going out on dates again, even though the attentions were to me and the dates were my dates. Thaddeus never let on how he really felt about her; he was sweet and friendly and she never suspected he couldn't stand her. Every now and then he would give my arm a subtle pat or squeeze my hand under the table, or we'd catch each other's eye to reaffirm that he and I were together against the world.

One night at the movies, after She had been chattering inanely all the way downtown in the car ("How do Mongolian people know if they've given birth to a baby with Down's syndrome?"), as soon as Thaddeus settled in with his arm around me, he whispered in my ear, "What an absurd stream of consciousness she's got," and we chuckled privately and I felt a wonderful new surge of confidence. Absurd. I could appreciate the absurdity of so many things now. (And I knew what stream of consciousness was.) I could divorce myself from the world and my sister in little ways that made the difference. It was exactly as if he had given me magical powers. Thaddeus protected me with his insights and love, and words. I could think "how absurd" and instantly feel *separate.*

How grateful I was for Thaddeus; he was my lifeline, my sanity, my proof that I was lovable, worthy, someone.

I couldn't refrain from touching him when we were together, imagining him when we weren't. Every now and then a painful thought would intrude: If we could really be alone, it would have happened by now. Maybe he can't or won't or doesn't want to be part of a grotesque sexual group; I couldn't blame him, in fact I felt relieved and glad. I would have hated him if that's what he had wanted. Oh, but will we ever do it? Will he get tired of this eternal dating and good night kisses and stop calling, stop wanting to be with me? I tried to quash these terrible thoughts, let myself be happy with what I had. It was more than I had ever really expected to have. I thought he loved me. I knew I loved him.

And then one night, after several weeks of seeing him regularly on his night off, phone calls every single day, thinking about nothing but him, cutting classes to meet him in the afternoons, sharing movies and dinners with She and Roger—one night he kissed me with unexpected urgency, and I felt him harden up against me right through my coat. He broke away and then he asked my brother-in-law if he could come in with us because there was something he just had to talk about or he'd burst. Just when I knew I couldn't wait any longer, here he sat on the couch, holding my hand tightly so that I could feel his pulse racing, talking not to me but to my keepers.

"I want Sandy very much and I think she wants me," he

said quietly. I felt suddenly queasy; it was the first time I had ever felt joy and wouldn't you know it would make me sick to my stomach? I breathed deeply through my nose. Then I stopped breathing at all, waiting for what would happen next. It couldn't be this good, it couldn't go on being this good. Surely he would say something awful now, to make it all vanish . . .

"And we've got to go to bed together soon or we'll both explode," he went on. Roger, embarrassed, nodded and knit his eyebrows together to show that he was thinking deeply about the problem. She was deadly quiet. There was something in this for her, too. I had never wanted to touch Roger and I hardly ever looked at him much when he made love to her. But this was new, a different equation. Someone wanted me now. I had to be taken into account. But more importantly, there was Thaddeus. Was She thinking about Thaddeus? Would she dare to include herself in as part of the deal?

I didn't want to think this way. This was the result of sexual starvation. I would be healthier once this conversation was over and we had found a way to be together. Just the two of us—oh, please, please God, if you exist and if you ever made a miracle, make one now. Make it just the two of us, Thaddeus and me. We love each other, God.

"Hey, Roger, help me out," Thaddeus said. If he was really expecting Roger to come up with an answer, boy did he have the wrong customer. But he knew Roger by now, so this had to be a gambit. I waited, wondering if my stomach would ever decide which way was up.

"Well, Thad, gee, I don't know what to suggest," Roger said unhelpfully. Nobody ever talked about sex out loud in his family. Roger had a collection of pornography hidden in his bottom drawer that he sometimes showed to Sheila to "get her hot"; a book by Frank Harris, some Oriental prints, and a couple of French magazines. That was as public as he'd ever gone on the subject till now. I was kind of enjoying his discomfort.

"Could I—could we stay here?" Thaddeus asked politely. He held my hand tighter, with both of his, as if he were afraid of being turned down.

I was dying to say something—after all, this was about me, too—but Thaddeus knew exactly what he was doing. I let it all unreel before me. Now that I knew he wanted me, I wasn't worried about anything in the world. Suddenly, I felt great. If his way didn't work out, I would figure out my own way of getting what we wanted: what we needed, what we had to have, what it was right for us to have.

"Uh, well, sure. I mean, if it's okay with Sheila, it's okay with . . . and if it's okay with Sandy, of course, well then it's okay with me. Sure. Heh-heh."

"They're not even married!" Sheila pointed out. This brought down a stunned silence for a moment and then even Roger decided to ignore it. We were all waiting for She to go on to point number two. "And what are we supposed to do, sleep four in a bed?" she added indignantly. But she was not really indignant at all. I was right; she did want it. She wanted Thaddeus.

"Well, we're already three," Roger said. So he had noticed, after all.

"Then it's settled," I said. I wanted to get up right then and rush to the bedroom and get started. But Thaddeus smiled at me and I melted down again and then I couldn't have moved off that couch if it had been on fire. He kissed me, gently at first and then more seriously, more passionately. As if no one were there but the two of us. It was wonderful. When we stopped, I saw that Sheila and Roger were pretending not to look at us. "Let's go to bed," I whispered in Thaddeus's ear.

"Well, can't we just stay here and sort of neck for a little while?" Thaddeus asked, in a perfectly normal tone of voice, which made us all laugh. Then Roger got off his chair and came around to the couch and asked us to move over so that he could squeeze in there next to She, and Thaddeus reached over and pulled the cord on the reading lamp so it was half dark in the room, and there we sat getting more ardent and more impatient every second. We touched each other and I opened his zipper and touched him there; he was throbbing and erect and I couldn't wait so I scooted on top of him, dragging She with me, but I didn't care and couldn't be stopped and then he was between my legs from behind with his hands and his cock and I couldn't bear it and off in the distance I heard Roger's little I'm-coming noise and I came wildly, shouting I guess, and then Thaddeus waited for me to calm down and relax and want it again, which only took a few seconds, and then he rode me evenly and slowly, not paying attention to the others, who had disappeared to another planet, not caring that they were finished, just slowly and gently moving it up between my thighs, against my lips, and then I felt his spasms and he clutched me as close as two people being one person could be and it went on and on and on and it only got better. It was a long time, it seemed, before we started moving around, gathering our clothes together, kissing each other little sweet kisses on the mouth, cheek, forehead, hair, chest, breast, shoulder, hand, fingers, and then we were finally awake and conscious again.

"Wow, I haven't done this since I was in high school," Thaddeus said. He laughed, and after a second we all did.

"Me either," Roger said.

"Oh, you never laid a girl on a couch!" She scoffed, and Roger swore that he had, once or twice.

"I could love the hell out of you," Thaddeus whispered darkly in my ear, and I clutched at him, not believing it, knowing how much I loved him and knowing nobody could ever love me that much.

Sleepy now, we all moved into the bedroom like little

kids clutching their teddy bears. Roger went in to check on the baby while Sheila and I got our faces washed and our teeth brushed. I had to really search the medicine chest to find my diaphragm; it was buried under an old shaving mug and a box of cotton balls.

"A little late for that, isn't it?" She pointed out.

As I closed the cabinet door, I looked at my reflection. I was shocked to see an almost beautiful face. I was smiling a satisfied, loved-woman smile, like Merilee Potter back in high school. I couldn't believe myself. I had nice eyes and my nose wasn't bad at all and my lips were full and well kissed, and without my glasses I looked almost attractive, blurred and soft and smiling.

"Come on, we can't hog the bathroom," She said crossly. We went into the bedroom. How lovely it was to see Thaddeus there, in his T-shirt and trousers, barefoot and a little shy. I went right up to him and kissed him on the mouth, and then She pulled at me and we crawled under the covers, snuggling down into the exact middle of the bed so there would be room for the two of them on either side.

Roger came in from Millie's room and offered Thaddeus a robe, but my darling smiled and said he never used one. Then Roger offered him first use of the john, and Thaddeus nodded and went in there. I could feel She tugging and burrowing, ready for sleep and pretty obvious about it. Well, once was Roger's limit, we all knew that. But I'd never felt more wide awake in my life. I was wild with anticipating, knowing I'd be sleeping with Thaddeus all through the whole night.

He came back in his shorts, hung his trousers more or less carefully on the back of a chair, and before I could move to block She's view of him, he slipped out of his jockey shorts and climbed in next to me. He put his arms around me and lined his body up against mine so we touched at every possible place. She tugged me away. I pulled her in my direction. There was quite a bit of wiggling and maneuvering and finally Thaddeus started to chuckle, and then I saw the humor of it and I started to giggle and then Roger came to bed in his striped pajamas and turned out the light and we were still giggling and he started, too, and finally She joined in laughing and we all lay there rocking the bed with our giddiness. Finally, we quieted and when Roger and She were asleep, Thaddeus fucked me oh so gently and silently and splendidly, and not wanting to move made it all the better, and then I fell asleep in his arms.

It was the happiest I had ever been, or would ever be.

In the morning, She opened her eyes and looked over on my side of the bed and shrieked, "Get him out of here! Get him out of here!"

Thaddeus and Roger woke abruptly. Roger shifted automatically into his comfort-Sheila mode and started petting her on the arm. This only made her madder, as he would have known had he been really awake. Thaddeus looked as if he couldn't figure out where he was, and no wonder, it sounded like the dangerous ward in Bedlam. I tried to hold my arms around him, but he shied away from me, too, in his confusion.

"What's the matter?" he shouted.

She was ranting and shoving at Roger, who now seemed to be trying to assume a fetal position without actually lying down. We were all sitting up in bed in a row like the "Triplets" scene in *The Bandwagon*, only there was one too many of us, of course.

"I want him out, out of my bed and my house! Who the hell does he think he is? Oh my God, Roger, look what she's done to us! I'm so mortified, if anyone ever finds out about this I'll kill myself, I swear I will! Ohhhhh . . ." The screaming dissolved into an inarticulate wail.

"Honey, what is it? What's wrong, darling? Oh, sweetie, talk to me, tell me what's wrong suddenly?" Poor Roger, he was really out of his depth.

Thaddeus knew. He leapt out of bed and started pulling his pants on. He looked at me and I understood, or hoped I did, that he was just going to get out of there as fast as possible because it was the only way to shut her up. It was for my sake as well as his, for everybody's sake, but it didn't mean anything had changed between us just because I had a mad sister.

I just lay there and watched him getting ready to leave. Tears rolled down my cheeks. He bent down and kissed me quickly on the lips, provoking a renewed howl from Sheila the She-Devil. He turned to wave 'bye at me before he left the room, but then he was gone and I heard the front door slam.

"Honey darling, what is it? Tell Rogie, let me make it all better. Alka-Seltzer? Cup of coffee? Tell Roger."

Maybe Roger-Dodger would learn something from proximity to a real man, a real loving lover, I thought. I was starting to get a headache. She's hysteria was building. She was tensing her body and that hurt my back. I tried to get up, but she was stronger than I in this. The delicious private stickiness between my legs was starting to feel cold and messy. I wanted a shower. I wanted her to shut up. Her yelling was making us all sick. I could hear the baby start to cry in the next room.

"How could you allow such a thing in our bed, in our house? It's no better than a barnyard. She's an animal, my sister is a whore and an animal. A stranger in our bed! Ugh, I feel filthy and it's all her fault. He's not even Jewish! He's not even circumcised! A girl can get cancer from that! Just because I had one too many and wasn't responsible for once, I depended on you, and look what you let happen! A fucking uncircumcised waiter in our bed!" She pushed Roger away and he fell backward off the bed and the drawstring in his pajamas yanked open and they fell around his knees and he had trouble getting onto his feet, trying to cover himself with one hand so I wouldn't see, but at no time in my life could I have cared less.

"How would you like it if somebody saw him leaving here

226

at this hour of the morning? Don't you think the neighbors would all just love it knowing that we were doing sick, dirty things in here, four of us in a bed. Oh sure, those Jews in that apartment out in the garage, look what they're up to now! I feel dirty, I feel sick, and it's all her fault and yours. How could you let her do this to us?"

Was it the location that bothered her? Maybe she wasn't actually trying to put a stop to my love life, just move it to another tent. I thought about Thaddeus; right now he was sitting on the subway, trying to figure out what had happened. He'd never be back; why should he? If he was sane, he wouldn't want anything to do with me. And if he didn't want anything to do with me, I didn't want to live. I started fantasizing on my perennial problem: how to kill Sheila. I hadn't thought about it since Millie was born, but now I didn't care. The baby would be better off without a mother like that. If killing my sister would mean my death, too, maybe Thaddeus would regret leaving, regret it for the rest of his life. He could search forever for someone like me, but how futile that grief-laden search would be. The poor, dear man . . . but that would be his own fault, for deserting me in his one moment of weakness.

The important thing was that the world would be rid of Sheila. I saw this as a public service. And I had one enormous advantage over any murderer I'd ever read about: I didn't have to concern myself with being found out. Usually in this fantasy I composed a note, explaining carefully and fully why I was doing this, listing all the grievances I had from all the years, pointing out that being a forgiving soul, I couldn't even remember most of them. The thing that cut off the daydream was inevitably my dissatisfaction with the note itself; it needed another draft, and then it needed being put down on paper because I couldn't remember the best parts, and of course there was no way I could commit this to paper, so it usually trailed off and ended right there.

But the morning She drove Thaddeus away from me, the note didn't matter. I didn't care whether the world knew the great wrong that had been done to me by God or fate or biology or my mother. I just wanted to get the deed done. I wanted my sister dead and I wanted to lie there for as much time as was left to me and look at her dead and be glad. Poison was no good. I didn't want to die in the bathroom while she retched it all up and recovered in time to call someone to cut her loose from my corpse. Gas would kill us both at the same rate, so I wouldn't have time to enjoy my short happy life alone. No, it would have to be an act of violence. I would have to shoot her or stab her or hit her over the head with a hammer. Good. I was just in the mood.

Roger was trying coffee as the consolation of the day. I could hear him in the kitchen and smell the good stuff brewing. "Let's get up," I said tentatively.

She renewed her bitching, louder. "You whore. You'd sleep with anything in pants, wouldn't you? You'd bring some stranger—some WAITER—to MY home and let him sleep in the same bed with us and not care a damn for me and my reputation and my *baby!* You are really rotten, and if Billie knew what you did to me, she'd die of shame. I'm just sick from waking up and finding that—that MAN in my bed! How can you do this to me? How could you? You're so selfish, you don't care what you do to my reputation, and I have to live here and I have a child, a little, innocent baby girl to worry about. Who's ever going to marry her, with an aunt like you bringing strange men into her own mother's bed . . ."

"Oh shut up. You can't stop me from living my own life."

"I'm not talking about your life! It's *my* life I'm talking about! Look what you're doing to my life! I'm the one who has a husband! I'm the one who's been through pregnancy and the hell of childbirth and I'm trying to build a decent American family here and you're just trying to ruin everything for me because you know nobody would ever marry *you*! It's a good thing my Millie isn't old enough to know what went on here last night, although she could get a trauma from it anyhow. You're supposed to be so goddamn smart, well, you're trash, that's what, just plain ugly trash. You think that waiter wanted you for your brains! Hah! He just saw that you were an easy lay, that's all. Pathetic is what you are. You disgust me. You make me sick."

Absurd, I told myself. Thaddeus, who loves me, and I both agree that this person is absurd. I tried sounding remote, uncaring, untouched. "Listen, if you're winding down now, how about let's take a shower?" Wonderful. It didn't sound anything like I was feeling.

She sat up and yanked me over to get out of bed on her side, and we stood under a hot shower for a long, long time. She was still ranting. I was still plotting, although I started to sing just to give her something else to be pissed off at. She couldn't stand hearing me sing. I knew all the lyrics to practically every song I'd ever heard, including hymns and coal miners' union songs and "Heil, Heil, Right in the Führer's Face," which is what I sang that morning. She ignored it, so I segued into something happy; that ought to get her. " 'He loves me, sings the April breeze, he loves me, echo the hills,' " my alto vibrated against the bathroom tiles. " 'It's spring again, and birds on the wing again start to sing again, that old melody . . .' "

"God, you're a bitch," she said as we were toweling ourselves.

I'm going to kill you, I thought silently. I think I really am. If he doesn't call me by nine o'clock tonight, I will honestly kill you. I don't have the guts to stick a knife into your flesh, but I can hit you over the head with a hard object. Yes, I can do that. I really can. I really will.

I was terrified, suddenly, cold with fear, because I knew I meant it.

21
My Romance

He must have been thinking of me every minute since he left and called the minute he got home. The phone rang while we were having our glum, silent breakfast. Even the baby was solemn; having lived with her mother for four whole months, Millie knew when to lay low. She blew quiet bubbles with her Pablum instead of spitting it with the usual gusto. Roger got up to get the phone and I heard him say, "Hi!" warmly and then, remembering, suddenly cold: "Would you like to speak with Sandy?"

She groaned and I dragged her with me as I scurried for the hallway. I grabbed the phone from Roger.

"Hello. Good morning," I said breathlessly.

"Hello, love."

Thaddeus's voice on the phone vibrated some cord within me on a purely physical level. I needed to sit down, but of course She was hogging the chair. I sort of knelt down.

"I was afraid you might not call me again," I said with

my usual tact and reverence for the subtle nuances of romantic banter.

I was rewarded with a nice low chuckle. "She's a real bitch, isn't she?" he said.

The "Alleluia" chorus from the *Messiah* flooded my head, with ringing lucid boy sopranos thanking God. Hallelujah, hallelujah, someone understands what I've been going through, what I've had to put up with all my life, this handsome, gentle, tender, brilliant, sexy man is *on my side!*

"Oh, Thaddeus!" A stupid sigh and his name were the best I could do just then, and even I was aware that it belonged in a balloon over my head. She made gagging noises. I didn't care. Thaddeus was on my side. I could cope with anything now. She would never be able to get to me ever again; I'd never again feel frustrated or care that I was misunderstood. What a dope I'd been all my life to bother about what those small-town small-minded self-appointed judges of the world thought of me just because they happened to be my mother and sister and all the ducks exactly like them. Hadn't I always known there was another world, my world, and here it was! I had found where I truly belonged, at last. Thaddeus loved me; his opinion was the only one that mattered now or ever would.

"I guess we're going to have to work something out so we can be together," he said softly in my ear.

"Yes," I murmured. "Oh yes."

"Maybe we could borrow an apartment from someone, for certain nights of the week. Would that be all right with you? I wouldn't want to do anything that would upset you."

"Not me. I'd go anywhere. You mean the other party." We'd have to work out a cleverer code than this. I was blissful, but my brain wasn't working very well. I wondered if happiness made you stupid. She made a piggish snorting noise and I hoped he hadn't heard her. I waited for his answer.

"She'd have to go along with it, wouldn't she? I mean,

once in a while. My God, don't you even get half your life to yourself?"

"Yes, well of course I do. It's just that—" Dare I say it out loud; would she punish me with hours of retribution? Recklessly, I dared, keeping an eye on the little hall mirror to see how she took it. "She can be a real pain sometimes," I said. "If she doesn't want me to do something, she can really make it tough. I just don't want you to have to put up with—"

He interrupted me, to my enormous relief. She was staring me down so fiercely I thought the mirror would crack. I concentrated on his voice. "—what you have to put up with all the time? Oh, my honey, my darling girl. You mustn't worry about me. I'm not going anywhere until you tell me to. Okay? Got that?"

I couldn't say anything. My throat filled up with emotion, and tears overflowed my eyes. I loved him so much I could hardly breathe. I had no idea what reaction all this was getting from my sister; I shut my eyes as the tears brimmed over, and for that miraculous moment she wasn't even there.

"Sandy, does it really matter so much to you when she acts like that? I got a small dose of how awful she can be, but does it affect you, really? I mean does it change what you do or how you do it—do you give in to her a lot, is what I'm trying to ask, I guess."

"No. No, I really don't. In fact I suppose I should more than I do. We—we fight. A lot. It's awful." My sister's whole body was trembling with rage, and I looked everywhere but in the mirror now.

"Will you let me help you?"

Would I!

"If you really want to," I told him. I was immediately sorry I hadn't said, "Yes oh yes I want your help." What if he took the out I was offering? I held my breath.

"I do if you love me," he said softly.

"Oh. Oh yes, that's positively true. Absolutely, emphatically true," I told him.

He laughed, a small private laugh, just for me. "Well, you're certainly not like any other girl I've ever known. I love this conversation. We're secret agents talking in code."

"You don't mind?" I asked anxiously.

"I love it. Okay, listen then, I'll see what I can do. I've got finals in two weeks—don't you?—and then we'll figure out a way. Okay? Will you wait?"

"Affirmative."

"You're great in bed, you know that?"

Trying for a voice in the more or less normal range, I cleared my throat and said, "Uh no, I didn't know that."

"And it's going to get better. You'll see."

"I don't see how it can, but—well, thank you very much. I'll certainly look forward to that. Yes indeed. And . . . thanks for calling. I only would have killed myself if you hadn't."

I got his warm little chortle as a reward. Then he said, "Am I great in bed, too?"

"Oh my gosh, yes. Oh sure. Absolutely. The best." I was embarrassed, for some reason. Why did such a paragon, a perfect man, need to hear a loser like me telling him he was great? How extraordinary that he was offering me up his vulnerabilities. I would love him all the more. I did already. I felt my love swelling inside me like a balloon, crowding out everything else. I looked into the mirror. Yes, I could even feel generous toward my sister; there was no room for petty emotions like hate anymore—only this enormous love now. She had her arms folded and her eyes closed. Could my fullness be filling her, too—could Thaddeus's love infuse us both and change everything between us, for us forevermore? Then she opened her eyes and the hate was still there. I looked away.

"You've had a lot of guys to compare me with?" Thaddeus was asking.

"No, not a lot." Maybe that wasn't what he wanted to hear. "Thaddeus? Almost none, actually." I laughed, a little nervously, so he could take it as a joke if he wanted to. But he didn't say anything for a long minute and I started to panic. Sheila was tapping her bunny slipper impatiently.

"Hey, there's really nobody like you. You know that, don't you?" Thaddeus said finally. This of course could be taken two ways, and naturally, the wrong way immediately popped into my head, but for once I held my tongue long enough to let my brain work. I decided he meant it kindly.

"Yes, I know," I said. "And the same goes for you."

"Study hard and make me proud, okay? And I'll see you right after finals. We'll celebrate. I'll line up that apartment. And if She doesn't like it, I'll deal with her."

"That'll be . . . wonderful." I was a mite disappointed that we had to wait until after finals, but of course he was right. Thank God I could count on him to be the sensible one.

"Hey, Sandy, when's your birthday?"

"August fifteenth. Why?"

"Good. I've got plenty of time to save my money."

I laughed. "You're funny. I'm not after you for your money."

He laughed too. "And a damn lucky thing that you're not. So I'm funny, huh?"

"Yes."

"But nice?"

"Yes."

" 'Bye, love."

" 'Bye . . . love."

I hung up and had a crazy impulse to hug my sister. I needed to hug somebody. I wondered if that would be physically possible. I turned to her, but in the mirror I could see her scowling. It was a lousy idea anyway.

Suddenly, books didn't absorb me as they had always done before. That had changed along with everything else in the universe. I'd open a book—even one I was dying to read—and there would be Thaddeus's mouth or his eyes or the back of his hand. Nothing could distract me from my daydreams

234

of him. I thought a lot about this phenomenon: I was no longer a loner. I couldn't convince myself it was true. I'd believe it when finals were over and we started spending real time together, days and nights and maybe ... maybe he would marry me and then the whole world would know that someone was on my side. I'd never have to be the third wheel again in my own bed ... and off I'd be on a daydream of Thaddeus all over again.

I got a C in geology, but it didn't even matter. It only made me more human. Only a semester before I had been inconsolable (not that anybody had tried to console me) over an A minus, but now I knew how much else there was to life.

The first night after Thaddeus's last exam, we all went to Foo's Garden to celebrate. We drank gin fizzes and toasted ourselves over and over again to each of us in turn, to Millie at home, to our host, Foo, and his sweet-faced wife, Li, who came out of the kitchen beaming and nodding and blushing at our compliments. We drank to geology (boo), Ovid in the original (yea), Greek comedies, Jane Austen, Will Shakespeare, Roger's boring case, the State of Massachusetts bar, to Li's duck with green peppercorns, to the gin itself, the drinks we had just finished, and the drinks to come. My fortune cookie said, "Don't cut off your nose, despite your face," and we laughed so much (even though I wondered for one stark minute whether there was a Chinese person working in a cookie factory who somehow knew my most intimate thoughts) that the other customers stared at us. So we toasted them, too. It was a lovely evening until we got in the car.

"Where we going now, troops?" I asked lazily from the backseat.

"Home," Roger answered fussily. "It's nearly midnight."

"Why don't you let Thad out at the T station so he doesn't have so far to walk?" She suggested, with a loud yawn.

"He's coming home with us," I announced. I looked at the

back of Thaddeus's head, but he didn't turn around. What a nice strong head he had, what fine thick hair, what perfect ears, what a sexy neck. I hoped he never cut his hair any shorter than it was right now, about three weeks overdue for the barber. It was perfect.

"The hell he is!" She snapped. She had been giggling from all the little drinkies up till then.

"Thaddeus?" I called tentatively. He didn't turn around. "Hon, remember what we talked about before—borrowing someone's apartment—remember? Did you have any luck?"

"Not yet," he said, still facing forward. "It's okay. I'll go home. I wouldn't want to upset your sister again."

There was something accusatory in his tone, in his not turning to look at me. I felt horrid, guilty of something I didn't even know I had done. But yes, I did know. I hadn't stood up to my sister. Well, I would now.

"Stop the car, Roger!" I said loudly and firmly. I meant it, and I meant for everyone to know I meant it. Roger slowed the car and looked back fearfully.

"Don't you dare stop this car!" She shouted. "I'm tired and I want to go home. She's crazy. Just keep on going, Roger."

I opened the door on my side. It scared everybody. Now Thaddeus turned around, to stare at me as if he'd never seen me before. We were doing about ten miles an hour. "Stop the car or I swear to God I'll jump and take your goddamn bitch wife with me," I said calmly in Roger's ear.

He pulled up. We were on Commonwealth Avenue. All the good burghers were asleep, all the houses dark.

"Thaddeus, tell me honestly. Do you want to sleep with me tonight or not?"

"Yes," he said, simply and blessedly. "But I won't let either one of us in for another morning-after like the last one. We have a right to be together, but it seems we have to have your sister's permission to enjoy it."

He was more than half turned around toward me now, looking straight into my eyes by the light of the streetlight. "I'll tell you one thing," he said, and this was just for me. "If I had you alone, Sandy, I wouldn't stand for any more of this shit. You and I would have a little talk and you'd either stand up for yourself or we'd be quits. But I can't say that to you in front of your sister and brother-in-law, can I? It sounds rotten, doesn't it? Only you know I say it out of love, don't you?"

There was a long silence before I realized they were all waiting for me to say something. "Yes," I agreed quietly, not absolutely sure what I was agreeing to. I just wanted Thaddeus to look at me the way he had before, with love in his eyes, and some lust too. What did I have to do or say to get that back? I'd do it. I'd say it.

He touched my face with the tips of his fingers and then got out of the car and just walked up the street away from me. We watched him until he was out of sight.

"Good riddance," my sister said.

"Shut up!" Roger snapped. This surprised Sheila so much (and me, too) that there was actually a moment of silence before She let him have it full-blast, non-stop all the way home and into the house and to our lonely bed. I lay there awake and I think Roger did, too, for hours and hours, long after the person between us had bitched herself to sleep.

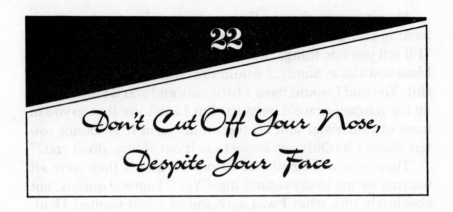

22

Don't Cut Off Your Nose, Despite Your Face

I lay awake and thought about how I'd let him down. I decided, sometime in the middle of that long night, that it would be a very fine thing if I were the one to come up with a place where Thaddeus and I could make love. If Sheila didn't want us in her bed, she'd damn well have to come to ours, and if it was someplace sordid, it would bother her a whole hell of a lot more than it would me.

I started asking casually among my classmates, people I studied with or ate with: Where do you live, in a dorm, in an apartment? Oh really, how marvelous, your own apartment. Oh, you have three roommates and your mother comes very frequently and unannounced from Philadelphia and stays there, too? There didn't seem to be any undergraduates with apartments they could lend or rent out for a couple of hours now and then.

"This is disgusting," my sister said. "I know exactly what

you're up to. What makes you think I'll go along with it anyway?"

"You'll have to, that's all. It's your fault I have to live in that stinking garage with you and Roger. If it weren't for Millie, we'd be living on my campus half the time."

"And I suppose you think all the Wellesley girls let themselves get laid all the time! Boy, you certainly have a low opinion of women!"

"The healthy ones must have healthy outlets for their healthy desires," I said.

"You're warped. You think everyone is as immoral as you."

"Well, you weren't exactly the blushing virgin when you got married, were you?"

"Roger and I never made love till we were married."

"Sheila, this is me you're talking to. I was there, remember? What was Millie, an immaculate conception?"

"No. She was two months' premature."

"Jesus."

Thaddeus didn't call me for three weeks. I thought it was over, and with it my life and all hope. Sheila had destroyed my only chance at happiness and I was not going to let her off easily. Roger-Dodger tried to make peace between us, but he nearly got what balls he had left busted for his efforts, by both of us. We wanted to be alone to fight it out.

Billie, who for no knowable reason had now decided she wanted to be called Mom, phoned us every Sunday, mostly to complain that we never wrote to her. Once she caught us at a terribly low ebb; it had been two weeks since I had heard from Thaddeus. Of course she didn't know a thing about him. I couldn't tell her I was in love with a waiter who wasn't Jewish, and She didn't want to rock that particular boat, for her own reasons. But when the phone rang and it was Billie, I burst into tears and she heard me.

"What the hell's the matter with you?"

239

"Mom, there's got to be a way to separate us. I can't stand it anymore! I can't live like this! Please, Billie—Mom, I mean—please find a doctor, please find someone who'll do it!"

My sister yanked the phone away from me. "Yes, you'd better, Bill—Mom, because I think Sandy's going to kill me. She is so jealous because I'm married and have a baby, she can't stand it!"

This made me howl with the injustice of it, and we were reduced to the two brawling, babbling babies we always had been. Maybe were were homesick for the chance to be ourselves again. I kicked She and she pinched me harder than she ever had. We both sobbed and pleaded with our poor mother, who was surely wishing she had never called, let alone given birth.

"You stop that this minute! Great big grown girls! Don't you care what you're doing to me, I'm going to have a heart attack. I can't take this. I feel sick from it! Why can't you love each other? Sisters should love each other. Why can't you be like other girls, other sisters who love each other? Why you two always have to be different from everybody else is beyond me. You're just trying to make me sick and miserable. Well, you've succeeded!" Now *she* was crying.

"Oh, Mom, I'm sorry. Please don't cry. I didn't mean to make you cry! You're not really sick, are you? You okay? You are, aren't you, Mom? Billie? Please? I'm sorry."

"Billie! I'm sorry, Billie! Mom? We're sorry we made you cry."

"Yes, Mom, we're both sorry. See, we're not fighting anymore. It's all right. Okay, Mom?"

She kept on weeping and we sat there with the phone between us. Neither of us wanted to put it down or to put it to an ear, either. Roger sighed, came over and plucked the receiver from the couch.

"Hello, Billie?" he said in his most jovial voice. "I've got a new joke for you! Here it is, are you ready? It's pretty raunchy. I guess I must be the only fellow I know with a mother-in-law I can tell really spicy stories to, ha ha, are you ready? That's good, okay then. A very drunk lady—well, she wasn't a lady, obviously—a very drunk gal staggers into a bar and sits on a stool and says, 'What kind of beer do you have?' and the bartender says 'We've got Schlitz and Budweiser,' so she says, 'Give me a Schlitz,' and she drinks it and orders another and another and finally she passes out, konk, right on the floor. So the bartender looks in her purse and there's no money, nothing to pay for the beers. So the guys in the bar all decide they will take her into the back room and, you know, give her what-for, and each one will chip in fifty cents and that way they'll get enough together to pay for the beers she drank. So they do, and then they toss her out on the street. Okay? So the next night the same woman comes in again, and she sits down on the stool and she says to the bartender, 'What kind of beer do you have?' and the bartender can't believe it, but he says, 'We've got Schlitz and Budweiser. And she says, 'Better make it a Budweiser. Schlitz makes my cunt hurt!' "

We could all hear Billie laughing like a maniac on the other end of the wire, until she started to cough and sigh and gasp and wheeze, and then she said with a final whoop, "You'll be the death of me! What a son I've got! You're a pip, Roger, you slay me!" and we knew it was going to be all right.

I waited another week and then I couldn't stand it, I had to talk to him. Even if She was right (and Roger agreed with her all the time now, so it was useless trying to get an opinion from him), even if Thaddeus had lost all interest in me, even if it had all been my imagination, I had to know. I called him.

"Oh God, it's good to hear your voice," he said.

"Really?" I tried not to sound sarcastic, but it came out before I could mold it into a softer sound.

"I haven't called you because I haven't been able to find

a place for us. There isn't a room in all of Boston, including the suburbs."

"Don't you know there's a postwar on?" I joked limply. He had said it was good to hear my voice. That more than made up for my sister's muttering about "crawling so low as to call a guy . . ." I cupped my hand over the mouthpiece so he wouldn't hear her.

"I can't stand to be with you knowing I can't have you, not anymore," he said in that low erotic vibrato that made my juices run.

"I—don't know whether to believe you or not," I confessed.

"It doesn't matter. Believe what you like. I only know how I feel. How do you think a guy feels when he can't let himself love anyone because he won't have any money for five or six years down the line? I wish I could rent a suite at the Ritz, but what good would that do? Your sister wouldn't let you go with me anywhere, would she? She's holding out for marriage or nothing. I know that type. Anyway, she's pissed 'cause I'm not Jewish, isn't she? What a crock! Thank God you're nothing like her."

"No, I'm not."

"I miss you, Sandy."

"Can't we just—go to the movies or something? Have dinner? You have to eat dinner and so do I, couldn't we just do that together once in a while?" I knew I was starting to sound desperate, pathetic even. I didn't care. I turned my back to the hall mirror.

"I'm saving every dime now. I'm sorry, Sandy. It's not just the sex, believe me. I'm just not spending any bucks at all, for a while. I've got to get through school or be a bum the rest of my life. I can't afford to—"

"I'll pay!" I hadn't known I was going to say that. I was farther gone than I knew, but I didn't care.

"Oh, my God!" my sister moaned.

"Sandy . . . love . . . you're so honest and straightforward, and so generous and loving . . . but I can't let you do that."

"Is your night off still Sunday?" I asked.

"Yes."

"Well . . . how about some duck with green peppercorns Sunday night?"

There was such a long pause I thought I'd lost him. I held my breath. "You're sure, Sandy?"

"Oh yes. Yes, yes, yes."

"Then I'll be there. Or should I pick you up?"

"We can meet there. Seven o'clock?"

"Fine. Sandy?"

"Yes?"

"Let me talk to Sheila."

"WHAT?"

"Come on. I know what I'm doing. I hope."

"I hope so too. Just a minute, I'll see if she can come to the phone." I giggled. I was going to see him and that was all that mattered now. I had soared from deep misery to glowing anticipation in less than a minute. "Thaddeus would like to talk to you," I told She.

She grabbed the phone. "Hi."

I don't know what he said to her, but I could hear the ice cracking and then she agreed that Sunday night would be okay, and she signed off with a little throaty giggle of her own in my lover's ear and hung up the phone.

"Well, you got your date, if that's what you wanted. How low can a person sink?" she said. I just ignored her. She was absurd.

Our dilemma was settled that Sunday night in a pattern that became an ecstatic routine. A couple of dry martinis and then a switch to gin fizzes, a lot of laughs over dinner, and when Sheila got drunk enough, we'd weave on home and fall into bed—or sometimes onto the living room couch, as soon as the baby-sitter was gone.

243

Thaddeus made love to me and Roger did his thing to Sheila. We two could have gone on and on; there was no end to the delights and surprises and just plain tender good feelings of our lovemaking. But after a little while—a very little while—we'd be aware that Roger and Sheila were finished and just lying there, or Sheila would grumble and I'd be aware of Roger watching and get kind of self-conscious, even in the dark.

Thaddeus asked about my scars. I told him the truth, that I had tried to hack us apart when we were little. He bent his beautiful head and kissed every old wound on my body.

One night Thaddeus's hand touched Sheila's skin and stayed there, but since he was still deeply engaged with my body I didn't mind, and She didn't flinch but in fact she moved closer to us, and pretty soon we were all just rolling together and feeling good all over and murmuring and keening, and Roger got hard again and fucked Sheila as Thaddeus was doing me, long and easy thrusts, deep and slow and joyous; he was watching and learning from Thaddeus and our rhythms began to jibe, and then their hands were everywhere and Thaddeus took Roger's stiff cock and steered him to She's clitoris with it and my sister had her first orgasm and we all kissed each other when she finally eased down from it and then She and I did whatever they wanted, except that she wouldn't take either of them in her mouth and I would; even tried both in my mouth at the same time once, but it didn't work, and I was surprised but not upset to see Thaddeus take Roger in his mouth and then Roger returned the favor and I knew that was what he really liked most and Thaddeus had brought us all this extraordinary gift. Love was the only possible name for it.

But he always had to leave in the middle of the night. No matter how thrilled she was at finally discovering what all the fuss was about, no matter how transformed she became during the act of lovemaking into a giving person, when it was over She was herself again and Thaddeus was never allowed to stay all night. That was our compromise, an understanding come to without words or discussion.

I began to have dreams I had never had before, about being alone with Thaddeus: checking into a hotel, riding in a gondola in Venice, having dinner in our own house with incredibly well-behaved children we both adored all around us. Some of the dreams turned bad, of course, but I still remember the good parts. I had no sister in those dreams.

Thaddeus had not yet said "I love you" in exactly those words, and as the weeks and months went by with our regular Sunday nights and nothing in between, I began leaning on him a little, to reassure myself. I'd ask if we could go to a movie, offer to cut a class to meet him for lunch. His answer was to remark on how bright I was, how I never seemed to need to study, and how he wished he were that brilliant, but he couldn't afford to miss a single class. Or I'd ask him to come to Filene's with us because I wanted his opinion of a dress She wanted me to buy, but he told me shopping gave him hives. I fell deeper and deeper in love and felt more and more deprived in the vast stretches of time we weren't together.

I read novels and short stories and advice in women's magazines about women who were too possessive, too demanding, too smothering: "Why Men Stray" and "Does He Take You for Granted?" Sheila was reading them, too; for once we had something in common. Roger was becoming more and more her slave, amiable to the point where I wanted to shake him by the shoulders until his head rattled. He never initiated sex now, never even asked She to look at his porno books; he just waited, as we all did, for Sunday night and Thaddeus.

The first time Thaddeus hit me was six or eight weeks into our happy new lives. He was getting dressed to go home. It was after three in the morning. He was sitting on the side of the bed. I reached out my arm to caress his chest, but he was just buttoning his shirt and my hand got in the way. He shrugged away from me. He didn't mean anything by it, but I couldn't bear it, not after sharing him with the others and wanting so desperately to have him to myself. I sat up and pushed myself into his arms, hugging him as tightly as I could. This meant that Sheila was thrown up against him, too, and first thing I knew she was hugging him from his other side.

"She, don't make him go. Please. Please, Thaddeus, stay the night. Sleep with me all night, please?" I begged.

It happened so fast I didn't know what it was. There was just this overwhelming whack on the side of my head. I cried out in pain and let go of him, clutching at my head to contain the hugeness of it. I thought the ceiling had fallen in or that someone had thrown a huge rock through the window, hitting me squarely. Thaddeus was on his feet, and I thought he was leaping to my rescue; I felt a surge of love over the crashing waves of pain. But he was glaring down at me.

"You're disgusting when you beg," he said coldly.

I stared up at him, shocked and . . . afraid. Sheila was trembling; I guess I was, too. My head reverberated from the blow. I was disoriented; I didn't understand what was happening. But She did.

"You didn't have to hit her," she said.

"Goddamn freaks," he muttered.

My Thaddeus!

Twenty minutes before, he had been deep inside my body, tender, gentle, patient, loving me. He had loved me so much he could even love my sister. What had I done, what had I said to turn his love to hate so suddenly and so violently? What vile poison in me had transformed my handsome beloved darling into Mr. Hyde? He was right; I was disgusting. Tears poured down my face, but I wasn't making any sound. The agony was too profound for that.

Thaddeus left the room and in a minute or two we heard the front door close. The whole thing had taken only a breath of time and Roger had not even waked up, unless he was just pretending. Sheila started to lie down, but I told her I had to wash my face. When I looked in the bathroom mirror, I saw my left cheek turning red and swelling. My head throbbed. I splashed cold water on my face and took two aspirins. She was silent, but I could see in the mirror that her lips were pinched tightly together, disapproving, like Billie's. When I turned out the bathroom light and we made our way back to bed, She whispered ferociously, "What the hell did you *do* to make him so mad?"

"I don't know," I sobbed, and then the tears started again and wouldn't be stopped. I watched the dawn light our room. When I heard Millie winding up for her morning yelps, I reached over She's sleeping body to rouse Roger. He got up obediently and went to change and feed her. I lay with my eyes wide open and my hand on my cheek until he had dressed and left for work. Millie's happy sing-song from her playpen finally woke my sister. We got up without speaking and followed our morning ritual in our usual silence. There didn't seem to be anything to say, although I would have welcomed a bit of human sympathy or understanding. I tried to think of someone I could call and meet to talk with: a friend from school, a relative, an acquaintance, a professional counselor, but I came up blank.

The phone rang around noon. She started to answer it, but I grabbed it away from her.

"Hello?"

"Sandy . . ."

"Yes."

"Oh God, I'm so sorry, I'm so sorry. I don't know what happened to me. I would never hurt you. Not you, of all people. Are you all right? Oh God, please . . . Sandy?"

"What happened, Thaddeus? What did I do?"

247

"It wasn't you, love, it was me. I just went nuts, I don't know. It never happened to me before, I swear, and I promise you it can never happen again. I'd kill myself before I'd hurt you, don't you know that? Oh God, I feel so bad. Honey, did I hurt you?"

I looked in the little hall mirror at my cheek. Yes, it hurt. It was discoloring fast and was so swollen my glasses were sitting crookedly on my face. I took them off. I looked like a blurred Rocky Graziano.

"Sandy?"

"No, you didn't hurt me, Thaddeus. Anyway, it's okay."

"Really?"

"Yes."

There was a little hesitation, a little pause, and then he said what I had been hoping and almost praying that he would say one day.

"I love you, Sandy."

I couldn't respond at all for a minute. I choked up and suddenly I was crying buckets.

"Sandy?"

"I love you too, Thaddeus," I sobbed happily.

My sister turned around so fast she wrenched my shoulder. She made a face at me in the mirror: It said I was wrong and stupid, a traitor to my sex. Poor dull Sheila; how could she possibly know what it felt like to be loved so much that you roiled up the deepest, most secret emotions of a sensitive man, a wonderful man? All right, my lover had a terrible flaw, but who among us did not? I felt something oddly like—well, relief, because he was not, after all, perfect. I had never quite believed before that I had a right to love him.

He loved me!

We had a kiss-and-make-up dinner, the four of us. In the booth at Foo's, Thaddeus touched my discolored cheek with rueful fingers and I damn near cried again, but then we were all smiling and laughing and everything was the way it had been before. At home in bed, Thaddeus was gentle with me and almost unbearably sweet, as if I were suddenly made of delicate and precious crystal. We were all very nice to each other that night, putting something back together, trusting it would hold.

And so we'd make up, and weeks would go by with absolutely delightful dinners and movies and drives and concerts and punting on the Charles when the weather got warm, quiet evenings at home, when She and I would cook—and our nights got better as even Roger dropped his inhibitions and She turned out to be madly passionate and we came to know each other's most intimate preferences and pleasures.

And then Thaddeus would be swept away by one of his terrible seizures and it would happen again.

I could no more give him up than I could separate from my loathed sister. I loved Thaddeus and he *needed* me. And if there was one thing I was qualified to understand, it was rage. I knew; I understood. It seethed up, it boiled over, it was impossible to control. Because I alone could empathize, I was the only one who could help him. His apologies broke my heart; he was so desperate to be forgiven and reassured that he was loved no matter what. I understood that.

Roger, the perfect brother-in-law, counseled me (at She's prodding); "You shouldn't allow yourself to be treated this way."

"I know."

"I'm not telling you what to do, you're a grown-up and you have to make up your own mind. I'm just telling you what we think is best for you."

"I know."

"We don't like to see you hurt."

"I know. Thanks."

Of course I knew what I should do. Anyone with a smidgin of self-respect or common sense would end it after the first blow was struck. But self-respect was one of the things that came between lovers; pride killed passion, even the B movies knew that. I saw it every day in my sister's marriage. Our love was infinitely greater than that. And yet how could I allow myself to be punched, beaten, spat on (oh, yes), and called vile names? No matter how great the love, something was wrong with a woman who let a man do that to her.

It always happened after lovemaking. Suddenly thrown onto the bed or the floor, I would lie there in shock and pain, with Sheila screaming beside me and Roger ineffectually plucking at Thaddeus to pull him away. Terrified and hurting, I would swear to myself this was the end, wonder what I'd ever seen in him anyway, how I let myself get degraded to this point. Sometimes I'd vomit, trying to regurgitate the bullshit tenderness, the lying love words, the sick sex. He would call me a freak, an aberration, a monstrosity, a sport of nature, a deviant perversion of what a woman should be, unnatural, a grotesque, a Jew. Sheila once kicked at him when he was shouting like that at me, and his rage turned on her. He twisted her ankle until she screamed with real pain; she never interfered again. Roger would be at the telephone then, trying to get up nerve to call the police, or else he'd just be standing in the hallway, shaking, with his hands covering his face.

But as soon as Thaddeus left the house, no matter how low I felt, how bad the pain, how vile the taste in my mouth and the blood, the emptiness frightened me more than the beating. If She or Roger tried to reason with me then, I screamed at them to shut up. No one could say anything against Thaddeus to me, not ever.

After a few times of being too visibly bruised to go to school, I dropped out, in the middle of the spring semester. This, at least, pleased Sheila. We became full-time parasites, with lots of time to go to hairdressers and shop for new clothes and play canasta with other bored young wives in their early twenties.

I planned to start writing a novel. But the days went by and I didn't. I thought about Thaddeus all the time now that there were no distractions. I thought about how I should demand more from him—more time, more attention, more proof that he loved me. Then I'd start shaking inside from the fear that he would walk out of my life and nothing, zero, emptiness—the dreaded abyss—would swallow me: I would become my sister. All I had to make the difference anymore was Thaddeus and how we loved each other.

23

Goodbyes

"Wow, what happened to your eye?" asked a neighbor we didn't know very well. We were in the cereal aisle of the supermarket.

Before I could say anything, my sister answered for me. "Don't you know what a klu—stumbler Sandy is? She's always bumping into things and falling down and banging herself on the head with something. It's a good thing I've got excellent balance myself—I used to be a dancer, you know— or I'd be all bruised, too. And my skin's a lot more delicate than hers."

After a bad night, She would tell me I was a masochist and that I should call the police and have Thaddeus put in jail, but then other times she'd say he was too good for me. I noticed she kept right on flirting and fooling with him herself. She was so stupid she figured as long as he was hitting me and not her, it meant he liked her better.

She was having her own problems these days. She had started saying awful things about Roger to her neighborhood friends, snickering about the way he made love (telling them old truths, not recent ones) and complaining to everyone that he'd flunked the bar exam after doing nothing but studying for a whole year. She started having two or three little drinkies every afternoon before Roger came home.

I just kept my mouth shut. I had changed, too. I found it was getting easier to pretend She wasn't even in the room with me.

My own temper seemed to be a thing of the past, for the most part. I was almost completely in control of myself and proud of it. I almost never did anything angry or violent anymore. Well, there was the night we were in a bar and someone played a record of a slimy-voiced crooner singing "You're Nobody Till Somebody Loves You" and for no reason in the world I threw my beer glass, still full, at the jukebox. It didn't mean anything; I just hated the stupid song.

One Monday after a bad night, Thaddeus came to the house without calling first. He just walked in, around dinnertime, and began kissing my nose where it was swollen, sweet little butterfly kisses, tender and heartbroken. He had real tears in his eyes.

"Oh God, I'm so sorry, so sorry, I must be sick, I should be locked up in jail or in a looney bin. Oh, Jesus, sweetheart, I can't believe I did this to you. I love you, you know that. Don't you? Don't you? Oh, baby, do you know how much I love you?"

"Yes I know, darling. It's all right. I know. I love you, too."

We got the baby-sitter and went out that night, leaving a half-baked casserole in the fridge. Thaddeus had called in sick on his job ("I am sick," he said, "knowing what I did to you."). We didn't go to Foo's Garden, though. I guess we didn't ever go there when I had a perceptible shiner or bum nose. Anyway, that night we went to a fish place along the docks. Thaddeus was being extra sweet, extra funny and attentive, and pretty soon we all felt happy and jolly. A few drinks, a good dinner, witty conversation and loving glances, hands held under the table, anticipation of the lovemaking to come. Two nights in a row; he really loves me very much, I was thinking. This is special, this is one night that can't possibly end in pain and sadness.

And then Thaddeus said, "You know something? I'm getting really bored with Harvard."

"When a man is bored with Harvard, he is bored with life," Roger said.

"That's London," I corrected him. "How come, Thaddeus? What's wrong?"

"I need a change. Boston is really just a small town with delusions of importance, and Harvard is a distillation of all the worst things about Boston. And snobbery. And conventionalism."

"And excellence in all things," protested Roger.

"Boredom in all things," Thaddeus pronounced.

"What are you saying?" I asked him, suddenly chilled.

"Let's drink to me," he said. He raised his glass and waited until we had all clinked. "I've applied to transfer to Cornell, and my acceptance just came through this morning. Cheers. I'm on my way to Ithaca."

He drank his beer and I sat there paralyzed. There are three moments in life I'll never forget. When I heard the news about President Roosevelt dying, I was in Schlosser's music store in Sioux City, in a soundproof glass booth. A man with tears streaming down his face walked by and we opened the door to find out what was wrong. Nearly twenty years later, I was in T. S. Martin's balcony when someone told me that President Kennedy had been shot. She and I were picking out new underwear. When Thaddeus said he was leaving Boston, I was in a booth at Deep Sea on Fisherman's Wharf; I had just taken a bite of swordfish and was trying to swallow it. My throat closed up on me.

"Kind of sudden, isn't it?" Roger asked. "I mean, you never said anything about transferring. Anyway, why on earth would you want a degree from Cornell instead of Harvard?"

"Well, since you ask, old buddy, and since it's just between us, here in the family, I'll tell you. I'm sick to death of elitist snobs. I don't want a degree from Hah-vahd because I don't care much for adding my name to the long, distinguished list of upper-crust exploiters of the working class. I'm going to switch from English Lit to animal husbandry. Who knows, maybe I'll end up contributing something to society."

"Are you a Communist?" Sheila asked. There had been a lot of talk about Communists lately and Sheila had vague fears for herself.

Thaddeus smiled that endearing little crooked half smile and said, "No, I just talk that way. Listen, I'm just pulling everybody's leg. Fact is . . . old Crimson's asked me to leave."

We were all three shocked into silence. We stared at him. I wondered what the joke was.

"Why?" Sheila asked, finally.

Thaddeus shrugged. "I'm not the Harvard type, I guess. They just found out what I've known all along. I haven't been feeling myself since I've been there, not really. I wonder if you know what I mean."

He was looking only at me. My answer was important to him. I hated to let him down, but I didn't know what the hell he was talking about. I shook my head, no.

"I've felt sometimes that I was pretending to be someone I'm not. Out of my element. If it hadn't been for the war and the G.I. Bill, I would have been lucky to get to college at all, maybe worked my way through Fordham or City College or some state university. I'm not a Harvard boy, that's all. Well, it's not as if I'm going to work in the salt mines. Cornell is a terrific school."

We all agreed that yes, it was. I felt dizzy. I had to spit the unswallowable fish morsel into my napkin. Thaddeus was going to leave me. Boom, just like that. He'd be in Ithaca. God knew where Ithaca was. I knew there was one in Greece, but this one had to be closer than that. It was the end, though. I knew that for certain.

"Where is Ithaca, exactly?" I asked carefully.

"Upper New York State," Roger explained. "Northwest corner. High above Cayuga's waters. That's a river."

"Then I guess we won't—see each other—anymore," I said. My ears seemed to be plugged up or something; my own words sounded very far away.

"Oh damn . . . no! I'll tell you what I've been thinking, though. It'll be hard for me to get to Boston, but I can probably swing some trips to New York. Any chance you could move down there? I mean, hey, Roger, maybe you'd have a better shot at the bar in New York, you know, and Sandy loves the city . . . Sheila does too, don't you, hon? That way we could go on seeing each other, at least sometimes. How about it, Roger? Any chance of your relocating to New York?"

She and I and Thaddeus all looked at Roger, on whom attention (my God, a decision, they want me to make a decision!) translated into a forehead sweat. He just managed a nod and then, "Well, I could see about it, I guess . . ." She kissed him lightly on the cheek, leaving a lipstick stain.

"Oh boy, I'll be so glad to get out of Boston!" She raved. "New York is so full of interesting people and things to do and places to go—oh, the pace is so fast and all!"

"Nice place to live," I started, and Thaddeus finished it for me.

"But I wouldn't want to visit there." We tried to get jolly again, on the surface anyway. There was a hard, bad jagged lump deep in my gut, which I knew I'd have to deal with late in the night, after Thaddeus had filled us all with love and had gone.

We got home about midnight and kissed and fondled and copulated and cohabited and screwed and fucked and cunnilingused and fellatioed and sucked and sighed and shot and spasmed and sweated and nestled and cuddled until Thaddeus kissed me sweetly and left quietly just before daylight. Sheila babbled happily all through breakfast, despite the lack of sleep, about New York and how provincial she had always found Boston and how she was determined to have an apartment on the Upper East Side and Roger would certainly pass the New York State bar exams because look how many lawyers they had in New York, it must be easy as pie and—he told her in a shaky voice that he hadn't even asked to be transferred to New York yet, and it was highly possible, even probable, that the firm couldn't use him in New York and he'd already put in a year on the laws of Massachusetts and he had always heard that New York State bar exams were the toughest in the country and just maybe they had been too hasty about deciding such an important move and then She started crying and saying, "You promised," and so Roger went off to work knowing it was New York or bust as far as his marriage was concerned.

Sheila went right to the phone to call her mother-in-law, assuming, with her infinite gall, that Margaretha would be ecstatic to have us all back in close proximity. I would have bet hard cash that the old bitch would find some reason to be off to Europe again, but I would have lost. I guess I underestimated the power of a grandchild to suture frazzled family pride. Although I wonder, if little Millie had had a twin and the poor little darlings had been somehow stuck together . . . oh shit, why did I always spoil the party, even for myself? Especially for myself.

Everyone was all huggy and kissy when we arrived in

Riverdale, car piled high with stroller, high chair, crib mattress, sheets and blankets, baby pillow, bottles, sterilizing equipment, clothes, toys, and a forty-year supply of diapers. Margaretha and Mr. Moritz and Mindy all came out to greet us as we pulled into the graciously curving driveway like Okies crossing into California. It was nice. We felt welcome.

Of course, they hoped we were only going to camp there for a couple of weeks, that it was just a visit. Roger had decided to wait and break the news in person that he had been fired when he asked for a transfer. Not that it was such a big deal; after all, with his Harvard education and family connections, he could join up with any law firm he wanted to, practically. It was just a matter of telling them; best done over a civilized sherry or late-afternoon tea.

So we settled in. I wrote to Thaddeus four times before he wrote back.

Dearest Sandy,

Sorry about the delay, but the p.o. really takes its time about forwarding mail and I got three letters from you all at the same time—just yesterday, although I see that they are dated a week apart starting four weeks ago. That must mean there is a fourth on its way, or my genius for mathematical puzzles fails me.

I moved out of The *Yahd* right after you guys left town; maybe it seemed too lonely with that phone sitting there where it had always sat and no you on the other end of it, no Sunday nights to look forward to, looking around the same old room and knowing you were gone made it unbearable. Not that you were ever there, were you? I always meant to sneak you in someday, ever since I heard that tale of how you were invited to MIT and couldn't go. I wanted to be the one who gave you all those adventures . . .

So I got the hell out of Boston, too. I'm making my way toward Ithaca slowly, which they say minimizes the bends. It's going to be hellish without you, I know that. Whoever said college years were the best of one's life? We had some lovely times, though, didn't we? And we will again, won't we?

But I guess you can't write to me for a while, till I get a more-or-less permanent address. The number I gave the Cambridge p.o. to forward my mail to is a friend's house. I'm there now but moving on. But look for a word every now and then—for every million times I think of you I'll try to send a postcard at least.

Best to She and Rog. Hope you are all having a great summer. See you soon.

Love,
Thaddeus

Curiously disappointing, although I too had adopted a breezy, unemotional style in my letters. I understood. I could follow the trickiest steps if my partner was a strong lead. And after all, I was in New York again only because he wanted me in the same state with him. Being in New York was great. Maybe in the fall I would try to register at Columbia or Hunter or the New School. Take some writing courses, start my novel. Stop obsessing about him.

I woke up and went to sleep with his voice in my head saying he loved me in that sweet sorry murmur. He really did love me. He wouldn't have hit me if I didn't mean so very much to him; he could have just walked away, but he cared and that made him hit out sometimes. I understood, I understood, I understood. Thaddeus would come back to me. In the meantime, wasn't I an expert on waiting?

"When are we going to start looking for an apartment?" I asked my sister.

"Are you crazy? Look where we are! You want to move out of a thirty-room mansion across the street from Toscanini back to a crummy mousehole of an apartment somewhere?"

I would have thought she'd want to have her marriage disintegrate in private. Well, I didn't give a damn. By the end of our second week in Riverdale, She had hired a nanny, uniform and all, to take care of Millie, and Roger had told his folks about losing his job and was already on rounds of lunches and drinks at the Harvard Club to talk with his dad's friends and his friends' dads about a new position. She and I spent at least three days a week, sometimes with Mindy along, shopping Lord & Taylor half the day and browsing Fourth Avenue for secondhand books the other half. We'd have lunch in dark little French bistros, drinking extra-dry martinis and eating snails in green garlicky sauce with wonderful crusty thick bread to mop it up. This was considered acceptable manners in a French restaurant. On Wednesday afternoons we went to Broadway shows. We always had to stand in the back of the theater, even if there was practically nobody else in the audience, because the fire laws wouldn't let them put chairs in the aisles. We both were totally transported by musicals, but sometimes if a play was straight drama and too talky for Sheila's limited concentration span, she'd bitch and moan and carry on about having to stand till people turned around to shush her.

Even with Ethel Merman singing, though, I thought about Thaddeus all the time. What had I done—or what had I failed to do—had I driven him away, ending the idyll for all of us?

Had I been too submissive? Too ready to forgive? Men get annoyed and bored with women who are too ready to forgive. Or was I too irritating, always bringing out his dark side? I had done things to make him so furious he was out of control, and then he had been embarrassed and ashamed:

Well of course no one could stand someone who made him feel that way! I couldn't get along with anyone in this world, not even my own love.

She always insisted on popping in someplace for a drinkie before heading home to Riverdale and Roger. (I thought it was mildly amusing that neither one of them could pass a bar, but there wasn't anybody I could share the joke with now.) Once I had two brandy alexanders and found myself thinking maybe I'd be better off if Thaddeus had never come along, if I'd never had even a taste of being loved. For a bizarre and foreboding minute I was thinking that he had done me a despicable, unforgivable wrong.

But I was hardly ever gloomy. There were always wonderful things to do in New York. Uncle Maudie threw a cocktail party in his magnificent apartment in the Waldorf Towers just for us. We went shopping at Bergdorf Goodman's and I spent ninety-nine dollars plus tax on a real silk dress with huge polka dots, a daring neckline, and a bow that was almost a bustle in back. When we talked to Billie on the phone that night, She told her all about our shopping expedition, and when she heard what my dress cost, my mother laughed loud enough for me to hear and she said, "Now, that's what I call putting a hundred-dollar saddle on a ten-dollar horse!" But I thought the dress looked okay on me.

The party was elegant and great fun, mostly. All the other guests were men of the homosexual persuasion, and even though everybody got pretty drunk, they were almost all terribly nice to us and went out of their way to be amusing. There's always one bad apple, though, isn't there? One who looked straight at us and said to his companion, "Oh my God, if Bergdorf's sells one more of those little hundred-dollar silk dresses, I'm going to spit up!" So I never wore that dress again; She had picked it out anyway.

Daddy and our mother came to visit, to see Millie and the sights of New York. I was worried that they might notice the permanent new bump on my nose, but they didn't say anything about it. We went out to dinner at a huge Italian restaurant where they give you too much to eat and it's too noisy and there are too many decorations. It was fun; you can't help feeling festive in a place like that. We were at a long table: Daddy, Billie, Roger, She and I, Uncle Maudie, Mindy, and a married couple my parents had met in Florida, Eddie and Bea Something.

After we had stuffed ourselves with antipasto, pasta, veal parmigiana, deep-fried zucchini, green salad, bread and butter, and heaps of other things I couldn't identify but ate anyway, it was time to order dessert and coffee.

Billie had already had her coffee with her meal, as people do in Sioux City. But now we urged her to try some espresso. She had never heard of it and therefore it must be no good, but she was feeling jolly from a few Scotches and a lot of wine and so she said what the hell, she'd try some. When it came, she took a sip and spat it out with a loud horrid sound: "Uhraughfft! yeachhu!" Not one sound but two. The first was from the unexpectedly bitter taste of the coffee, the second to make sure everyone understood that the first was intentional. It seemed to me that the cavernous room with its hundreds of gluttonous patrons suddenly went dead silent, one of those pauses that occur when someone has done something to stun everyone's sensibilities, sucking up all the oxygen. That was my mom.

Billie had our full attention. She had spat the black espresso halfway across the table onto the white albeit tomato-stained cloth. Now an explanation was due.

"Tastes like . . . uh . . . ergot," she said.

Silence. She had only compounded the mystery.

"I once tried to—uh—get rid of Sheila and Sandy here," she went on to explain.

Daddy laughed, and so did Eddie and Bea. Uncle Maudie laughed so hard he had to be pounded on the back by Mindy, who didn't know what was so funny but laughed politely anyway. An abortion, that's what we were supposed to be. Had she only half succeeded? ("Oh dear, I said abortion, not aberration!") Had the old knitting needle rammed us together instead of poking us out of there, like ear wax? If I ever heard an argument for legal abortion, this was it: Sheila and Sandra, living proof of what can go wrong with the back-alley, ergot-swilling, self-help fetus removal system. How much better for everyone if it had worked!

But I couldn't bring myself to look at my mother that whole night and all the next day, afraid she might see my anger. I did ask She that night how she felt about it, and She said she had no idea what I was talking about, didn't I even know when my own mother was making a joke?

When she was asleep that night, Roger got out of bed on her side and came around to mine. Maybe he heard me crying. Maybe he was just missing Thaddeus as much as I was. He tried to get in next to me, and honestly I was kind of flattered at the thought, but it was a terrible idea and I just patted his penis (soft) and said, "Sh. Go back to sleep." And of course, being Roger, he did.

Margaretha invited our folks to the house to have lunch (no other guests) and stay for the afternoon to play with Millie. She didn't have a party for them, but they didn't know that was supposed to be a slight. The rest of the time we spent driving them around to see the city—Greenwich Village and the Lower East Side and the public library and the Metropolitan Museum of Art and things like that. Daddy was fascinated with everything, but Billie refused to get out of the car and walk around or go inside anyplace except Macy's.

One evening Roger drove us all out to Coney Island, and we looked at it from the car. My dad had heard about hot dogs from Nathan's, so Roger got out with him and they brought some back to the car for us, but nobody could figure out what was supposed to be so special about them. Roger said if we wanted to see the ocean, we could just climb a little flight of wooden steps onto the boardwalk and there it would be, but Billie didn't want to bother, so she never saw the ocean. Daddy did, though. He loved it and said someday he'd like to take an ocean voyage; he had come to America steerage class when he was nine and he'd like to go back first-class before he got too old to enjoy it. Then he and Roger got to comparing world wars.

It was nice having them visit, knowing they had to go back to Sioux City and we didn't. Having them there for a week took my mind off Thaddeus for minutes at a time. I didn't get another letter from him. Several weeks after my folks had gone back home, I was still crying myself to sleep every night, silently, so as not to wake She or Roger. I would swear off him, like going on a diet. I'd promise myself not to think about him until after lunch. Or I'd vow that every other time he popped into my head I'd exorcise him out, somehow, and only think about him every *other* time in between. Trouble was, memory and longing wouldn't cooperate. I loved him and I hated him and I wished he were in my arms, except sometimes I wished he were dead—or I was.

And then, at last, he called.

24

A Night at the Biltmore

"Hi, Sandy. I guess you must have given me up."

"Hi. Oh no, not really. I mean, I figured you'd turn up someday."

"I won't say 'bad penny' if you don't."

I forced a nonchalant, gay laugh. "Deal." Then I asked, very casually, just out of idle curiosity, "Where are you, Thaddeus?"

"I'm in New York, love. Come and meet me?"

"Am I still your love?"

"Yes. Aren't you?"

"Yes. Where and when should I meet you?"

"How about under the clock at the Biltmore at five-thirty? That's supposed to be an old New York tradition, going back to a movie of the same name, I think."

"Today?"

"Unless you're busy or you'd rather not. I'll understand—"

"No! No, it's all right. It's fine. I'll be there."

"Good. See you then. I can hardly wait." I couldn't believe it, but it sounded like he made a kissing sound over the phone. Not his style, but deliciously nice. I melted into Silly Putty again, and I hadn't even seen him yet.

"I take it you made a date. How about consulting me before you make plans like that? I have obligations, you know."

"Oh shut up, Sheila. You want to see Thaddeus as much as I do. Almost as much, anyway. What should I wear?"

Roger had found a job in a corporate law firm, and She called him to tell him to meet us under the clock at the Biltmore at five-thirty. Just like that, no mention of Thaddeus. How nice, I thought. She wants to surprise him with the unexpected appearance of his dear, maybe his best, friend. I couldn't even think of the real word for it then. His lover. My lover. Her lover. Decline the verb to love in all persons. I love, you love, he or she loves, we love, you love, they love. Object of the verb: Thaddeus.

I sang all day, all the time we were getting dressed, driving to the station, parking the car, waiting for the train, getting aboard. I sang softly, to myself, as the train rounded Spuyten Duyvil and went underground at 125th Street and I sang until She said, "If you don't shut up, I'm not going. I swear it." I apologized.

The Biltmore was not such a terrific idea. People stared; they even pointed at us and came over to gawk as if they'd bought tickets as we tried to sink down onto a couch that faced the lobby and that damn clock. Some debutante types were hanging out there; every now and then, an Ivy Leaguer in a blue blazer jacket would come up and take one of them away. I wondered how they could tell each other apart.

And then Thaddeus! I felt too weak to stand up. I must have made some sound because She looked up from her magazine and quickly pulled us both to our feet.

"Thad!" she shouted. He grinned and quickly strode over to us. He looked so good I almost wept. I could feel love rushing back into me; was it possible I had almost lost it? In the few seconds it took Thaddeus to get to my side and take me in his arms and kiss me alive again, I knew I was saved from the very edge of nothingness. He was back and his arms were strong and firm and we loved each other.

"People are staring," my sister reminded us sharply. Thaddeus smiled down at her and kissed her on the cheek, but she shook her head and tried to pull us all out of there. "We're making a spectacle," she muttered. Her face was red and she needed a drinkie. She led us into the dark bar, where sentimental music was being played on a piano, and we all sank down together in a cozy heap and ordered drinks.

"Isn't Roger coming?" Thaddeus asked.

"Oh sure. Of course," She told him, manifesting her boredom with the very idea of Roger.

"Will he know to look for us here?"

"Yes," I said shortly. Thaddeus and She both laughed at me; I'm not sure why. Something about the way I said it. Wanting the attention back at me, maybe. I hated them sharing a laugh at my expense.

The drinks came and for a terrible minute or two it seemed we didn't have anything much to say to each other. At any rate, I didn't want to ask him stupid questions about school and so I couldn't think of anything to say at all. Sheila was smiling and swilling down a double, and Thaddeus seemed perfectly at ease in the silence, not looking at me or at anything in particular. It had been over eight weeks since we had been together, and maybe things just couldn't ever be the same again. Maybe I was wrong about the way his arms felt around me out there in the lobby. It seemed to me that he didn't even want to look at me.

"Penny for them," Sheila said, chipper as a Walt Disney chipmunk.

"Really?" Thaddeus asked, without cracking a smile. She nodded. He put out his hand. She laughed, opened her purse, rooted around on the bottom, and put a tarnished penny in his hand. He closed his fingers around it. He looked at me (he loved me!) and then back at her and he said, "I was thinking how can I possibly get them to sleep with me tonight, right here at the Biltmore, get a room and stay all night together. That's what I was thinking. Get your money's worth?"

Sheila flushed and nodded and took a big swallow of vodka. Thaddeus looked at me and my eyes filled up and all I could do was nod: yes, yes, yes, yes oh yes.

"I have a baby at home," She said.

"You have a nanny, too," I pointed out. "So how about it?" If she said no, I was planning to reach around and jab her eyes out with my swizzle stick.

"If you say, 'How about what?' " Thaddeus told her, to my delight, "the answer is, 'How about us all shacking up tonight?' " He looked at me then, his face so close I could feel his warm breath. "Right, love?" he half whispered, and I knew again that he really did care for me. I nodded and touched foreheads with him, too happy to talk.

Roger came into the bar, stood for a moment adjusting his eyes to the rosy darkness, and then saw us and headed over. His general-purpose smile, polite and hopeful, opened warmly as he shook hands with Thaddeus. Thaddeus did not stand up, which I thought was kind. He was a lot taller than Roger.

"Long time, long time," my brother-in-law said. He bent to kiss Sheila's cheek, nodded cheerily at me, and finally sat down. He ordered a double. "Got to catch up with everybody. Sorry I'm late. I was in a meeting."

"How are things going for you, Roger?" Thaddeus asked.

Before her husband could open his mouth, my sister exploded furiously. "Thad thinks we're going to hop right into bed with him. Just like that! All he has to do is whistle, no, all he has to do is put in an appearance, just show up and— boom! Everybody in the world drops dead just for the chance to sleep with him. He said he wants us all to 'shack up' in a hotel room, that's how he put it. Want to 'shack up,' Roger? God, that's insulting!"

Roger concentrated on his drink, saying nothing.

Thaddeus put his arm around me and said softly, "I'm sorry you feel that way about it, She."

"Well, you damn well ought to be!"

Then I spoke up, an announcement, loud and clear. "I will sleep with you tonight, or any other night, here or anyplace else in the world, and if my sister doesn't like it, she can lump it."

"Or hump it," Roger murmured, so quickly in his cups.

"Or dump it," Thaddeus added cheerfully.

"Or rump it," I said.

"Or—" Roger's next rhyme was interrupted by a drink thrown in his face by his wife.

"I'm leaving here," She said, and started struggling to get up from the table.

"I'm staying," I said. I grabbed onto the table with both hands. Thaddeus retreated slightly; not that he didn't want to help me, but I guess he was just appalled. Anyone would have been.

It hurt. The place where we are joined hurt because it was pulled and twisted. I was wailing like a baby and so was She, and now even in the dark recesses of the hotel bar, we could tell people were looking at us. Suddenly, Roger got up and left, practically at a run. I thought maybe he was going to the men's room to be sick. But then I saw Thaddeus slowly sliding out from the banquette—he was leaving, too!

"Don't go, Thaddeus!" I begged him through my tears. He just shook his head sadly. And then he was gone.

She and I stopped struggling. We both sat back, exhausted, weeping. My head fell back against hers. "Oh God," I said with a terrible sigh. "I wish I were free of you!"

"Where the hell is Roger?" She moaned.

"I don't think he'll be back," I told her.

"Oh, he'll be back. Where the hell is he going to go?"

"Maybe with Thaddeus. I don't know. They're both gone, and we deserve it."

"Roger's my *husband*!"

"Husbands have been known to go before," I pointed out wearily.

"Waiter! Two more. Make 'em doubles!"

"Thaddeus is the only man I'll ever love," I said.

"Cow crap. He never loved you, not really. Anyway, there's plenty more men."

"Not for me."

She looked me over critically in the smoked-glass mirror across the room. "Maybe not," she agreed.

"You're getting very drunk," I told her.

"I don't need you to tell me that."

"I don't need you, either."

"Well then, go away."

"Okay. You go away, too."

"Oh shut up."

I started to cry again. I wanted Thaddeus back.

What happened was that we were too drunk to go home. I don't know how we managed to pay the bar bill and get out of there (or had Roger paid it when he left, mad as he was; it wouldn't be out of character if he had). I do know that we couldn't find the front door of the hotel for a while, and then we decided that the intelligent thing to do was to stay there all night—someone had suggested it earlier, hadn't they?— so we must have asked for a room, I guess, because there we were in the middle of the night in a hotel room, sobering up and feeling sick. At least I was: dehydrated, thirsty, and nauseous. It was 2 A.M. and we hadn't had any dinner. I guess what we had done was pass out. And at two in the morning we woke up in this hotel room; no matter how fancy the Biltmore may have been downstairs, the rooms were not much more than a double bed, a chair and bedside table, and grimy windows looking out on a brick wall. And a bathroom, where I spent quite some time sitting on the nice cool floor (She grabbed the bathmat under her) with my head in the toilet bowl, trying to throw up with nothing in my stomach.

"I want Thaddeus," I moaned.

"Okay," She said. "Come on, then. We gotta make a phone call."

"Huh?" What trick was she up to? She didn't have hangovers; she never got sick. Was she going to punish me somehow? I didn't understand.

"I'm gonna get Thad for you, come on. Of course we have to take old Roger, too," she giggled. "Come *on!*" I let her pull me up, slowly so my head wouldn't start whirling again, and we went back to the bed. I tried to lie down, but She wanted to sit up. She picked up the phone and asked the operator to ring the number of the Harvard Club.

"Harvard Club!" I thought maybe she was going to order out for one of their special chicken club sandwiches, but I didn't think they delivered, especially at two in the morning.

"I want to speak with Mr. Roger Moritz, please. Oh, I know what time it is, thank you very much. Just ring his room. I know he's there. This is Mrs. Moritz . . . no, not his wife. Don't you think I know you don't put wives through? No, this is Mrs. Moritz his mother, and there's been a family emergency, so put me through or Harvard will be very, very sorry."

She waited. I waited. Then Roger was on the line, sleepy but honest. Her voice turned from harridan to honeybun.

"Hi, darling. I had to tell you how sorry I am and how lonely I am for you and how awful I feel. Please say you forgive me."

271

Roger must have said he forgave her.

"Honey? Guess where I am?"

Roger couldn't guess, apparently.

"In the Biltmore Hotel, honey, in room—uh—" The key was on the table near the phone. She looked at it. "Six-one-three. I miss you, sweetie. Can you come over here real quick like a bunny? And we'll do something nice that bunnies do!"

I don't know what Roger said then.

"Is Thad there with you?" She asked, still nice-nice. "Is he awake? Well, say hi to him, and, Roger honey, maybe he wants to come over, too. Sandy really wants him to."

I was stunned, amazed, thrilled. My head cleared miraculously. What a pal, what a sister! I loved her. I had always loved her, I saw that now. Okay, so we had had some misunderstandings. So we brought out the bitchiness in each other; I was as much to blame as She. From now on, it would be different. I would never forget what she was doing for me tonight.

"Is he coming? Is he coming? Is he coming?" I asked excitedly.

She made kissy noises into the receiver and then hung up the phone. "Not yet," she giggled. "That'll be up to you, won't it?" She was witty! She was a wonderful friend, a true pal, an interesting person, and I had never even noticed! She reached into her handbag and pulled out a pint bottle of vodka, about half gone. There was a glass in the bathroom. She drank a half glassful quickly and then poured another to carry around the room while we fixed ourselves up.

In about a half hour there was a tap-tap on our door. We had used the time to clean up our smeary makeup and redo our hair, get out of rumpled clothes, and assure each other (in our new camaraderie; Billie should only see us now) that our slips were sure-fire sexy. When Thaddeus and Roger walked in, we all smiled a little sheepishly and then fell onto the bed in a playful heap. The slips and everything else were abandoned on the floor.

Roger was the first to wake in the morning, as we later reconstructed things. He woke revolted at the scene: a hotel room, anonymous and drab, and three bodies sprawled in ugly positions, two of them physically joined together. The third was a man, a naked man whose body good little Roger Moritz had taken inside his own. He stumbled into the bathroom, where thousands of unknown people had stumbled before him, pissing and shitting and bathing and cutting their toenails and God knows what in that nameless room with the stained tiles, and poor Roger puked up his guts, all his sins against his class, against nature, against his mother and his money and his birthright. He wept and knocked his head against the yellowed tile wall, and that sound woke me up. I heard him sobbing in there, but I didn't know what to do. Should I comfort him? Could I? I lay there wondering, feeling pity for him, feeling the sensuous stirrings of my beloved Thaddeus lying curled around me. He was getting hard. I slipped him into me from behind, not knowing or caring if he was awake.

She stirred, too, and tried to stretch, but I was wrapped around my lover and couldn't, wouldn't move. She woke up and heard Roger.

"What's wrong with him?" She asked.

Yes, there was something different, desperate and singular, about Roger's cries, but oh, there was something major going on inside me, too, and I couldn't be concerned about my brother-in-law's regrets just now. Thaddeus began moving, just enough so I knew he was awake. But his erection began to fade away against the music of Roger's sobs.

"Damn," he sighed. "What's wrong with Roger?"

"Be a love and go see, will you, Thad?" She wheedled.

"No," I protested, clutching my thighs together to keep him.

Then Roger was quiet. We were all quiet. I think Thaddeus fell back to sleep. He slipped out of me, but I still didn't move. After a while, Roger came out of the bathroom. He was stark naked, but he stood in front of us as though he were in a conference room with suit and vest and tie and handkerchief in breast pocket folded just so.

"I want a divorce," he said.

She got up on one elbow. "WHAT?"

Roger started putting his clothes on. Boxer shorts. Garters to hold up socks. Socks. T-shirt. Trousers. "I want a divorce, and the sooner the better. You can have as much money as you want, but I've got to get out of this."

"WHAT DID I DO?" shrieked Sheila.

Thaddeus and I were disengaged now, propped up on elbows and staring at Roger in astonishment.

"What did she do?" Thaddeus asked sleepily.

"You stay out of this! You . . . you . . . cocksucker!"

"Wow," Thaddeus said. He snuggled down into the covers, to smother a guffaw. I was furious with him because he made me want to laugh, too, and I thought Roger deserved better than that.

"This is just sick, sick and horrible. I don't want to do this anymore. I don't want to be a sick person with a disgusting sex life. I want to be normal, and I want to be married to someone normal—"

That was it. Sheila threw a lamp at him, but she missed and the lamp went crashing to the floor. By now he was all dressed except for knotting his tie, so he just went out the door without looking back. She screamed, "Roger! ROGER, YOU GODDAMN WELL COME BACK HERE!" and she kept on throwing everything she could reach from the bed, including the Bible and Thaddeus's wallet, and then she collapsed in sobs and Thaddeus and I comforted her as best we could.

It had turned truly sordid and by now I wanted out of there, too, and I knew Thaddeus did. "Let's take a shower," I said as soon as She stopped for a breath, and Thaddeus agreed and together we got my weeping sister into the tub and turned on the water and the three of us stood there scrubbing ourselves (not each other; this was not for fun). She calmed down and we got out and dressed quickly and silently.

Thaddeus kissed me and said, "I'll call you," and then he was gone. We went back to Riverdale, and Margaretha told us she had had a long phone call from Roger and she was glad he had finally come to his senses. She hoped we would find an apartment for ourselves as soon as possible. The maids would help us pack.

25

A Fine and Private Place

I wanted to live in the Village, but She's alimony was paying the rent, so she chose. We took Millie, her nanny, and all her equipment and moved into an East Side building that had a vulgar lobby and obsequious doormen.

She told me I was the ruination of her marriage, and I believed her, although I did think she contributed to the general disrepair. But Roger's defection had brought down our house, and he wouldn't have gone if I had known how to keep Thaddeus. We had all depended on Thaddeus's happiness. I had failed him, and destroyed us all.

He didn't write to me, but once in a while the phone would ring and there was his warm and loving voice to churn everything up in me again. I lived on those calls. I tried not to be too loving, too demanding, or too casual. I tried to say things he would find amusing, attractive, compelling. I never dared ask if or when he was coming to New

York. We just chatted. Ho ho ho, old buddy, nice to hear your voice.

Roger came every Saturday to pick up Millie and on Sundays he brought her back. He and Sheila didn't speak to each other.

"Hello, Sandy, how are you?"

"Fine, Roger. You?"

"Fine, fine. Is the baby ready?"

"Tell my pervert husband she's been ready for half an hour."

"Tell my wife I'm sorry I'm late. The traffic was stalled all the way down from the George Washington Bridge."

"I'll tell her when I see her."

"Thanks, Sandy. I think I married the wrong sister."

" 'Bye, Roger. Have fun. Bye-bye, Millie. Wave bye-bye to Aunt Sandy? And Mommy? That's a big girl. Bye-bye, sweetie."

"Tell my poor little baby's father that if he doesn't get her back here tomorrow by four o'clock exactly, I'll have him in court Monday morning."

"Hey, Roger, your wife says—"

"Yes, I heard. Come on, Millie, bye-bye."

"Bye-bye."

My sister and I were finally on our own, with no parents or husbands to run interference. I had longed for this for years, somehow imagining that without the Greek chorus telling us what to think and how to live, She and I could work out our lives. I wonder what in hell ever made me think that.

My fantasies had included, or centered around, a career. Now I sat in a wrapper with black coffee and endless cigarettes every morning, reading the employment opportunities while She read the Bonwit ads. I imagined myself going on interviews, and I imagined what it would be like to have this job or that. They were *real* jobs, ones I could have handled:

Gal Friday to television producer; Assistant Editor, children's books; Entry Position in glamorous public relations field; Production Assistant, commercial films; copywriter for a small ad agency, must be creative . . . but I didn't have a college degree and . . . well, obviously I couldn't even go on interviews. I could only daydream.

Inexplicably, the city I loved had abruptly stopped loving me back. On our little day trips from Riverdale we had been tourists, looking and experiencing and enjoying the city. Now it was different. On our own, we were shark bait.

"Hey look, them two is Siamese whatchacallits!"

"Oh my God, Muriel, Muriel, take a look!"

"Do you see what I see? Are those women trying to fit into the same dress or what?"

Taxi drivers piled into other cars because they were eyeing us in the rearview mirror. Store aisles jammed with customers who stopped fingering the goods to crowd around and finger us.

Liberal types came right up and talked to us:

"You must have to get along with each other real well, huh?"

"How do you—you know, how do you—uh, is either of you married?"

"Do you mind autographing this piece of paper for my daughter, she'd be so interested."

"Would you consider participating in a benefit for a worthy cause? It'll be very tasteful and all you'd have to do . . ."

We started going to doctors again. It had been years since we last looked for help. Maybe there had been some developments, a miracle we had missed reading about. Again, we went through all the humiliating tests and the shame of being on exhibit to swarms of rubber gloves and white coats. There was a doctor at Columbia Presbyterian Hospital who thought he might know a way to separate us; he diddled for months, but in the end he said his insurance company wouldn't let him try it. Then he sent Roger a bill for $12,000. I enrolled at the New School to study creative writing, music theory, and French, but She almost always made me late getting there, and during the classes she'd sigh out loud or file her nails or pretend to be sleeping, and then one day she saw a cockroach along the wall and—believe it or not—she screamed and made a terrible scene right in class, and finally I just stopped going.

I began writing my novel, but it was so vicious and bitter and unpleasant I couldn't imagine anyone wanting to read it. You're supposed to have at least one sympathetic character. I couldn't think of anybody sympathetic.

She began to make friends or, more accurately, drinking buddies. There was a bar down the street from our apartment building where we soon knew all the regulars. I amused myself (not greatly) identifying them as your standard midway attractions: There was Bobo the Dog-faced Girl ("She walks, she talks, she's almost human") and Eely Jack the Snake Man ("crawls on his belly like a reptile") and Strongman Stan ("he could break your back with just two fingers if you made him mad") and the Fattest Woman in the World and the Skinniest Man and even a Bearded Lady. We fit right in. It was a very democratic group, after all: all colors and nationalities and ranks of life, as long as they had the price of a drink. I learned how to nurse a beer for hours. When She was mellow we'd go home, and when she fell asleep I'd read or watch Edward R. Murrow on TV or just lie there and wonder what I had done to drive love out of my life.

I was listening to Mozart on the radio and crying one rainy Saturday evening when Thaddeus called.

"Hello, is it Sandy?"

"Yes. Hi, Thaddeus."

"How are you, love? Sounds like you've got a cold."

"Oh no, I'm fine, never better. How are you?"

"I'm in New York."

279

"You are? You're here?"

"Yes. I was wondering . . . would you want to see me? If you don't, I'll understand. Or anyway, I'll try to. I know I've been lousy about calling or writing. I wouldn't blame you if you were mad."

"Lordy, no. Why should I be mad? Of course I'd love to see you. We both would."

Sheila was snoring quietly. The rain was dripping dismally down the windowpanes.

"Should I come up, then?"

"Up here?"

"I'm not far away. I could be there in a half hour."

"Sure. Okay, see you in a half hour."

"You're sure I'm not interrupting anything? You don't have any other plans? I know it's short notice. I don't know—you think a half hour is short notice?"

I laughed lightly. "It's as long as I can stand," I said truthfully, hoping he'd realize I was only joking.

"That's my girl. See you then."

"See you." I hung up and woke my sister out of her coma. She pulled herself together with amazing grace as soon as she realized what I was saying. She acted like it was her date, of course, but what the hell, let her think whatever she liked. Thaddeus was here! He wanted to be with me!

We scurried to get washed and combed and redressed from our undies on up. For once, She would have to be the third wheel. I took off the bra with safety pins and put on the one with lace. I felt sorry for my sister in a way, but after all, for years I'd been the Invisible Woman in her bed and now that Roger was gone, it was just her turn to be number three, that was all.

Oh, but would he still want me? It had been months since we'd seen each other. Maybe the spark would be gone. Maybe he'd just want to be friends.

I was saved from despondency by the bell. One of the doormen was asking if a Señor Todd-A-O could be admitted.

"*Si,*" I told him, and Sheila poured herself a quick vodka and slugged it down. What in the hell was she nervous about?

I opened the door and it was exactly the same as it had always been. He was beautiful, and dark and smiling. He was also soaking wet. My lips trembled and my legs went wobbly, and I opened the door wide and hung on to it to prevent myself from falling into his arms. He was wearing a sopping trenchcoat sexier than anything Bogart ever owned. His hair was dripping into his eyes; no sissy umbrella for him!

"Come on in," I said.

"I'll drip on the furniture," he laughed.

"Who cares?" I said.

"Take off your coat and hang it in the shower," She said, frowning.

I helped him out of it. He was wearing his good tweed jacket. "Fix yourself a drink," I told him over my shoulder as She and I hurried to the bathroom with the dripping raincoat.

When we got back, he had made three drinks and handed us each a glass. "To old times," he said.

"I'll drink to that," She said, and did.

"*Le temps perdu,*" I said, not meaning to be brittle or clever.

"And so they are," Thaddeus agreed. He looked sad, but I thought it was just put on. If he regretted the lost times, why did he let them get lost in the first place?

"Tell us all about Cornell," I said. She and I sank into the couch, and Thaddeus took the big chair facing us. I thought how cozy this dull room suddenly was, with the steady rain against the windows no longer lachrymose but now a contented sound, and us inside all private and safe. It only needed a fireplace. If we lived in the Village, we would have had one. But Thaddeus was here and that was everything. I was very happy.

"I'm too big a boy to be going to school," Thaddeus said.

281

"That damn war made men of us before we were ready and now we're expected to be schoolboys. I want to get on with my life."

"You'll be finished soon," I reminded him.

"If I can stick with it," he said. "Oh well, let's not be glum. It's wonderful to see you, finally. Both of you." He was being polite to my sister, maybe remembering how she carried on if she ever felt slighted. I appreciated that.

"You want to leave Ithaca?" I asked him. What a lovely idea. I hoped I didn't sound too hopeful, but I was already thinking what it would be like when he came to New York. Was it too much to hope he might consider moving in with me, I wondered.

"As fast as possible," he said. "San Francisco's the place. A lot of people I know are heading out there."

"San Francisco?"

"Oh, we were in San Francisco once," my sister piped up. "There was an earthquake and I thought the building was going to cave in. I've never been so scared in my life."

"Huh?" There hadn't been anything like an earthquake when we were there.

"Oh my God, don't tell me you don't remember that!" She scoffed.

"Well, you can't worry about natural disasters," Thaddeus said. "How about another drink?"

"Thanks."

"No thanks, I've still got some."

"I would love to take you girls out to dinner," Thaddeus said. "But I have to confess to the old G.I. Bill blues. I haven't got a dime."

"Who wants to go out in the rain anyway?" I said. "We can cook something—"

"We can order out," She broke in. "The doorman can go pick up something from one of the restaurants nearby. I have charge accounts at all of them and that way Roger pays for it! Isn't that perfect? He can buy us all dinner, and we won't even have to put up with his boring company!"

Thaddeus caught my eye and that same extraordinary covenant passed between us; we were inside each other's minds and hearts as if we'd never been away. I would have vowed all over again that he still loved me as I did him.

"Pizza?" She was offering. "Chinese? Mexican? There's an Indian restaurant but I don't think they'll make up plates to take out. Oh, and there's a Greek place, but I hate it."

"Pizza sounds good to me. How about you? Sandy?"

We both agreed. After an amiable rundown of Pete's Pizza menu, we even agreed on the topping. I was the only one who liked anchovies so I was outvoted on that, but Thaddeus and I won on the mushrooms.

We switched to beer when the pizza came, and we sat on the floor and enjoyed ourselves, although I worried that I might be boring him. It occurred to me that since my life was such a bust, I had nothing to say that could possibly interest this brilliant, wonderful, witty, and well-read man. Of course he never would let on if he were bored, would never hurt my feelings or anyone else's that way. It was just my own feeling. He was relaxed and sweet. After we finished eating, he snuggled up next to me and pretty soon we were kissing, and just so Sheila wouldn't feel left out, he reached over and sort of patted her behind while he kissed me. Then we moved into the bedroom and we all got undressed very quickly and fell onto the bed. I was grateful to Sheila for being so cooperative.

Much later, I wondered if he ever noticed that I was wearing a bra with lace on it.

He made love to me rather more quickly than he used to, because it had been so long and he was so hungry for me. (Could it be possible he had been faithful all this time? Don't be a total nut case, Sandra; would you have been faithful if you'd had half a chance not to?) But it was good and satisfying and he finished with lots of little kisses all over my body, and through it all She was being incredibly patient, even thoughtful, leaving me alone with my love. It was just the two of us: Thaddeus and me. It was good—no, it was wonderful. Well, no, it was just good, but we had all night for wonderful.

But then he turned to my sister and started caressing and kissing her, and pretty soon she was moaning and wriggling and he was on top of her and then he was inside her. He gave her an orgasm. Is there an opposite to *orgasm*, an antonym for that terrible noun, a word for that all-encompassing passion, those spasms—a feeling just as deep and filling and powerful but made of hate instead of love? I just lay there till it was over, staring up to where rain, reflecting through the windows, splashed across the ceiling with slowly drying tears.

When he had finally finished with her, sighing deeply, rolling off, She wanted a drinkie and I got up with her. The bedroom bar was empty, so we went to the kitchen and She got a fresh bottle of vodka and I picked up a knife from the cabinet. She didn't bother to notice what I was doing. When we got back to the bedroom, Thaddeus was asleep. We lay down beside him and pretty soon She was asleep, too. I was wide awake. I lay there with the knife cold alongside my left leg and Sheila warm alongside my right leg and Thaddeus separate and asleep, holding all the love I'd ever known or would ever know. I lifted up my hand with the knife in it and I raised up on my elbow and the rain had stopped and there was moonlight coming through the blinds and I could see just where his big artery was throbbing rhythmically in his throat and I sliced across it so neatly he never felt a thing. The blood was terrible, though.

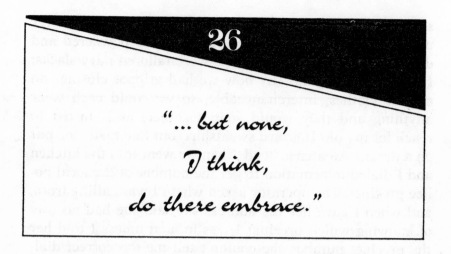

26

"... but none,
I think,
do there embrace."

When She woke up, she screamed and screamed until she realized it wasn't doing anybody any good and then she turned cold as January in Juneau and said, "What are you going to do about this?" There was a peculiar silence because it took me a while to understand. I was now in charge.

"I guess . . . call the police," I said shakily. It was happening to someone else. I stared and stared at him, but I wasn't really registering anything at all.

"I want all this cleaned up before Roger gets back here with Millie," she ordered.

"Sure."

We got out of bed as carefully as we could so as not to disturb Thaddeus or touch the soaked red sheets and pillow and blankets. There was blood splattered on the wall and on the table and lampshade and the telephone. We just got into the shower right away and stood there for a long time scrubbing and soaping and letting the hot water pour over us, hair and all. When we were dried and powdered and deodorized, we got dressed. She wore tailored navy slacks; I pulled on my jeans (by now we had gripper closings on all our clothes, interchangeable, so we could each wear anything and they would snap together) and started to reach for my old Harvard sweatshirt, but She made me put on a decent sweater instead. Then we went into the kitchen and I dialed information to get the number of the local police precinct. The operator asked where I was calling from, and when I gave her the address she said she had no way of knowing which precinct I was in, and unless I told her the precinct number she couldn't tell me the correct dialing number.

"Well, the thing is," I confided to her in a low voice, "I need to report a murder."

My sister screamed again, and I guess the operator must have heard her.

"You want homicide," she told me. She gave me the number, and I hung up on her and dialed it. It rang many, many times before someone answered. Fearful of setting my sister off again, I didn't say murder this time but that I wanted to report a problem. The homicide operator, whom I pictured as middle-aged, with her hair in rollers, wanted to know what kind of problem and was it urgent. I started to feel bad for wasting her time on a homicide that wasn't urgent. I said I didn't think it was exactly an emergency because the person was already dead. Sheila was shuddering, so my own teeth were starting to rattle. I grabbed the coffeepot off the stove and handed it to her, gesturing that she should start making some coffee, but she started wringing her hands like ZaSu Pitts and crying, so I saw I would have to do it myself as soon as I got off the phone.

I finally got to talk to a cop, who asked my name and address and phone number and whether I called in complaints very often and then he said, "You came in over the emergency number; is this an emergency?" and I said the operator already asked me that and then I gave up and lied, which seemed to be what they wanted.

"Yes," I said. "It's very urgent." What was urgent about someone being dead? "I just killed someone."

"Hold on a minute," he said.

He wasn't taking me seriously. He figured I was a crazy person, even though he'd never even seen me. Well, probably I was crazy, but that didn't mean he shouldn't take me seriously. Crazy people often do serious things.

He put me on hold and I waited. Finally, another man said, "Homicide, Detective Spielberg speaking."

I had to tell my name and address again and said I had killed someone and he said who and I told him Thaddeus's name and he said he would be right over and not to touch anything. I said, "No, of course not, everybody knows that much," making a joke to ease the tension, but he didn't get it. I hung up finally and made the coffee and some toast.

"Want an egg?" I asked my sister, but she shook her head.

"I hate you, I hate you, I hate you. Look what you've got me into," she kept muttering. She was kind of shuddering and keening, and it seemed pretty genuine. Had I found a way to reach the real Sheila underneath? It wasn't a trick I could resort to very often, but I did appreciate our having a genuine moment together, especially just then.

We were sitting at the kitchen counter when the house phone rang and the doorman announced Detective Spellburn.

"Sure," I said. "Send him up."

There were two of them: a uniformed patrolman and Detective Spielberg, in light brown trousers and dark blue jacket. I invited them in. They stepped into our living room and stood there staring at us.

"Are you—uh—Siamese twins, excuse the expression? I

287

don't mean to offend." Spielberg needed a shave; he was the type who always did.

"Yes," I said. She wasn't saying anything, just sniffling and trying to look innocent.

"Holy shi—" The cop whistled through his teeth. Then he took off his police cap. I didn't think they were supposed to do that, but I guess something about the situation made him feel reverent, or maybe just ill at ease.

"You called us?" Spielberg asked me, looking right in my eyes.

"Yes."

"Someone's dead here, so where?"

"In the bedroom."

"Would you lead the way, please?"

"I don't want to go back in there!" She yelped. "I didn't have anything to do with it. I was asleep and I woke up and there he was, and I'll throw up if I have to go in there!"

She made gagging noises, and apparently Detective Spielberg believed her because he just headed in the direction I pointed and the cop followed him and we waited in the living room until they came out. Spielberg had a shorthand notebook and a ballpoint pen. We all sat down and they started asking questions. I told them exactly what happened. I told him Thaddeus and I were in love, that he had spent the night with me, that my sister got in the way, through no fault of her own, and he had made love to her, not really meaning to, and I couldn't stand that, so I did what I did.

"Uh, did he rape you? Either one of you or . . . both of you?" Spielberg asked.

"No." He hadn't understood a thing I said.

Sheila just cried and blew her nose.

Spielberg said we'd better get a lawyer. Sheila dropped the bathos, grabbed the phone, and called Riverdale. She told Mr. Moritz I had done something horrible that she couldn't talk about in front of a roomful of police and detectives and he had to get us a damn good lawyer right away.

I twisted round to add a quick bit of crucial information. "A criminal lawyer," I barked into the phone. Spielberg nodded.

She hung up, but she didn't take her hand off the phone until it rang again a few minutes later. It was Roger's great-uncle Charles. He asked to speak with the detective. Spielberg almost clicked his heels when he found out whom he was speaking to, and he handed the phone back to Sheila with something like awe. She listened and wept pathetically for Great-Uncle Charles's benefit and then she said goodbye and hung up and told Spielberg that the best lawyer in the entire world would meet us at police headquarters, so let's just go and get it over with.

"I haven't done anything and you'd better not try to harass me. I feel like I'm going to have an asthma attack as it is, I can hardly breathe. I am an innocent bystander and you can get in big trouble for false arrest—or a whole lot worse, if I get sick from this!" she told Spielberg. "My sister can go to jail and rot there if she has to and I won't be sorry, but you'd better damn well not try anything with *me*."

I felt oddly peaceful, sort of floating above it all. It was like a movie; whoever had detectives and corpses right in their own apartments? It wasn't happening to me!

The cop stayed to wait for the guys from homicide, and Spielberg took us in an unmarked car (no sense of melodrama, Spielberg) to a building downtown. The lawyers were there already; a very impressive, tall and handsome older man, so well groomed he made my hangnails hurt, and a deferential young bureaucrat in a cashmere coat. They took us to a courtroom, where our man joshed a bit with the judge and bail was set at fifty thousand dollars. No problem, apparently; the young whippersnapper grabbed his crocodile briefcase and headed out of the courtroom. We waited for him in the hall with Too-handsome Silverhair, Esquire, who didn't seem to want to talk to us, at least not where anybody might see him. Junior Partner came back, his brief-case a little lighter no doubt, and they took us outside through a crowd of reporters, acting the way they'd seen it done in newsreels. We were hustled through the crowd into—of course—a waiting black limousine.

"Take me home to Riverdale," She said.

Our savior shook his head. He had a monumentlike pro-file, chipped rather than carved out of craggy rock. "You're to go back to your apartment and wait there until I tell you differently. Have your food brought in and speak to no one. No one, understand?"

"You can't tell me what to do—" She started, but he just glanced at her and she shut up.

"I'm afraid to go back there," She whimpered as the car swung into our own street.

"Prison's worse," God said. He opened the door and let us climb gracelessly over his feet to get out. Well, I mean, there was nine feet or so of room, but still, he could have gotten out first. He just stayed where he was. The driver handed us out and slammed the door noiselessly.

Thaddeus was gone when we looked in the bedroom, but it was still a bloody mess in there. Two plainclothesmen were standing around smoking cigarettes. They let us get some things from the drawers and closet, watching every move we made.

We slept on the Hide-A-Bed in the living room. The cops changed shifts every eight hours. They helped themselves in the kitchen or we all ordered up pizzas or Chinese or Mexi-can or ribs. No point in not being friendly, but the only thing any of them ever wanted to talk about was what was it like being Siamese twins. She called the lawyers and asked if we could have the place cleaned up. They said no. It was creepy, living like squatters in our own living room, with a couple of men hanging out in our bedroom around the clock. When I looked in there, I saw that the blood was turning into ugly brown stains, shabbier every day. The apartment started to stink, more from the cops' stale smoke than from the congealing blood and stuff. Every day lab technician types came and did things, I don't know what. We didn't watch what they did in there.

Finally, they said we could clean it up and the cops went away. We hadn't seen our regular cleaning lady since it happened, so we called a maid service. It took three visits. It was humiliating to sit there pretending to read or watch TV while horrified and disgusted women scoured and scrubbed and came back and forth out of the bedroom to stare at us.

But I was still numb and remote from everything on the planet earth. The only thing that got to me was when I realized, every once in a while, that Thaddeus was dead and I'd never see him again. Then I'd push that thought back, way back, and go on being part of the audience at these very interesting proceedings. My sister stayed hysterical throughout the entire time, and they gave her tranquilizers every four hours.

Years before, when Uncle Maudie had his scandal, the Moritz family had been able to keep it out of the papers, but their money and influence couldn't keep them out of this one. I was on the front page of *The New York Times* four times, and there were six other newspapers in the city then, three of them half-size tabloids, although nothing like what you see in the supermarkets these days. (Just recently, we were featured again, right between MOM PUTS BABY IN MICROWAVE, TURKEY IN CRIB and ELVIS IMPREGNATED ME FROM THE GRAVE, TEENAGER INSISTS.)

The number of people who were dying to talk to me probably soared into the thousands, but none of them were members of my family or Roger's or Thaddeus's. I finally got to meet his parents, at the inquest. His mother was large and his father was small but pleasant looking.

Roger's mother put on sunglasses and took a boat to a Buddhist retreat in the Himalayas, where there were no telephones or cameras. I liked knowing that she was sitting up on top of some remote snow-capped mountain thinking about me. It must have played hell with her meditations. I hoped that if she ever tried to leave there, her face would crumble like Margo's in *Lost Horizon*.

Thaddeus was dead. There was no one in the world anymore to love me.

Roger's sister, Mindy, must have wanted to call me or even come to see me, but somebody probably wouldn't let her. Mr. Moritz kept paying for everything, but he never said another word to me or his daughter-in-law, even when he saw us in court. At the inquest, She tried to run up to him with her arms wide open, but he turned and walked away as if he hadn't noticed two grown women soldered together coming toward him, with flashbulbs going off and yammering reporters moving with them every step they took.

I couldn't think about my mother at all. I couldn't bear to think how I had hurt her. When Daddy called, he said all she could do was cry and how did I feel being a murderer and was I trying to kill my own mother as well as that *shaigetz* I had slept with? Was I trying to ruin them both, was that what I wanted? I cried so hard when he talked to me that way I almost couldn't hear Billie shrieking and sobbing right next to the phone. "How could she do this to me? How could she do this to me? What have I done to deserve this?" They didn't come to New York; my mother said she couldn't put her face out the door for shame.

"Did you love this man?" I was asked at the inquest. I didn't see what that had to do with anything. It was irrelevant to the facts of the case. I had already said I stabbed Thaddeus to death; love was none of the coroner's business.

But the lawyers had drilled me thoroughly. I answered by rote.

"Yes," I said.

"And did he love you?"

"Yes," I said. Sheila snorted.

"How did you know that?" the inquisitor asked, not unkindly.

"A woman knows those things," I said.

"Why did you kill him, then?"

"I wanted him all to myself."

"Did you know it was wrong when you did it?"

"I don't know what I knew just then."

"Did you intend to kill him?"

"I don't know."

"Do you know now that it was wrong?"

"Of course." I hate being patronized. If the scorn in my answer was too obvious, well, it would only make it clear that any insanity on my part had been very temporary.

It occurred to me that prison would be a fine and private place, maybe even quiet. I could be happy, I thought, living in a cell if I had books and paper and a typewriter. I could really write my novel there. Once the guards and other inmates got used to us, there would be no strangers to stare. And with no expectations, I couldn't disappoint anybody ever again or be disappointed myself in anyone else. Solitude would be my salvation. I looked forward to it; I really hoped the brilliant and famous lawyer would screw up just this once.

Of course my sister would hate prison; she had no inner resources. She always had to have people around her, and small talk, and in jail they probably wouldn't let her have any of the things she loved, like clothes and hairdos and soap operas and gossip. But all that was so trivial and stupid that in fact I'd be doing her a favor. I'd actually be a missionary saving her banal soul by introducing her to deeper thinking, inner peace, the blessings of abandoned hopes.

But it never happened. We didn't even spend one night in

jail. The lawyers pleaded me guilty to manslaughter with extenuating circumstances. When you plead guilty, you don't need a trial. At the sentencing, our lawyer said that punishing me for my crime would severely impinge on my sister's civil rights. Since the Constitution of the United States places the rights of the innocent above all things—even the punishment of the guilty—we were let off. I was to remain free in order to ensure my sister's freedom. It was a bitter blow.

I desperately wanted to stay in New York forever, where people would forget about us just like they forget the name of the restaurant they've been going to for twenty years the minute the building is torn down. But Billie the Mother wanted to know when we were coming home.

I told her She and I both thought we'd like to stay in New York. Honest to God, I thought she'd be pleased that the two of us agreed on something. I also didn't think she'd want us back there embarrassing her every minute.

"How can you even think of doing that to me? You want people to say I'm ashamed of my own children, that I wouldn't have them back? You've got to come home and stay here, and I've got to take you in. That's the way things are supposed to be. We have to stick to each other."

An unfortunate choice of words, but I let it pass.

"Say something, Sheila!" I growled, thrusting the phone over my shoulder. I could hear my mom, now using logic and persuasion on the other end.

"Don't think I don't know what you're up to, you two. You haven't hurt me enough, have you, not yet. I know what you really want, and don't give me any of that concerts and museums crap. You want to keep on having your own SEX LIFE, don't you? Hasn't that gotten you into enough trouble yet? What's the big attraction in New York—it's not as if your friends were getting you anywhere socially!"

Sheila refused to take the receiver at first. The phone

dangled there between us, Billie's squawks getting dimmer as the cord played out.

With a loud martyred sigh, She hauled it in slowly. "Mom?" she ventured against the waves of sound. "Mom?" Louder. "No, we don't, Mother. We don't want our own sex life. I never even wanted it in the first place!" She started to cry. My mother was already crying. I was crying, too.

My sister could sob and talk at the same time and her nose didn't even run. "Okay, okay, we'll come home. Sure we do. No, we really, really do want to. Don't we, Sandy? Sandy says yes, she wants to come home, too. We just weren't sure you wanted us—well, no, I mean we knew you wanted us, but maybe it would be, well, you know, embarrassing. We still get an awful lot of attention from the press, and photographers go absolutely everywhere we do now. I can't let my hair go for a minute. Yeah, okay, we'll get the tickets and let you know what plane we'll be on. Can you drive down to Omaha to get us?"

"Well," She said to me after she'd hung up, "it won't be so bad. At least we'll be with our own kind."

So here we are, back in Sioux City, and sometimes it seems to me that I never left. Now that I have murdered someone, I am considered to be even more peculiar than before. On Halloween, the kids dare each other to come up on our porch and ring the bell. I don't care.

I hear that Louise Hansen has been married three times and now she lives in Los Angeles. I wonder if she ever found out the answer to her question about Orthodox Jews. If I ever see her again, I'll tell her it wasn't my fault.

Some of She's old friends, married and settled down in the old hometown, still invite her to luncheons and after-noon bridge games, and I schlep along. We go to movies on Saturday nights now instead of Saturday afternoons. Then we stop at the Green Gables for a snack, but they don't make those curly thin, crisp french fries anymore.

My mother was right all along: Reality is unlivable. Think about something else. *Casablanca* is on TV again tonight. The Germans wore gray and you wore blue. Round up the usual suspects.

Roger married a dentist, the daughter of old family friends. He sends Sheila a check every month. He used to let Millie come visit us in the summer for two weeks and then again at Christmastime. Being Jewish, we don't celebrate Christmas, and being in a small town we don't celebrate Chanukah, either. Millie hated it here. By the time she was nine, she was fighting with her mother all through the vacation, and after that she refused ever to come again. We haven't seen her in years. She has children of her own now. Sheila says Millie is a brat, spoiled by wealth and too much attention from her Moritz grandparents. She sends us a Christmas card once a year with a picture of what my sister calls the Maternity Scene on it.

My father is old, but he won't retire. What would he do at home?

My mother says she worries about what will become of us when she's gone. How will we manage without her? We were always such klutzes in the kitchen she shooed us out of her way, so we don't know how to cook or do much of anything for ourselves. She says these things right in front of the woman who comes every day to clean and do laundry and iron and cook and put up jam and weed the garden.

"My life is ruined," she says, "but that doesn't matter because I am a Mother and it's a Mother's cross to bear, worrying about her chicks no matter how badly they've hurt her." Then she consoles herself. "Well," she says, lighting up a Virginia Slim, avoiding our hateful eyes, "at least I can rest easy, knowing my girls will always have each other."

Twins' Recovery
Difficult

(from *The New York Times*, October 6, 1987)

Baltimore, Oct. 5 (AP) — Twins born joined at the back of their heads could remain hospitalized for up to six months as doctors deal with post-operative care that is as complicated as the surgery that separated them, doctors said.

The twins also suffered some brain damage during the surgery, the doctors added.

Since the 22-hour operation on September 6 that parted the twins, 8-month-old Patrick and Benjamin Binder have been besieged with complications, said Dr. Bejamin [sic] Carson, a pediatric neurosurgeon.

"Some days it looks like you can see the clearing, but some days it looks like you're deep in the woods," said Dr. Carson, who performed the delicate separation of their scalps, skulls and veins at Johns Hopkins hospital.

Since then, the boys from Ulm, West Germany, have made repeated trips to surgery—at least nine times between them—for skin grafts, cleaning of their wounds, insertion of new intravenous feeding tubes and draining of excess spinal fluid that their separate bodies now have difficulty absorbing naturally.

"The twins have had wound breakdown, problems with lungs, kidneys, liver, problems with everything," Dr. Carson said.

"Discouraged? I'm not," he said. "We knew we were in for a tussle."

The twins remain semi-comatose, sedated so they will not fully awaken while connected to tubes and life-support equipment. But doctors say the boys react to light and to sudden noise like a hand clap, move their arms and legs, have opened their eyes spontaneously to their mother's touch, and at times have made guttural noises that are not quite a cry.